CANTERBURY CANTICLE

ALSO BY H. BYRON EARHART

The Twin Destiny Series

No Pizza in Heaven

Faith Finds Forgiveness

Meeting the Devil

Devil Deja Vu

Canterbury Canticle

Byron's Memoir

At Grandma's House: The World War II Homefront in Havana, Illinois

CANTERBURY CANTICLE

BOOK 5 OF THE TWIN DESTINY SERIES

H. BYRON EARHART

Chula Vista • Columbus

Printed in the United States of America

Published by iCrew Digital Publishing

Website: icrewdigitalpublishing.com

e-mail: icrewdigital@gmail.com

ISBN: 978-1-946739-12-4. (iCrew Digital Productions)

iCrew Digital Publishing is an independent publisher of digital works. We support the efforts of authors who wish to self- publish in the digital world.

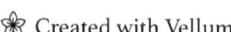 Created with Vellum

This book is dedicated to all the teachers who had the patience and persistence to nurture my appreciation for the diversity and richness of human life and culture.

PROLOGUE

Sleet pounded against the windows, waking Faith. She glanced at the clock. Just past three in the morning. As the December storm intensified, the wind howling, Scott's snoring provided a bass background to the high soprano screech of the tempest outside.

Unable to go back to sleep, Faith got up and slipped on a warm robe, wandering to the picture window overlooking Lake Michigan. She peered through the thick glass, but could not see her beloved lake.

She plopped in the lounger, trying to relax so she could return to bed and get some more rest. Her mind raced ahead to the next morning.

Faith looked forward to another Monday at Canterbury, the bright faces of the children greeting her with smiles. She reminisced, looking back at her long career at Horton Hotels.

Yes, other people considered her "successful," but she had never really been happy at the hotel. Not until she reunited with the twins did she blossom into a mature and satisfied matron.

Helping out at Canterbury, and then making the place her full-time avocation, turned her retirement into a wonderfully fulfilling experience.

Sleet slammed against the picture window. Specks of frozen rain piled up at the corners of the glass, forming an icy coating. She had no fears for safety in her high-rise condo, yet she felt a strange sense of unease.

Faith got out of the lounger, moving to the window, and pressed her face against the cold pane. The lake had always given her signs. In the pitch black night, it remained invisible, yet this unseen and voiceless body of water seemed to send a signal. Not a clear message, just a premonition. Maybe the lake was warning her about the weather. Or some other danger.

A true Chicagoan, she knew that in an instant the windy city could become the icy metropolis, making the roads impassable. She hated the thought of not being able to go to Canterbury. Faith resisted the temptation to check the forecast on her computer.

What would she do if bad roads kept her at home? The kids would be disappointed if she didn't show up for playtime. Sorting through alternative plans, she hit upon an idea that pleased her. That helped her settle down and get back to bed.

She snuggled next to Scott, still asleep and wheezing softly, the spousal lullaby that helped her return to dreamland.

1

I n the morning, still tired from her interrupted sleep, Faith didn't hear Scott get up and dress.

He nudged her. "Hey, hon, come to the kitchen table, we need to talk. I've got a cup of tea for you."

She yawned, and made her way to the kitchen. "What's up?"

"In two words, ice storm. The mayor has asked everyone to stay off the roads. Schools are closed. You won't be able to go to Jeremy's place."

"I was awake in the night. The sleet woke me. I wondered if it would get worse."

"What will you do about Canterbury?"

"Early this morning, half asleep, half awake, I came up with an idea. I can Skype to one of the residents, and have her use a lap link to the big television. This gal, Colette, is the sharpest computer techie there, so I'm sure she can do it. We'll have story time in place of playtime, from a remote location."

"Great idea. Listen, I've got to go to the office. They're probably shorthanded, with some people stranded at home." He gave her a peck on the cheek and left.

The kitchen clock said a quarter past seven, a little early, but

Faith knew Colette and her little tyke Carla usually lined up about that time for breakfast. Faith called Colette on her cell phone. "Hi, it's Faith. Because of the ice storm, I can't come in today, but hope you can help me out." Faith explained the Skype maneuver, and Colette agreed to set up her laptop with a link to the lounge TV.

Still tired from her early morning rude awakening by the sleet storm, Faith figured she could take a leisurely hot bath and still have plenty of time to pick out a few story books for playtime at ten.

Relaxed and refreshed by the hot water in the tub, Faith dressed and then decided to call Jeremy at Canterbury. She let the phone ring until it switched to the message machine. "Jeremy, call me when you get a chance. I won't be in today—you know—ice, but I've set up playtime with Colette, using Skype and the TV."

She made a cup of tea and sat in the lounger. The lake appeared dark and foreboding, with occasional whitecaps. She felt like calling the second line for the academy. After a half dozen rings, a breathless voice said, "Canterbury Academy, Maisie speaking."

"Good morning, Maisie, sorry I couldn't join you for breakfast, but my husband and the mayor laid down the law about driving on ice. Did Jeremy make it in?"

"Uh, no, he didn't."

"I guess the ice must really be bad to keep him away."

"Well, no. Actually, Melanie called and said he didn't feel well."

Faith bolted upright in the recliner. "What's the matter?"

"She didn't say. Hey, I have to go. Maria couldn't come in, we're making do for lunch with all volunteers, and some of these gals don't know a potato peeler from a potholder."

Faith hung up and speed-dialed Jeremy's house. Melanie answered.

"Hi, Mom, I saw your name on caller ID. You probably want to know about Jeremy. This past week he felt tired, and stayed in bed most of the weekend. Today he said he just couldn't make it in to his office."

"Melanie, I know you're a good caregiver, and don't mean to preempt you, but tell me, how is his color?"

"That's one thing that concerned me. He's rather peaked, and no appetite."

"Fever?"

"Low grade."

"In that case—"

"I know where you're heading, Mom, and I asked him if he had any pain. He said he had a deep-down soreness in his back."

Faith sighed. "Well, here's the maternal diagnosis. I think it would be advisable, as soon as the roads clear, to take him to urgent care."

"I thought of that, too. Jeremy objected, telling me it would be stupid to risk an accident for something that probably will get better on its own."

"Melanie, I agreed to do playtime from home at ten, connecting Skype up to the TV. But by eleven or so, I'll call you and we can figure out a plan."

"Thanks Mom, I appreciate your concern."

"I don't want to bother Jeremy. Just tell him to rest and drink plenty of water."

FAITH REVERTED to her hotel vice president take charge mode, booting her computer and preparing her hour of remote playtime. At ten, reading to the children, and showing pictures from the books to them, kept her preoccupied. The kids yelled for another story, but she begged off, promising she would see them soon.

Turning off Skype, she pulled up the local weather forecast. The main roads had cleared up, but side roads still had patchy ice.

Faith dialed Melanie. "How's the patient?"

"Not too good. Fever's a little higher, and he's listless."

"Here's my plan. I stick to the main highways, drive to your house, and watch the kids while you take Jeremy to the nearest ER. Well, it's your call. If you want to stay with the kids, I can drive Jeremy."

"Why don't you babysit. They'll love that, and I can get the care directions from the doctors."

"Uh, maybe I'll pack a few things. You know, just in case. The roads might get bad later."

"Uh-huh, good idea."

Faith called Scott, knowing he'd be busy and she'd get his answering machine. She left a message, explaining the unexpected trip to Oak Park, and told him she'd call as soon as they found out anything about Jeremy. She threw a few changes of clothes, pajamas, and toiletries in an overnight case, and headed for the car.

The roads to Oak Park didn't seem that bad. She restrained herself and drove under the speed limit, even though she wanted to hurry.

Pulling in to Jeremy and Melanie's drive, she saw Beth and Mark perched in the front window, waiting for her. She gave them hugs and kisses, while looking over their shoulders at Melanie's troubled face.

"Mom, you were right. He seems to be getting worse, fever a little higher, and no appetite or energy."

When Faith saw Jeremy, she tried not to show her concern for his pale appearance. "You sure picked a bad day to get sick."

He tried to smile. "Oh . . . I'll be alright, but I can't outvote two strong women."

He put on a robe and overcoat, letting the kids help him with his boots, then shuffled out to the garage with Melanie.

FAITH FELT glad to have the company of the kids to keep her mind off Jeremy. After they had lunch, she called Scott's office. Again, she got the answering machine, and gave him an update.

The children had no idea how sick their father might be, and she didn't discuss it. Distracted, Faith had to scramble for something to help pass the time. She told them to get out the cardboard theater and finger puppets, and play-act "What I want to be when I grow up."

Mark got a little fussy, so Faith had him sit in her lap and watch Beth do a version of her favorite cartoon in the theater. Soon he fell asleep and she just held him, glad to have his warmth next to her.

When he woke up, Faith made hot chocolate with marshmallows. The phone rang, startling Faith so much she spilled some of her hot chocolate. The kids laughed.

Glancing at caller ID, Faith recognized the *Trib*'s number.

"I called as soon as I could. We're shorthanded. I won't make it home until quite late. But hey, give me the news on Jeremy."

"Melanie hasn't called. The roads are slippery, so I imagine ER is crowded with car accident victims, who come ahead of low-grade fever patients."

"How does he look?"

"Terrible. About like his pasty complexion when he had bad kidney function."

"You think that's what it is?"

"I don't know what to think, and hate to predict."

"What are you going—"

"Scott, call coming in. Maybe it's Melanie. I'll phone you soon."

"Hi, Mom, I'll give you this quick, then need to get back to Jeremy and the doctors. You were so right! The preliminary diagnosis is possible kidney infection—maybe nephritis—because of his past condition. They're testing blood and urine, to match an antibiotic for whatever bug he has. And . . . they want to keep him in the hospital for a day or two until he's stabilized. I hate to ask you, but—"

"No worry, I brought a small bag, just in case. You stay by Jeremy's side. No need for you to get on the roads late tonight. Maybe you can catch some naps in a lounger."

"Thanks so much. There's plenty in the fridge for supper."

"Don't worry, we'll make do."

Faith started to call Scott, when Beth interrupted her. "Is Daddy sick?"

"Yes, he is, and he's in good hands with the doctors. They want him to stay in the hospital tonight to make sure he gets well right away."

Beth went back to the cardboard theater, using gloves on both hands to talk to each other about Dad being sick but going to get well.

Faith called Scott and brought him up to date. He joked, "Are you joining the visiting nurse brigade? Well, hang in there. Better to stay off the roads. Hell, I may just crash here on a sofa. Could be freezing rain tonight, and even if I got home okay, might be stuck there tomorrow. Give Beth and Mark a hug from Grandpa."

"Scott, I'm scared."

"Hang in there, babe, we've been through worse."

Faith had the children help with preparing supper. After loading the dish washer, Faith read stories to them. When Mark fell asleep, Faith carried him in to his bed, and then read more stories to Beth, tucking her in a little after nine.

Faith sat right next to the phone, waiting for the call she anticipated. Melanie phoned at half past nine. "He's resting better now. They gave him something to make him sleep. His fever is down slightly, but we won't know if the antibiotic is working until tomorrow."

"That's good to hear. By morning they should have a better diagnosis and plan of treatment. You must be stressed out with all that waiting around. Try to get some rest. The children are in bed. We had a nice day."

"Thanks so much Mom . . . for everything."

Faith turned on the news, but only half watched it. Finally, she switched off the TV and placed a prayer call to Harriet and Mary, asking them to intervene for Jeremy, and to give her strength.

She double checked all the doors, and then climbed into bed in the guest room.

2

Faith tossed and turned, too uptight to fall asleep. When she did doze off, she entered a haze of nightmares. Jeremy appeared in scene after scene, sick, in the hospital, and bedridden at home. Then the setting shifted back to the past struggles with Doug, the devil who would not release medical records. Faith revisited the long negotiations with Doug, and relived the episode when he posed as a flower delivery man at the condo, and she opened the door to a leering Doug. She saw again his eyes getting bigger as his voice echoed in her head.

She woke with a start, looking at the radio clock on the nightstand. Two o'clock. For a moment she didn't know where she was, and automatically reached over to touch Scott. That reminded her she had stayed over at Jeremy and Melanie's. She thought of the children, walking to each of their bedrooms, making sure they were covered.

Returning to the guest bedroom, she got back in bed and finally dozed off.

IN THE MORNING she woke to the sound of soft crying. Beth stood next to the bed, sniffling. "I went to Mommy and Daddy's room, but they're not there. Where are they?"

Faith reached out and held Beth's hand. "Honey, they had to spend the night at the hospital, so that Daddy can get better."

"C'n I get in bed with you?"

"Sure, Beth, let's make this a pajama party."

Faith pulled back the covers so Beth could crawl between the sheets. Grandma was as glad as Beth to have warm body to body contact for physical reassurance. Faith dozed off with her arm around her granddaughter.

When Beth roused, Faith gave her a kiss on the forehead that prompted a smile.

Beth laughed. "I like pajama parties. Let's do it again."

Faith appreciated the humor. "I know what. Now let's have a pancake party. Don't wake up Mark, we'll surprise him."

They went to the kitchen. Faith had Beth mix the batter while she heated a skillet. When they had the first stack of pancakes ready, they got Mark up. Entering the kitchen, he yelled, "Pancakes, yay!"

With breakfast out of the way, Faith had the kids turn on the TV to their favorite morning programs. Then she waited by the phone, knowing Melanie would call after doctors made rounds.

Faith picked up on the first ring. "Good morning, Grandma, how are things on the home front?"

"Fine. Toasted cheese sandwiches for lunch, spaghetti and hot dogs last night, pancakes this morning. Keeping them well fed keeps them happy. They'll want to talk to you, but first give me the latest."

"It'll be a day or two before the antibiotics kick in, but they think they have one that will combat the infection. Fever's down slightly. He did eat a little this morning."

"That's good. You didn't say—I'm guessing they want to keep him for a few days."

"Right. At least until his fever is gone. Maybe two or three days.

Then they say he should have bed rest at home for a few weeks, could be a month."

"I can house-sit and baby-sit for as long as you need me. Gee, do you need to come home for a shower and change of clothes?"

"Let's see how long this hospital stay is. I won't come home today. Maybe tomorrow."

Faith turned the phone over to the kids, who pumped their Mom with all kinds of questions.

WHEN THE KIDS went back to watching television, Faith switched into high gear. Calling Felicia, she asked her to hold while she hooked Agnes into a conference call. "Gals, I only have a few minutes, and will give this to you as quick and straight as I can. This is not about the ice. Jeremy's in the hospital, some kind of infection. It could be a flareup of his old kidney problem. I'm at Jeremy and Melanie's, taking care of the kids.

"I've tried to get my priorities in order. First and foremost is Jeremy's health. I'll stay with the kids as long as they need me, a few days, possibly a week. Second is the smooth functioning of the Foundation. That's important so that Jeremy doesn't worry about it, and doesn't try to come back to work too soon.

"It's essential to keep Canterbury running well, not fall into a slump in its first year, just when we're doing so well.

"Jeremy may have to be in bed for a month, so we need to figure out a division of labor to keep the academy operational. I don't mean to play mother superior, but here are some ideas I came up with to make things work. I have to lay them out quickly before getting back to the kids. You two think this over, and get back to me with your ideas.

"Whatever we do must be cleared by the board. They already named me unpaid Founder and Counselor, so they should approve me as interim head of Canterbury. I can handle all of the decisions and paperwork that would come to Jeremy. Felicia, you've been so

good at finances, it seems logical for you to be in charge of donations, dealing with new donors, and keeping in touch with past
donors. You can oversee the budget. Agnes, we have a good start on
programs for the residents, so it would be good for you to make
sure we maintain the current activities and continue to recruit
volunteers.

"I apologize for this abrupt and bold proposal. Let me say again,
this is just a proposal—to get the ball rolling. When you have time
today, send me an email on how you see the situation and how
you'd like us to handle it. My idea is that as soon as Jeremy gets
home, and I'm freed up to be at the academy, the three of us can put
our heads together and come up with a plan. Well, I need to get
back to the kids. Any quick comments?"

"Felicia here. First things first. Jeremy's health. You're right,
that's our number one priority. After that, we can sort out the issues
of the academy when we get together. Give Jeremy and Melanie our
best wishes."

"Okay, this is Agnes. Jeremy is fortunate to have you as a
backup. I mean, not just for his family, but also for Moms and Kids.
I don't want to take up your time, just put in my 'ditto' to Felicia's
comments."

"Thanks so much, you two, I knew I could count on you. I'll
update you with emails on when Jeremy will come home and when
we can get together as a threesome at the academy."

Faith turned around to see Beth waiting to talk to her. "Tell me
again, when will Daddy and Mommy be home."

"As soon as Daddy gets better. The doctors are doing their best,
and they need the medicine and nurses at the hospital to help him
get well."

Beth's lips curled down in a frown.

"Hey, kids, I know what we can do. Let's make get-well cards for
Daddy. Beth, bring paper and crayons to the kitchen table and we'll
get to work."

They spent more than an hour making their cards. Faith folded
computer paper in half and folded it again to make a blank card.

The children drew flowers on the front, and Faith helped print their get-well messages inside.

Melanie called mid-morning, telling Faith she'd come home that afternoon, eat supper with them, and then return to the hospital in the evening. "I need a shower, and will pack a travel bag with clothes. I don't even have a toothbrush here."

Faith checked the fridge, getting low on essentials. She asked the kids what they wanted for supper. Mark insisted on pancakes. Beth agreed if they could have sausage with it. She had them accompany her to the store to get groceries, and pick out their favorite breakfast cereal.

That afternoon the two young ones left the television to watch out the large window for their mother's car. They hooped and hollered when they saw her drive up, and hugged her as soon as she opened the door. She sat on the couch, Mark and Beth on each side of her. The kids gave Melanie the get-well cards to take to Jeremy.

After Melanie had answered all their questions, Faith rescued her. "Kids, I think Mom wants to take a shower and pack some clothes. You two help me fix supper. Beth, you're good at mixing batter, and Mark, you set the table."

They had a nice meal. Mark piped up, "Mom, Grandma makes the best pancakes!"

Melanie stayed until Mark fell asleep, and then tucked in Beth.

Faith ushered Melanie out the door. "I'd like to talk with you, but it's getting late, and you need to be on your way to the hospital."

Melanie lingered with a long hug. "I don't know what we'd do without you."

Faith felt she deserved some down time with a cup of tea. Then she turned on her laptop and scrolled down to the messages from Felicia and Agnes. They must have talked on the phone, sending similar messages. They encouraged her to take care of the kids and Jeremy, and not to worry about the academy until the three could get together.

Relieved, Faith called Scott. "Hon, do you know this is the first time we've been apart overnight since you made the detective trip to Peoria?"

"Well, I was thinking, this situation takes me back to my bachelor days. Alone, but in much nicer digs. Hey, how's Jeremy?"

"When Melanie was here the kids wouldn't leave her side, so she didn't say anything. I'm sure she'll let me know after the doctor's rounds tomorrow. Scott, everything's fine here. The kids are super. Still, I'm worried about Jeremy."

"Hang in there, babe."

"I miss you at night. This morning I rolled over to snuggle, and when you weren't there, I realized where I was."

"Same here. I miss you, but you're doing what you have to. Before you know it, you'll be back here."

3

Jeremy stayed in the hospital until the weekend. Mid-morning Saturday, Melanie drove him home. He had trouble getting in the door, mobbed by the kids. Beth cried. Mark put his arms around a leg and wouldn't let go.

Faith and Melanie chuckled at this warm greeting.

Faith tried not to stare at Jeremy, noticing his pale face and rather gaunt appearance. She managed a, "Welcome home, Dad."

While the kids sat with Jeremy on the couch, Melanie and Faith went to the kitchen to fix lunch.

Faith placed her hands on Melanie's shoulders, looking into her eyes. "Tell me, is it nephritis?"

Wrinkles spread across Melanie's forehead. "The doctors couldn't give me a simple diagnosis, and I can't provide you with an easy answer. Nephritis comes in many forms and many stages. Basically, it's inflammation of a kidney, and it's serious when it becomes acute or chronic. Untreated, it can become acute or chronic. Hopefully we've caught his infection—a cause of this inflammation—early enough to prevent structural damage to the kidneys. Only time will tell, and that's why rest is important, and some change in diet—like less red meat."

Faith gave Melanie a hug. "I didn't mean to put you on the spot, but Scott's going to want to know. And let me assure you that I'll do everything I can to help you with the kids and with the academy. I won't go into the details now, but Felicia and Agnes and I are going to look after the academy so that Jeremy can take his time getting back in the saddle. Even after he rejoins Moms and Kids, we'll be handling some of the work and stress."

Melanie burst into tears, putting Faith in a tight bear hug. "Thanks so much . . . for the kids . . . for Jeremy . . . for everything."

Beth and Mark ran into the kitchen asking if lunch was ready.

Faith figured the Goodman household needed some family time, so she threw her clothes in her bag and left. Mark yelled after her, "Come back soon and make pancakes."

They all laughed at this culinary farewell.

Driving to the condo, Faith called home.

"Hi, Faith, good news?"

"The good news is that I'm on the road, be there in a half hour or so."

"Have you eaten?"

"No, I left Jeremy and Melanie to have a well-deserved family reunion."

"I had a late breakfast. Should I fix something, or do you want to go out?"

"I'd take a sandwich—anything—and a reservation for my favorite seat overlooking the lake."

Before long she made it home, was in the door and in Scott's arms. He ushered her into her recliner, a sandwich and cup of tea on a tray table.

"Babe, decompress. How was the week with the kids?"

"Wonderful to be with Beth and Mark. Great kids. Pleasant times. Makes me regret all the more that I couldn't share such moments with Jeremy and Jon."

"Precious memories."

"Yes, but . . .."

"But you worried about Jeremy. What can you tell me about his condition?"

"You know about nephritis?"

"I looked it up on several sites, and talked it over with the science editor who covers medical issues. Can be quite serious. You know it's irritation or inflammation of the kidney. Depends on how severe and how long it goes on."

"Right now, they don't know how bad it is. The important thing is for him to rest. I didn't have the opportunity to tell you this, but I've already been planning for Felicia, Agnes, and me to take over some of Jeremy's workload. We'll handle all of it for the month or so when he's at home—bed rest—and I think we need to take over some of his tasks on a permanent basis."

"Smart girl. Let me know how I can help."

"Glad you volunteered. Otherwise I'd shanghai you. My idea is to bring in Jon and Rachel on a regular basis. Jon already chimed in, said the children at the academy need more contact with men. Soon we'll see if we can snag you for some regular time in this family business."

Faith had gobbled down her sandwich. She got up and sat in Scott's lap. "Do you have any dessert?"

"That could be arranged." He led her into the bedroom and they shared a lovely last course to the lunch.

Faith slept for an hour. "I didn't realize how tiring it is to take care of kids."

"Double trouble, what with worrying about Jeremy."

They spent the rest of the weekend catching up with each other, walking the beach, wondering out loud about Jeremy, and running over Faith's plans for the academy.

~

Monday morning, Faith called the second line at Canterbury, figuring she would get Maisie.

"Canterbury Academy, Maisie speaking."

"Hi, Maisie, I'm running late. Could you save me something for breakfast, and if you have time, could we chat while I eat?

"Sure thing. Are you in the car?"

"Right."

"Hang up and pay attention to the road. I'll have something for you."

When Faith walked in the Academy, the children crowded around her. "Miss Faith, we missed you." "Where were you?" "Don't go away again."

"Hey children, it's great to see you. I'll see you at playtime, but Maisie saved some breakfast for me, so I've got to go to the kitchen."

She walked through the dining room to the kitchen, where Maisie had her meal waiting for her on a small work table. "If you want to talk, this is better than the dining room."

"Great. I guess you know it may be a month or so before Jeremy can work. He's my main concern, but I want to keep the academy running smoothly so that he won't worry, and won't have any problems when he comes back. I'll level with you, Maisie. You have your finger on the pulse of this operation more than anyone else. What's the mood here?"

Maisie straightened up in her chair, glanced at the ceiling, then looked right at Faith. "Hmm. No shilly-shallying around. Well, what I hear is that the place has kind of divided into two different camps. You know, when Jeremy was here, we took him for granted. Now, with him gone, some of the residents think the academy may not survive. They wonder what they'll do and where they'll go if the academy folds. Others think this place is here to stay. Colette, the one who used her computer to help you with playtime, said you'd never give up on the kids and moms. And Louann, who Agnes helped with writing—and the other gals she's tutoring—they said to be patient and see if you and Jeremy will work things out."

"I suspected as much. I need to check in with the office soon, but will let you in on something, strictly QT. Felicia, Agnes, and I are going to take up the slack for Jeremy while he's recuperating—maybe a month. And as soon as the three of us can put our heads together and finalize these plans, I'll have a get together in the all-purpose room and let everyone know. Thanks for a super breakfast and a rundown on the rumor mill."

Faith hurried to Jeremy's office, fending off children's questions. "Hey, get ready for playtime. See you then."

Jeremy had hired Jackie Jones as secretary, a super-efficient assistant. Entering the office and shutting the door behind her, Faith asked Jackie, "How bad is it? A ton of mail and a hundred phone calls to return?"

Jackie laughed. "I sorted out mail and messages into three categories: take care of now, look at later, and handle whenever."

"That's very helpful. It looks like you and I will be working together for a month or more. I appreciate that kind of take-charge efficiency. Today I can't let the kids down, have to do playtime. After that, I'll sort through the 'take care of now' mail and calls. After lunch I'll try to whittle down the backlog, writing replies and giving callbacks. Give me the pile of must do mail."

Faith opened and scanned a dozen letters, prioritizing letters from state agencies and prime donors. She lined up these letters on the right side of the desk, so she could answer them in the afternoon.

Jackie interrupted her. "If you don't get to playtime now, the children are going to break down the door."

Faith felt like the pied piper leading her faithful as she proceeded to the dining room. "Who can drive a truck?"

Most of the kids had blank expressions of their faces. Leonard shouted out, "I can drive a truck!"

She led the boys and girls into the large room and had them line up chairs. Leonard grabbed the first chair.

"Okay, kids, driving a truck is serious business. You know, trucks bring us milk, bread, potatoes, and other things to eat. The mail trucks bring us letters. Tanker trucks bring us gasoline for our cars. Semi-trucks have louds horns that they blow. Let's see if you can make that noise. Raise your arm and pull down on that horn. Beeeep, Beeeep!"

The kids gave an anemic beep, and Faith urged them to belt out a louder sound.

"Now, Leonard, tell us what kind of truck you're driving, a little pickup truck, a large tanker truck, or a huge semi-truck. Where are you coming from, what are you hauling, and where are you taking it?"

"Uh, I'm driving a semi. And . . . I come from the country. From a farm. And I got lotsa cows in my truck. And I'm taking them to town, so we can all eat hamburger."

The kids giggled.

"Can you blow your horn? Real loud."

He belted out a BEEEEP! BEEEEP! Faith had the other kids join in.

Then Leonard went to the end of the line of chairs, and another child became the truck driver. The moms gathered around, and had fun prompting their child with suggestions.

After every youngster had a turn at truck driving, they played back the performance on the television. The children and their mothers laughed and hollered so much that Faith turned around, expecting the noise to bring Jeremy out of his office. Then she did a double take, realizing he was at home.

After playtime, Faith had a half hour to plow through more mail, before heading to the lunch line. She looked up Colette, thanking her for helping set up playtime with a lap link on the ice day. They sat together for lunch. Faith wondered, "Where did you pick up your computer skills?"

"I had a basic introduction in high school, and started with programming in junior college, but had to give up school when Carla came along."

Faith talked to Carla, a fair skinned, black haired beauty. Then she told Colette, "Jeremy's twin brother Jonathan will be coming to the academy to tutor, and can help you with programming. You know who Jonathan Rockwell is?"

"No, never met him."

"He's the founder and president of Jontronics."

Colette put her fork down. "Oh, my God."

"Listen, we've got some junior college schedules, and you should think of taking an online programming course. He could help you."

Faith excused herself and went to the office, scanning the rest of the "take care of now" pile, and began answering letters, with the opening line, "Because Jeremy Goodman, the Head of Canterbury Academy is ill and will be out of the office for a while, I am answering some of his mail. I am Faith Armstrong, Jeremy's mother, and with him, co-founder of this project." She highlighted and copied this sentence, and used it in the initial paragraph of a number of letters as she worked through the pile of correspondence.

Later she contacted Felicia and Agnes for a conference call, asking them to come to the academy Tuesday afternoon to brainstorm the handling of Jeremy's absence.

At four o'clock Faith told Jackie, "I'm too frazzled to write another letter. It's better for me to hit the road before I get too tired.

"Young lady, you've worked hard today and should head for home."

Driving to the condo, she felt a mixture of tiredness and satisfaction, like she had experienced after a long day at the hotel with too many meetings.

Faith arrived home a few minutes before Scott.

"Well, Miss Academy Headmistress, how was the first day on the job?"

"Exhilarating and exhausting."

"Too tired to go out?"

"Almost too tired to think about eating."

Scott made some sandwiches while Faith put her feet up in the lounger. "I have a right to be tired. I supervised a fleet of truck drivers today."

She told him about the children at playtime driving trucks.

"You're getting dangerous."

"I'm running out of ideas, and can't wait until you come and play with the little ones."

They talked away the evening sitting in the recliners, discussing Faith's plans for Agnes and Felicia to help her run the academy.

4

Tuesday morning, she was up early and made it to Canterbury for early breakfast. Maisie scolded her. "I would have saved breakfast for you."

"Thanks, but I've got too much work to take care of this morning."

She got in line with Colette and Carla. Faith held her arms out. Carla looked at her mother and then came to Faith. After a quickie breakfast, Faith excused herself and went to the office to take care of the last urgent letters.

Jackie came into the office. "Sorry, know you're overloaded, but you asked for the list of callback numbers, so here they are."

Faith ran down the list of numbers and began making calls, apologizing for the delay in answering, mentioning Jeremy's illness, and responding as well as she could to each query.

At half past eleven, Faith wandered across the lounge, looking for Felicia and Agnes. She found Agnes and Louann sitting next to each other, engaged in a lively conversation.

Agnes looked up. "Hi, Faith, we were talking about Louann's next course, another writing class, or maybe an introductory computer class."

Faith shrugged. "Either one. The important thing is to continue the good work."

Louann beamed. "Look at this red badge on my blouse. Agnes gave it to me for completing my first online course."

"Congratulations."

They passed time until Felicia showed up. Faith apologized. "I'd like to take you out to a nice restaurant, but I think it's best if we eat lunch here and save time for our discussion. While they ate, Faith brought the others up to date on Jeremy's condition, and the nature of nephritis.

Walking into Jeremy's office, Faith announced, "Here we are, the three of us. I know we can make this work, hold the academy together until Jeremy returns. And I'm ready to hear what you think of our future. Oh, yes. I had a talk with Maisie yesterday morning. She tells me the residents' grapevine is spreading rumors about Jeremy's absence and wondering if the academy is going to disappear. Some say yes, others think we'll weather the storm. I'd like to get the board's approval—if you agree—that our threesome can take the place of Jeremy. That would give me the green light to call all the residents together and assure them that Canterbury will stay afloat and continue to provide a safe haven."

Felicia nodded. "Well spoken. Your ideas are right on target. You know Agnes and I are old friends, and talk regularly. So we agreed —but I'll let her put in her two cents—that we're one hundred percent behind your plan, and today we just want to brainstorm on how to move ahead."

Agnes leaned forward in her chair. "Yes, yes, and we think it's good to get the ball rolling, contact the chair of our board, Father Murphy. If he goes along with us, Felicia and I as board members are votes for this move. Surely Bill Ludwig will say yes."

"It's very good to hear strong support from you two. The past week I've been babysitting and on edge about Jeremy's medical condition, which made it difficult for me to think straight about the academy. I appreciate your input. Hmm . . . how about if I call Father Murphy now?"

Agnes and Felicia looked at each other, nodding in silent agreement.

Faith placed the call, but Father Murphy was busy and she asked his secretary to have him phone later.

"Well, gals, maybe the best way to start out is to assess our present situation. I was only away for a week, but want to make sure I'm on the same page with both of you. Agnes, how are the programs going?"

"I tutored last Tuesday and Thursday, helping residents with their online writing courses. I'm glad to continue with tutoring. You know, like with Louann, who was so proud about her red badge. We're doing well with this educational venture, thanks to you and Amelia paving the way. Frankly, what we need is a broader program."

Faith cheered, "Good work! Yes, we need some diversity in the program. Jon and Rachel said they're willing to help us with computer mini-courses. Rachel can give introductory how-to sessions, and Jon can help more advanced students. Yesterday I told Colette if she signed up for an online programming course, Jon would help her."

Agnes smiled. "That's wonderful. Here's an idea I haven't mentioned—offering basic business courses, you know, sales and marketing, like a business administration program. I'd like to see us train residents how to apply and interview for a job. We need to recruit volunteers for such instruction."

Faith breathed a sigh of relief. "That reassures me the academy is poised to move ahead in education and training. Felicia, how are we doing with the financial picture?"

"We're doing well, have enough money now, but believe me, we can't rest on our laurels. You and I need to massage all the past donors to make sure they continue to support us. Let me mention, while you were baby-sitting last week, I came in and looked over all the books. We seem to be in good shape. One thing I wanted to ask you . . . this is a little sudden, what can you tell me about Jim Anderson?"

"You mean how he fits in to the big picture?"

"Uh, yeah, his history."

"He started out handling donations and finances for Jeremy in his One Way religious program, and did a good job, so Jeremy brought him along to Moms and Kids. Is that what you wanted to know?"

"But you didn't have him take on the major fundraising?"

"No. I had a frank talk with Jeremy, told him Jim might be good for paying the bills, but he didn't have the personality or skills to raise major sums. Jeremy agreed."

"What's your quick assessment of Jim?"

"Back in my hometown of Canton, we'd say he' not the sharpest knife in the drawer. He can handle the day to day essentials, but shouldn't take on a major financial drive."

"But he does oversee all purchases, bills, and even some expenditures to residents."

Faith chuckled. "Yeah, that's why you hardly ever see him. He stays in his little office, taking care of daily and monthly invoices."

"He doesn't handle financial transactions with residents."

"No, of course not. You know we never charge residents for anything, so there's no need for him to take money from them."

"But Faith, you do help residents financially, don't you?"

"Only when they transition. When one of our moms is ready to leave and begin independent living, we give them five hundred dollars, what we call 'startup money.' That helps them with the first month's rent and grocery money."

"How is that handled?"

"Well, I never mentioned it to you, but Jeremy and I realized that for these women to go out on their own, they'd need to be financially independent. Jim Anderson helps every resident set up an individual savings account with the bank we use. What little money the gals have from welfare, family, or the father of their child, they deposit it in that savings account. They can't really qualify for a checking account while they're living here, but when they leave and establish a residence, and hopefully have a job, the bank is ready to give them a checking account."

"You and Jeremy really thought this out. And you only give them five hundred in start-up money."

"We'd like to do more, but we figure that's all we can afford, to enable us to help more individuals."

"I saw the name of Brigitte Barton in the books. You helped her?"

"Yes, when she transitioned. Uh, why do you ask about her?"

"I'm just getting a total picture of the money situation. But you don't give her or the other women cash."

"Oh, no. Jim does a transfer from our account directly into their account. You should be able to see that on the bank records."

"You're right. Uh . . . I did see that on some of the monthly statements."

"Wow, Felicia, while I was taking care of grandkids, you really went over the books."

"Well, that's what you asked for."

"With all your questions, you seem to be on to something— what is it?"

"Let's meet again on Thursday, after I've had more time to look at the records."

They said farewells in a three-way bearhug.

FAITH REENTERED JEREMY'S OFFICE, taking a seat in the chair behind his desk. Thoughts rambled through her brain.

A good meeting. Three strong women will move Canterbury forward.

But Felicia's persistent questioning about Jim Anderson and finances made me wonder what Felicia had in mind.

A phone call interrupted her reverie.

"Father Murphy here. Sorry I couldn't talk to you earlier. And right away, let me say how sorry I am to hear that Jeremy is laid up. Any news there?"

"Thank you, he seems to be doing better, is home now."

Faith summed up her proposal for her threesome to oversee the academy until Jeremy could return. He accepted the idea, and offered to run it by Bill Ludwig, just to make it official. That pleased Faith, yet her mind got stuck on Felicia's questions. These queries stayed with her on the way home, and she mentioned her puzzlement to Scott, who joked, "Hey, look at the bright side. The Canterbury troika had a great meeting, and the three of you are set to move Canterbury forward."

5

The following day Faith had an early breakfast at the academy, schmoozed with residents, and took care of correspondence and phone calls. She had asked Julia Kaminski and the new social worker, Donna Smyth, to stop by her office. Julia offered a brief report: several residents had plateaued and neared transition, so she recommended looking over the list of applicants for newcomers. Donna gave an update on her interviews, most doing well. Julia admitted they had fallen a little behind with contacting transitioned women.

"Julia, how is Brigitte Barton doing?"

"Seems to be doing well. Has a job in a department store, and hopes to move up the ladder."

"She was in our first group at the old hotel. I remember interviewing her. Jeremy and I had reservations about her, because she came in with a juvie record. I felt reluctant to admit her, but Jeremy thought we should take a chance with her."

He reminded me, "Mom, these young women have gone through a lot—abuse, broken homes—and worse. The only way they can go is up."

"I'm glad he persuaded me to accept her, because it looks like she's doing well."

"You can talk to Brigitte yourself. She's coming by Monday, has a day off, and her little girl misses the excitement of the other children."

"Good. I'd like to speak with her."

MID-MORNING, Father Murphy phoned, assuring Faith that he had called Bill Ludwig, and he agreed to Faith's plan. "Bill has a high regard for your executive abilities."

Faith wasted no time setting up a conference call with Felicia and Agnes, asking them to come in before eleven on Thursday, so she could arrange a meeting with residents after playtime. Faith wanted all three of them to be present and say a few words to the women, letting them know the academy would fare well while Jeremy recuperated.

Felicia mentioned, "I'll come in early Thursday morning so I can review some more records and be ready for a more complete financial accounting in the afternoon."

"Good. I'd like to have a clear picture of our financial standing so that we can focus on educational programs."

Faith had Jackie post notices for a special meeting in the all-purpose room at eleven on Thursday.

FAITH FELT satisfied that the troika, as Scott had named them, seemed to click and work well together. She joined the lunch line and sat with some residents she didn't know too well. After lunch Faith returned to the office, wrote a few letters and made some calls. She felt so tired, she wished she was back in her carpeted hotel office and could take a horizontal break. She decided to go home early and beat the rush. It was tempting to stop by to see

Jeremy, but maybe she'd do that Friday. She had pangs of guilt for neglecting Scott.

She got home early enough to retreat to her recliner, cover up with an afghan, and take a good nap. She felt refreshed when Scott came home, and they went out for a German meal at Berghoff's. The rest of the evening they lazed in the recliner, snuggling and chatting. Faith got so comfortable she fell asleep leaning on his shoulder. He woke her and they went to bed.

GETTING a good night's sleep gave Faith the energy to go to the academy early for breakfast. Felicia surprised her by joining her in line. They split up after filling their plates, so they could talk with residents. Felicia ate quickly and hurried to Jim Anderson's office to check records. He had the day off for one of his children's school events.

Faith checked in with Jackie, who had no urgent tasks for her, so Faith spent time getting acquainted with some new faces, and waiting for playtime. She felt relaxed knowing someone else was in charge that day.

Agnes finished an early tutorial, then joined Faith during play-time. A little before eleven, Felicia still had not shown up. Faith asked Jackie to find Felicia and have her come to the all-purpose room for the special meeting.

Felicia hurried into the room to join Felicia and Agnes. Faith opened the meeting.

"Greetings to all you moms and kids! It's always good to see you. Today I wanted to call a special meeting to give you some information and let you ask questions. The main reason for this get-together is to let you know about Jeremy. You probably heard most of this, but let me repeat it if you haven't heard it.

"Jeremy has a kidney infection that put him in the hospital for about a week. He's better now, at home, but will need at least a few weeks, possibly a month or more before he can come back to the academy. While he's away, the board of Canterbury Academy for Moms and Kids has named me interim head. I'll oversee the activities of the academy. The board appointed Felicia interim director of finances. She'll make sure the academy has the money needed to continue operations. The board asked Agnes to be interim head of programs. Some of you know her for her tutoring. Her job is to keep up those activities while she explores a more diversified educational plan. She'll tell you about that. Now let's hear from Felicia."

Felicia joked, "They named me interim director of finances, but they might just as well have called me Miss Moneybags. We're all fortunate to have such a wonderful facility for Moms and Kids. What you must know is that it takes a lot of money to keep the place going. I can assure you that our financial picture is very good now. And we are constantly looking for new donors and supporters. We'll keep the academy going while Jeremy is away."

Faith announced, "Next we'll hear a few words from Agnes."

"I know most of you, have had the great experience of tutoring some of you, and look forward to working with more of you in the future. The tutoring and writing program has gone so well that we want to expand it to computer instruction, some practical business mini-courses, and how-to sessions on applying and interviewing for jobs. Soon I'll be posting sheets to see who is interested in these possibilities, and then we're going to recruit volunteers, people from the area with experience in these fields. All of these programs are part of Moms and Kids, free to everyone here."

Faith spoke again. "The three of us will run the academy until Jeremy gets back. Now it's time for questions."

The residents seemed satisfied with the meeting. A few asked about the timing of the new programs. Agnes said she'd get the new instructional sessions up and running as soon as possible. Faith encouraged them to do what Amelia and some others had done—take online courses.

Faith promised to provide occasional updates on Jeremy's condition.

That ended the meeting, and everyone hurried to get in line for lunch. The troika split at lunch, and continued informal discussions while eating.

AFTER LUNCH, Faith ushered Felicia and Agnes into the office.

"Gals, that was a great meeting. If I read faces accurately, we set everyone at ease."

Agnes piped up, "It was a smart idea to have a formal meeting and clear the air."

Faith looked toward Felicia. "Well, during the meeting, Agnes practically gave an update of the future of the program, so we don't need to hear that again."

"Felicia, you've been poring over the books very carefully. That's something Jeremy and I haven't done, so I'm interested to know what you found out."

Felicia blinked, cleared her throat, then spoke slowly and firmly. "Ladies, we have a problem. A serious problem. One we have to deal with right away."

Faith, wide-eyed, blurted out, "A problem? But you said our finances are rock-solid."

"Yes. The problem is not finances as such. It's a person."

Faith demanded, "Who?"

"Jim Anderson."

6

M outh agape, Faith gasped for air. Exhaling, she cried out, "Jim! Not Jim!"

Felicia stared at her. "Yes. Jim. A problem."

"Not a financial problem."

"Yes. A financial problem. A major financial problem."

Faith held her hands over her eyes. "I . . . I've known him for such a long time."

"You've known him longer than I have, but I examined the books, so I know him better than you do."

"Well, out with it. What did you find?"

"I started comparing receipts and checks from six months ago. I noticed a discrepancy in the monthly payment for the meat supplier, a check for a hundred dollars over the receipt. I figured that could be a typo, but then I checked this meat supplier's receipts for the next five months, and it's the same story, he 'kited' the monthly check for a hundred dollars more than billed."

Agnes frowned. "So he paid the meat man too much. How did that benefit Jim?"

Felicia turned toward Agnes. "My best guess is that it's a classic kickback scheme. Either Jim had something over the meat supplier, or threatened to use a different supplier, or split the hundred with him."

Faith began to hyperventilate, frightening Felicia. "Are you okay?"

Faith nodded. "I'm alright. It's just such a shock. I don't know what to think. Or do."

"Honey, if that set you back, you haven't heard the kicker. I scanned some large ticket items, including the five-hundred-dollar start-up transfers for transitioning residents. I ran into an anomaly —Brigitte received six hundred."

"No!"

"Yes, and you say you and Jeremy never authorized more than five hundred for start-up money?"

"No. Never. I don't know about buying meat, but I'm sure about the five-hundred-dollar limit for helping residents in transition."

"Faith, I'm sorry to dump this on you, but it's a real problem, and has to be taken care of."

"Yes, sooner or later we'll have to deal with this."

Felicia clamped her jaw and bit her lip. "Sooner, not later."

"Can't this wait until after Jeremy comes back?"

"Definitely not. We don't know how this will play out, but I hear that recently you've been through some courtroom scenes. If a judge called you to the stand, first the judge would ask when you found out about this, and if you had waited a month or so to do anything about it, the next question would be why you didn't do something right away. If you don't take care of a problem promptly, you become part of the problem."

"All this has my head spinning. What do you think we should do?"

"Let me be clear about how serious this is. Canterbury Moms and Kids is a young project that is thriving, with a bright future. One scandal like this could dry up donations and scare away support. So, two things. One, the 'kiting'—call it what you want —'padding'—has to stop. Two, we need to handle this carefully, quietly, with no damage to the academy."

"How do we do that?"

"The most important thing now is to keep the lid on. That means not talking to anyone about it, not even spouses."

Faith frowned. "Ouch."

The next step, I think, is to bring in Bill Ludwig. Can you handle that, Faith? You know him."

"He's very good, and if there's a way to do this legally and quietly, he'll know how."

"Good. I suggest we close the meeting and let Faith contact Ludwig. And until we have a solution in place, not a word to Jim Anderson. Or to Brigitte Barton. Or the meat man."

Faith mumbled, "Okay . . . I guess . . .."

Felicia got up and walked across the room to Faith, giving her a hug. "Sorry to have to tell you this, but we have to face it. Frankly, the future of the academy depends on it. Some accountant or auditor eventually would come up with this. And one thing we haven't talked about, but for the sake of Jeremy's health, we don't want the threat of a major scandal stressing him out."

Faith closed her eyes, tears trickling down her cheeks. "No. No. You're right. We can't leave this mess for Jeremy."

The ladies did a triple hug and parted company.

Faith picked up the phone and dialed Bill's office, knowing she'd get a secretary. "This is Faith Armstrong, a client of Bill Ludwig. I have an urgent problem related to the Canterbury Academy. I'd appreciate a callback at his earliest convenience. Oh, yes, I'm at the academy now."

She waited in the office until four thirty, stewing and fretting. She couldn't stand the fact that Felicia said even spouses couldn't know about the scandal. She picked up her jacket and started to leave when Bill called.

"First things first. How's Jeremy?"

"He's doing better, thank you. Slowly but surely."

"Now what's so urgent at the academy?"

"While Jeremy's away, Felicia took over finances, and has definite proof that our financial officer has been stealing money. I guess it's called 'skimming,' paying our meat vendor a hundred dollars a month over the invoices for the past six months. And we're not sure how to handle the situation carefully, so as not to stain the academy with a scandal and that would ruin our donation stream."

"You people are in a mell of a hess, and it won't be easy to take care of this. Tell you what, I'm extra busy tomorrow, but if you three ladies—you're in this together, aren't you?"

"Yes."

"If you can come to my office tomorrow at 4:30, we can explore the best way to handle this."

"Thanks so much, Bill."

"Better wait to see what we can do before you thank me."

Faith left messages for Felicia and Agnes, saying she hoped they could make the appointment.

7

A little after four Friday afternoon the Canterbury troika sat in Bill Ludwig's outer office. A half hour later as he ushered a client out of his office, he glanced at the women. "I'll be with you ladies in a minute."

He reappeared with a thirtyish man in tow. "This is Brad Ashford, who'll be sitting in with us. Meet Faith, Felicia, and Agnes."

They stepped into Bill's office, Brad taking a seat next to Bill.

"Ladies, it's always nice to see you, at the academy or here in the office. I'd like to be more sociable, but my first obligation is to present some legal niceties. I have to put it into the record that Faith, a long-time client of mine, asked me to help her with a concern she has at Canterbury Academy. She is my client, I am her attorney. We may discuss various matters, such as Canterbury Academy, but I do not represent the academy. If the academy chooses to seek legal representation, they will need to find another lawyer. As a board member of the academy, it would be a conflict of interest for me to serve as its legal representative."

Listening to Bill, the three women nodded.

Bill continued. "If, after we discuss the situation at Canterbury

Academy, you three women wish to draw up any legal papers, Brad is here to provide assistance. He is familiar with criminal law and what is usually called 'white collar crime.' Brad, let's hear from you."

"Thank you, Bill, and thanks to you three for trusting our firm to help you resolve a troublesome issue. Bill has given me a brief overview of your concern, but I need to hear you describe the situation that brings you to us."

Bill had taken his Mont Blanc pen out of his shirt pocket, writing notes on a legal pad. He suggested, "Faith, why don't you tell us what you mentioned to me, and then Felicia and Agnes can add their comments."

Faith hesitated, frowning. "We come here reluctantly, forced by circumstances beyond our control. Because my son, Jeremy Goodman, head of Canterbury Academy, became ill and unable to run the institution, the board named the three of us to temporarily take over the day to day operations. The board appointed Felicia to oversee finances. When she began to check the financial records, she discovered serious discrepancies between invoices and payments, and brought these to our attention. It's best to let Felicia sum up these irregularities."

Felicia, staring at a spot on the opposite wall, shifted her gaze to Bill and Brad. "As Faith just mentioned, we come here reluctantly, but out of a sense of duty to protect and preserve the valuable work of the academy. When Faith asked me to review the financial picture of the institution, I had no reason to suspect something amiss. To my surprise, I found a major inconsistency, a monthly check for meat products that was a hundred dollars more than the invoice. I thought this might be a clerical error. I then checked the next five months of payments to this meat supplier, and found exactly the same discrepancy.

"This raises serious questions that I cannot answer. Who benefited from these hundred-dollar overpayments? Did Jim Anderson, the financial officer who wrote the checks, benefit from the overpayments?"

Brad sputtered, "Uh, Felicia, you double checked these figures?"

"Yes. I triple checked them."

Bill raised his eyebrows. "And you have record of these inconsistencies."

"Yes."

Bill continued, "And you can provide us with these records?"

"Yes."

"Well, please provide these records as soon as you can."

Felicia picked up her large purse. "I have them right here. She pulled out an accordion folder with a sheaf of papers. "The first sheet is a log of six months of meat supplier invoices, with the check numbers, the amounts of the checks, and dates that match each invoice. The extra papers are copies of the invoices."

Brad grabbed the papers, and quickly riffed through them. "Wow, you have the goods."

Bill smiled. "Felicia, I've occasionally tried to get Faith to join our investigation team. Maybe when this episode is over, you'd like to consider joining us. Where in the world did you learn to do this work?"

"My dad was a prosecuting attorney. Sometimes he brought work home, and I helped him order his documents. When he handled a case in court, I enjoyed watching him present his evidence to the judge and jury."

"Very impressive. Jim Anderson apparently stiffed the academy for $600. That's not petty larceny. Hmm, anything more?"

Felicia added, "Well, we found one overpayment to a former resident who was supposed to receive five hundred dollars for 'transitioning' to independent living but received a check for six hundred."

Brad held his chin in his hand. "Have you confronted Jim Anderson or this resident?"

Felicia shook her head. "No, we wanted to discuss this with your office first. Frankly, we're not so worried about the amount of money as we are concerned that a scandal would ruin our reputation and dry up donations."

Bill chuckled. "You women are as smart as a trio of mother superiors. Being a board member, I know you have a multi-million-dollar endowment, and sizeable annual donations. So, six or seven hundred dollars is chump change. Yeah, and Jim Anderson is the chump. I think I see where you're going with this, but I'd like to hear it from Faith. What do you want us to do?"

Faith looked back and forth at Felicia and Agnes. "We don't have a clear plan. We're not out to *get* Jim Anderson, have him arrested and go to jail. That would be counter-productive to our main goal of protecting the reputation of the academy. Well, it would be nice to get the money back, to balance the books. What's more important, we want to keep this quiet. We don't know how to do this, which is why we came to you before we talked to Jim Anderson."

Brad smiled at Bill. "I wish all our clients were as savvy as these ladies."

Bill chuckled. "Okay, the day's getting late, and Brad and I need to get home. I have a quick and dirty solution, but first I need to hear more about the perp we're dealing with. Usually guys steal from work for one or all of three things—drinking, women, and gambling. Faith, give me a thumbnail sketch of Jim's weakness."

"Sorry to disappoint you, none of the above. He's pretty squeaky clean. If I had to guess the reason behind his larceny, it's his move to Chicago. I overheard him talking about his situation. In Springfield he had a small house with very little equity, and when he came to Chicago, couldn't muster up the down payment for a decent house, so he's stuck in a so-so apartment. He and his wife are unhappy in a rental situation, and would like to have a nice house."

Bill told Faith, "The offer for a job in our investigation unit still stands. Excellent cameo of Jim. And I can expand upon your picture. I bet Jim has squirreled away all of his pilfered money in a savings account, his "down payment account." That would make it easier for us, because he could cough up the money. Now, here's the quick and dirty. In a few days Brad can write up a paper where Jim

admits he took money from the academy, and he agrees to reimburse all that he took. In exchange, the academy agrees not to file
charges. Hey, that way, it all stays out of the papers. Brad's draft of
the statement can be emailed to you Monday. We'll send it to your
private email account, Faith, because we don't want it to float
around the academy. You three can review it, and then we'll have to
decide when to confront Jim Anderson. How's that?"

Faith gushed, "Oh, Bill, I think that's just what we were looking
for. Well, I'm speaking for myself. What about it, Felicia and
Agnes?"

Felicia laughed. "My dad always said a plea bargain often is the
best bargain."

Bill picked up his Mont Blanc pen and put it in his shirt pocket,
ending the meeting. "Now let's get the hell out of the loop."

Faith turned to the women. "Why don't you wait out the rush
hour with me while we eat dinner?"

Felicia and Agnes agreed to this plan.

8

A s the three women left Bill's law office and got in an
elevator, Felicia suggested, "Some place close, not a fancy
restaurant with a long wait."

Agnes mumbled, "Uh-huh, I need to get home, too."

Faith chuckled. "I know a corner café not far from here. Years
ago, when I started working at Horton Hotels and had little money,
sometimes I stayed in the loop for a musical event or lecture, and
got a light meal at this place."

In a few minutes they were sitting in a booth in The Loop Café.
Each of them called home to tell their husbands they'd be late.

Faith ordered a bowl of chili and a large dill pickle.

Agnes joked, "Hey, girl, are you PG, or what?"

"I've been under high stress for several weeks, and this is my
decompression splurge."

Felicia and Agnes got sandwiches. While eating they rehashed
the meeting with Bill.

Felicia teased Faith. "The way you pick good lawyers, now I
know why you were an executive vice president."

Agnes added, "I've never been in a meeting with a lawyer who
was so quick and decisive. He cut right through the sh... stuff and

got right to the point. Protected himself with the upfront legal mumbo jumbo, while also watching out for our best interests."

Faith smiled. "We've been through a lot together. Well, we don't have much time, so let me bring up something we didn't settle with Bill. We didn't discuss Brigitte. The other day I was talking with Julia Kaminski—you know, our social worker—and asked her how Brigitte is doing. Julia said Brigitte's got a good job in a department store and has a chance of moving up. And in fact, she has Monday off and her little girl misses the academy, so she'll be bringing her by for a visit. I told Julia to have Brigitte stop by my office. That was before I knew about the meeting with Bill. Now I can't back out of meeting Brigitte, because it would look fishy. Here's what I have in mind, let me know what you think. I'll just play it cool, ask her how her transition is going, what her plans are, her possibilities for moving up in her store. I won't say anything about Jim Anderson or the overpayment to her."

"Way to go," Felicia said.

"Yeah," Agnes agreed.

They finished their meal and went their separate ways.

WHEN FAITH WALKED into the condo, Scott called out from the kitchen, "How much does Canterbury pay you for overtime?"

"Sorry, dear, but we had to run some academy business by Bill Ludwig, and I invited the gals to eat a meal with me while they waited for the traffic to ease up."

"That's okay. I had a sandwich and a beer."

Faith settled in the lounger and half watched news.

Scott turned to her. "Hey, honey, you've been quiet, kind of moody. Still bummed out because of Jeremy?"

"That threw me into a tailspin. Hey, why don't we plan to visit them for lunch Sunday, maybe bring in pizza?"

"Sounds good to me. I can take the kids out and you can have some quality time with Jeremy and Melanie."

Faith called Melanie and set up Sunday for lunch.

Melanie gave her the name of their favorite pizza place, which had nice vegetarian selections. "We're still avoiding red meat."

Faith chuckled. "We should probably cut back on meat, too."

SATURDAY MORNING SCOTT left early for the newspaper. Faith made a cup of tea and retrieved her journal, taking it to her lounger. She sipped the tea for a few minutes before opening the booklet and writing.

TROUBLE.

What's the worse trouble—shenanigans at Canterbury, or keeping the news from Scott?

Scott knows something's wrong, but thinks it's worry about Jeremy.

Canterbury is a double problem.

I still can't believe Jim Anderson is a thief.

Bill Ludwig may help us quietly take care of Jim if the money is returned. I expect he'll have to leave Canterbury and find another job.

We would never be able to trust him again.

Brigitte—the other problem. I think Jim manipulated her, because of her juvie record. We have to salvage Brigitte, can't let Jim's mistake be her mistake.

MORE TROUBLE!

Jeremy is always on my mind.

Saint Harriet and Mary, help us through these difficulties.

FAITH COULDN'T WAIT for Scott to get home. She booted her computer and looked up information on nephritis, mostly a repeat of what she already knew about kidney infections.

She went to the picture window to view a dreary, cloudy day.

Late morning, Scott came home and started to take off his raincoat.

Faith grabbed him by the lapels. "Why don't we take a walk along the beach?"

"Are you kidding? It's cold and starting to drizzle."

"I need a lake fix. A walk on the beach will recharge my batteries."

She got her raincoat and they took the elevator to the front entrance. The doorman asked, "You want a taxi?"

Scott waved him away. "Not unless you find one that takes us along the beach."

They returned after a half hour, and Faith heated them bowls of steaming soup.

LATE SUNDAY MORNING they ordered veggie pizza from Jeremy and Rachel's favorite pizza joint, and drove out to Oak Park to pick it up.

Beth and Mark greeted Faith and Scott at the door, yelling, "Yay, pizza!"

Faith looked closely at the parents, noticing the stress on Melanie's face and Jeremy's general fatigue. After a quick lunch, Scott loaded the kids in the car to take them to a fast-food restaurant that had an indoor playground.

Melanie joked, "Scott's always in tune with the kids. They've had cabin fever being cooped up in the house. They needed to run and work off some energy."

"What about you two?" Faith asked.

Jeremy tried to smile. "We're hanging in there. Tell me about the academy."

"We have what Scott calls the Canterbury troika. The board approved me as interim head, and named Felicia interim financial director, and Agnes interim program director. How does it feel to be so indispensable that it takes three people to replace you?"

Jeremy laughed. "I bet it's better run with three capable people."

They chatted about the academy until Scott came back with the kids. He had taken video footage of them clambering up, over, and through all of the equipment, and they wanted to see the playback on the television. While the guys viewed the video, Melanie and Faith went to the kitchen to fix hot chocolate.

"Melanie, tell me, how is Jeremy doing?"

"All I can say is it's a slow process, and will take more time. At least a month. I'm glad Canterbury is in good hands, because he needs a break from any kind of stress."

Faith hugged Melanie. "Felicia and Agnes will help me keep Canterbury running smoothly, so that Jeremy can get well."

After hot chocolate, Faith told Scott, "We should go now and let Jeremy rest."

On the drive back to the condo, Scott put his hand on Faith's. "Hang in there, babe, we'll make it through this dark valley."

"Dear, I need your support now more than ever."

9

Scott's videotaping of the kids in the fast-food playroom gave Faith an idea. Monday she took the video camera to Canterbury and had everyone—kids, residents, and staff—give brief get-well messages for Jeremy. The next time she went to Jeremy and Rachel's, she'd play it for the family.

Faith sat at Jeremy's desk, conflicting emotions clogging her brain. The anticipation of receiving Brad Ashford's legal paper about Jim Anderson excited her. On the other hand, the meeting with Brigitte Barton filled her with dread.

She had checked her personal email several times, and finally Brad's draft appeared. She speed-read his introductory paragraphs and jumped to the legal document:

I, James Anderson, of sound mind and of my own free will, make the following statement. As the financial officer for Canterbury Moms and Kids Academy, I misappropriated at least $700.00 of academy funds. I will reimburse the academy for this $700.00 (and any additional funds that may be discovered to have been misappropriated). The academy has two months to discover any such losses.

The academy, having been reimbursed for all misappropriated funds, will not file charges against me.

Signed,
James Anderson Date
Faith Armstrong, Interim Director, Canterbury Moms and Kids
Academy

FAITH BREATHED A SIGH OF RELIEF. No threats. No recriminations. No name-calling. And if Jim signed the paper and returned the money, no scandal would stain Canterbury's reputation.

Faith forwarded Brad's email to Agnes and Felicia, asking for their comments.

Jackie stuck her head in the office, saying Brigitte Barton asked to see Faith.

"Show her in."

Brigitte walked in. "While my daughter is in playtime I wanted to drop by. Julia said you'd like to see me."

"Yes, I understand from Julia that you've made a smooth transition, and that you have a good job in a department store."

"Well, it's a beginning, and with any luck I can move up the ladder."

"It's young women like you who do well that make us happy. We at the academy are glad to help you get a good start."

Brigitte had been relaxed, but when Faith mentioned the academy helping her get a good start, Brigitte looked down at the floor, and squirmed in her chair. "Yes, without the academy, I don't know where I'd be today. Well . . . and my daughter, too."

"It's good to see you Brigitte. Go watch your daughter in playtime. And come back to see us again sometime."

They shook hands and Brigitte left.

Faith thought back to her days in hotel work. Sometimes body language is louder than spoken words. Faith saw the unspoken guilt in Brigitte's uneasy squirming. One thing they would have to clear up with Jim Anderson was the unaccounted for extra hundred dollars transferred to Brigitte's account.

As Faith expected, Agnes and Felicia had been watching their email, and promptly replied with their hearty approval of Brad's draft. Faith sent them a response that she would ask Bill when he and Brad could come to Canterbury to confront Jim.

After four o'clock, Bill called. "So you liked Brad's statement."

"Succinct, firm, diplomatic. Yes, all three of us loved it."

"I'll cut to the chase. I think we should go ahead with this as soon as possible. We have the evidence, so we should move forward with it. I think Brad and I should come to your office to meet with you three ladies. We're free Thursday afternoon. Can you ask Anderson to meet with you and other board members, say two o'clock. Don't give away our position. Just tell him while Jeremy's recovering, you need a better picture of academy finances."

"Okay. One other thing, Bill. I talked to the transitioned resident, Brigitte, without saying anything about the extra hundred dollars. She acted nervous. My hunch is that Jim used her juvie record as blackmail, told her if she didn't go along with the overpayment, he'd tell her employer about her past."

"I don't doubt that you're right. When we talk to Jim, we'll get around to that. Mind you, we won't mention Brigitte upfront, just ask him if there are any other hundred-dollar overpayments we don't know about."

"Right. Well, I'll call Agnes and Felicia to lock in Thursday afternoon. If there are any problems, I'll email you."

"My dear, I'm beginning to enjoy this caper. It pleases me to see dirty scoundrels get their just desserts."

Faith called Agnes and Felicia, who both agreed to the Thursday meeting.

WHEN FAITH RETURNED to the condo, somehow she restrained herself and did not divulge any of the Canterbury machinations to Scott. Several times he asked her, "How ya doin'?" He seemed to blame her moodiness on Jeremy's condition, and she didn't correct him. Because she did worry about her sick son.

Faith felt glad she had Scott's support, and the day to day tasks at the academy to keep her busy until the crunch meeting with Jim.

~

THURSDAY MORNING, she was surprised when Jim Anderson dropped in to see her. "Uh, Faith, is there any reason we have to meet this afternoon? What's this about?"

"Jim, I've already got three board members scheduled to come, so we need to have this meeting. To discuss the financial situation of the academy."

"Okay, if you insist. I hope you make it brief so I can get back to my paperwork."

"Yes, we'll make it as short as we can."

Bill and Brad had suggested that the meeting start with Felicia mentioning the discrepancies she had discovered, and ask him to explain them. Depending on what he said, Brad and Bill would ask specific questions, hopefully leading the way to an admission of guilt and signing of the legal document admitting misappropriation of funds.

Thursday afternoon Jackie and Faith had brought in extra chairs to Jeremy's office. Faith sat behind the desk, Agnes and Felicia sat in front of the desk to one side, Bill and Brad occupied chairs on the other side. Directly opposite from Faith, they reserved a chair for Jim. When he entered the room, he looked around, and blanched.

Faith, fiddling with her pen, said pleasantly, "Take a seat, Jim, we waited for you before starting the meeting."

10

F aith looked directly at Jim. "Oh, you know everybody here but Brad Ashford, a colleague at Bill's firm. He'll be sitting in with us today."

Jim turned and grunted, "Uh, yeah."

Faith announced, "For the benefit of Jim and Brad, let me say a few words about the state of the academy and why we're meeting today. Our head, Jeremy, is still recuperating, so Agnes, Felicia, and I are helping hold the place together until Jeremy returns. I'm overseeing the institution, and held a general meeting for all the residents to assure them that Canterbury is in good shape and will continue to operate as normal while Jeremy is away. Agnes is supervising the programs, like tutoring, and has plans to expand the educational and training activities. Felicia is in charge of the endowment and major donations and finances in general. She says our endowment is looking good, and we will continue to look for new donors.

"We need to know about the daily and monthly transactions, how the academy is doing paying its bills. That's why we asked you to come, Jim, to give us a report on how we stand with expenses and payments."

Jim had been twisting and turning in his seat. "Uh, gee, I wish you would have told me beforehand, and I could have brought a spread sheet and shown that we stay on top of all expenses."

Felicia leaned forward in her chair. "Why don't you tell us how you receive and pay bills."

Jim shrugged. "Nothing to tell. The bills come in, I pay them right away."

Felicia nodded. "Some bills, like for deliveries, are handed over in person, some arrive in the mail."

"Yeah, like that."

Felicia continued, "And usually you pay them by check."

"Yeah, that's right."

During this exchange, Bill and Brad sat back in their chairs, just taking in the conversation.

Agnes asked, "So all bills are paid?"

"Sure. By the end of every week, all incoming bills are taken care of."

Felicia nodded. "Do you go back over bills to make sure of the amounts?"

Jim frowned. "Carpenters measure twice and saw once. I check twice and pay once!"

Felicia chuckled. "That helps us avoid mistakes. Most of us still have erasers on our pencils in case we make mistakes."

"I prefer not to make mistakes."

"Yes, it's better not to make mistakes, so you don't have to correct them. I was looking through the records a few days ago, while you were out of the office, and came across something I'd like to ask you about. It's an invoice from Otto's Wholesale Meats, from six months ago, August 30. It's for $435.16. I looked at the checkbook, and found a September 2 check in the amount of $535.16 which seems to pay for that invoice. Is that right?"

"Well, I'd have to double check and make sure."

At the mention of Otto's Wholesale Meats, Bill and Brad turned their heads toward Jim and paid close attention.

Felicia continued, "If the meat company received an overpayment of a hundred dollars, they surely would have repaid it, right?"

"Uh, if it was an overpayment, yes. I'll have to look at that."

"I happened to make a copy of the invoice if you need to see it."

"I can do that back in my office."

Felicia pulled a sheaf of papers from her oversized bag. "Well, I can save you the trouble of going back to your office. I have the invoices for this meat company for the next five months and the corresponding checks are all written for a hundred dollars over invoice. The dollar amounts are both in numbers and spelled out. That seems to be something deliberate, not a mistake."

Jim had a wild-eyed look, and began breathing rapidly. His voice broke as he mumbled, "Like I said, I'll have to look over those figures."

Jim's squeaky words got overpowered by Bill's baritone phrases. "Jim, you're an accountant, and you just said you doublecheck all payments. Six straight months of hundred-dollar overpayments don't need a second look. They call for an explanation."

Brad chimed in. "Once, a mistake. Twice, a circumstance. Three times or more, a pattern."

Jim started to open his mouth, but didn't say anything. He gasped for breath.

Faith broke the awkward silence. "Jim, you are our financial officer. We expect you to explain these discrepancies. Here and now."

Jim glared at her. Voice trembling, he muttered, "That's not fair. You didn't tell me . . . that I'd have to go back six months and remember every invoice . . .."

Felicia shook her head. "No, we're not asking you to remember every single invoice. We're only asking you to explain why you overpaid a hundred dollars to the same vendor six months in a row."

Beads of sweat dotted Jim's forehead. He cleared his throat. "Well, tell you what, I'll go back to my office . . . like I said, and look over the books, and come back tomorrow with an answer."

Bill spoke slowly and firmly. "Jim, we all know the answer is not in your office. All you need to do is look at yourself and say what you did these last six months."

"It . . . it's not that simple."

Brad added, "Make it easy on yourself. You're not proud of what you did. Tell us what you did. Get it off your chest."

As tears trickled down Jim's cheeks, Bill encouraged him. "Take your time, think about it, and then tell us what you did."

Jim shut his eyes, brushing his sleeve across his face. "You don't know how hard it was for us to move from Springfield to Chicago. My wife and I, the kids, too, were excited to move to the big city. We didn't get a good price for our house in Springfield, only netted about twenty-five thousand from it. When we came house hunting here in the city, we didn't have the down payment for a house, and had to settle on a crummy apartment."

He hesitated, sniffling. Agnes chimed in. "Housing is tough in any major city. Much tighter and more expensive than Springfield."

"My wife is so unhappy she's talked about going back down-state, even if it means moving without me."

Faith broke in. "A divorce?"

"She's danced around it. Rents are high, and we can't save much toward a down payment. I told her I'd try to scrounge up some money so we could have our own house again."

Brad nodded. "So that's why you began skimming money from the meat supplier."

"Uh-huh. It seemed just a small amount out of a large budget. And I told myself, once I had the money for a down payment, I'd stop."

Bill shook his head. "At a hundred bucks a month, you'd be years away from that goal. You must have had your sights on larger stakes."

"Believe me, I've never done anything like this before, and I was just seeing if something like this could work."

Brad said, "So you overpaid Otto, and he gave you the hundred bucks as a kickback."

Jim shrugged. "Apparently a lot of companies are familiar with this—'the price of doing business.'"

Bill leaned forward and made eye contact with Jim. "You realize how serious this is, don't you?"

Jim whimpered, "Yes."

Faith said gently, "Jim, we didn't contact any authorities. We wanted to make this as easy as possible for you and for the academy."

Jim began sniffling and crying.

Bill volunteered, "I imagine you kept these six hundred dollars in a separate bank account."

Jim raised his head. "That's right. And I figured if there ever was a problem, I could just repay the money."

Bill agreed. "An insurance policy."

"I guess."

Bill shrugged. "That's better than spending it on some frivolous luxury."

Faith opened her mouth to speak, then stopped. "Uh, Jim, we're trying to help you here. So far, we've discovered six hundred dollars that you diverted from academy funds to yourself. Is that all you took?"

A terrified look on his face, Jim answered, "Yes, that's all."

Bill, a half-smile on his face, asked, "Are you sure? Take your time and think about that answer again."

"What do you mean?"

"Simple. Did you take anything other than the six hundred dollars from the meat supplier?"

"No."

Felicia pulled several sheets from her purse and began reading. "Transfer of six hundred dollars to Brigitte Barton for transition start-up. Jim, you handled this transfer, didn't you?"

Jim had his hands over his face, almost doubled up. When he straightened up, he sobbed. "That was terrible. I didn't feel so bad about using the meat man, because a lot of places are pulling that. But it was mean to take advantage of Brigitte. I knew she had a juvenile record, and didn't think her employer knew about it. So, I told her if she gave me back the extra hundred dollars, I would forget about her teenage arrest."

Faith's eyes flashed with anger. "Jim, we've been extra nice to you, too nice. But now I'm going to tell you what I think. Yes, it was terrible for you to take academy money, funds that we could use for unfortunate young women and their children. But threatening— actually blackmailing—Brigitte, that was despicable."

"You're right. I hated myself for it."

Bill shot glances at Faith, trying to catch her attention. "Well, people, I think we've arrived at a point of clarity. Jim admits that he took money from the academy, and is prepared to pay it back. Is that right, Jim?"

He nodded his agreement.

Felicia mentioned, "Jim, we didn't do an exhaustive search of all the academy records. If there are any other discrepancies, we'll expect you to pay them back."

He shook his head. "That's all of them."

Brad announced, "We have here a paper we drafted, antici-pating that you had misappropriated funds and would be willing to reimburse them." He showed the paper to Jim, who quickly read it.

Faith asked, "Do you agree to that?"

"Yes."

Brad said, "Think about this over the weekend, and if you are ready to reimburse the money, sign the paper and return it to Faith on Monday."

Faith tried to smile through her frown. "You've put us all under a lot of pressure. Not only your own career, but the reputation of the academy is at stake." She sighed. "Meeting adjourned."

Jim hurried out of the office. The others shook hands, hugged, and congratulated themselves on a tough meeting with a good resolution.

Alone in the car driving home, Faith had second thoughts about how hard they had been on Jim.

If only he had come to us and told us he needed the down payment for a house, I'm sure we could have worked something out.

11

Faith felt relieved she could go home and tell Scott about what had dragged down her spirits. She beat him to the condo and got out the wine glasses to celebrate.

When he opened the door, she met him with a bearhug. "If you were Father Whitmore, I'd say, 'Bless me, Father, for I have sinned.'"

"Is this a gross sin, a mortal offense, or just a minor, venal sin?"

"I don't know how to grade it, but I feel guilty about it and want to confess."

"Well, spill the beans."

"This past week or so it wasn't just Jeremy's sickness that depressed me. When Felicia checked the books, she found out that Jim Anderson, our financial officer, took academy money by padding the books for the meat supplier. Our Canterbury three-some decided that we'd have to keep the lid on the affair, and tell no one, not even our husbands. We did bring in Bill Ludwig and one of his lawyers, and confronted Jim today. If he'll agree to repay the money he took, we won't file charges. The important thing is that the academy escapes a scandal and a stain on its reputation."

They talked the evening away, as she filled him in on all the details. He laughed. "You know, the few times I met Jim, I didn't really like him. The word that best describes him is 'mousey.' And frankly, that's the way he carried out this penny ante scam. I mean, the academy has millions of dollars, and he risks his job and maybe jail time for peanuts."

Scott grabbed Faith and held her tight. Then he made the sign of the cross, and announced, "Go and sin no more."

FRIDAY JIM TOOK the day off, not a surprise to Faith. He probably needed the extra time to make his decision on signing the paper. She had not wanted to face him two days in a row.

Faith enjoyed a ho-hum, no stress day at the academy. She left early, got home ahead of Scott, and had the wine glasses ready. When he came home, they shared some white wine. She suggested taxiing to Happi Sushi. They had Japanese beer and eda mame, then sake with the sushi. A little tipsy, they had made a wise decision to taxi to the restaurant, and took a cab back to the condo.

They went to bed early, pleasantly full of sushi and liquid spirits.

SATURDAY MORNING FAITH let Scott make his run for the newspaper before she got up. As her tea water got hot in the microwave, she fetched her journal and opened it to the last entry.

Sitting in the lounger, she ruminated on the past week before beginning to write.

TROUBLE.

Trouble handled.

Trouble defeated?

Maybe.

Too much stress.

Hope for the best Monday.

Thanks to Saint Harriet and Mary for help in facing the trouble.

ON THE SPUR of the moment, she thought about going to Oak Park and having a pancake brunch with the Jeremy and Melanie. She phoned Scott, who responded, "Great idea. I can be home about eleven, we can take off then. Why not see if Jon and Rachel can join us."

"Depends on if anyone has a cold—Melanie is protective of Jeremy."

"Righto. Handle it however. Gotta go."

She called Melanie and got her okay. "I've talked to Jon and Rachel, and they're all healthy."

WHEN SCOTT RETURNED from the newspaper, he and Faith got in his car and headed for Oak Park. Melanie and Rachel had already mixed up pancake batter. Before they fried the pancakes, Faith asked for a prayer circle, giving thanks for her wonderful family, and asking for divine help in Jeremy's recovery.

With so many present, Faith and Rachel each fried stacks of cakes. The kids loved it and so did the parents. When they cleared the dishes, Faith surprised everyone with her video from the academy, full of well wishes to Jeremy. He got weepy viewing all of the warm fuzzies.

After lunch Scott took the kids on a repeat of the exercise path, with calisthenics mixed in at intervals. They came home forty-five minutes later, exhausted.

Faith exchanged glances with Scott. "Yeah, babe, we better get back into the city."

Sunday morning Faith went to church. As she left the service, Father Whitmore whispered, "Long time, no see."

"Sorry, Jeremy's sickness has kept me extra busy. I'd love to talk to you, will try to find time when your schedule is open."

She and Scott went for an hour and a half walk after lunch, and then a long nap. They enjoyed a glass of wine watching night fall on the lake. They viewed an old Bogart and Bacall movie before bed.

Monday morning, refreshed after a peaceful weekend, Faith got up early and had breakfast at the academy with residents. She lingered over coffee, talking to many of the young women and their children. One resident she ate with wanted more information on online courses. Faith was counseling her when she saw Jim Anderson walk in. He seemed to be a different person from the Friday Jim, who had been overwhelmed by the double team of the troika and the legal duo.

On Friday, his shoulders slumped, and he appeared defeated. Coming through the door today, he held his head high, chin up, nose in the air. Faith shuddered, thinking he looked like he was bruisin' for a fight. He headed right for her table, announcing confidently, "I'd like to see you as soon as you have time."

"Sure, Jim, let me finish talking about an online course to this resident."

"Give me a ring when you're free."

Faith went back to Jeremy's office, and figuring she might as well deal with Jim, called him.

"I'll be right there."

When he entered, she was toying with her pen, ready to write on a legal pad.

With no upfront pleasantries, he launched into an obviously rehearsed speech. "Last Thursday you ambushed me, caught me off guard, and outnumbered me. Today it's one on one and I've had the weekend to think things over."

Faith interrupted him. "Did you bring the legal paper Brad gave you?"

He retrieved the folded paper from his shirt pocket and threw it on the desk. "Here, you can take this piece of paper and . . . give it back to Brad."

She unfolded it, seeing he had left it unsigned. "You're not going to sign it?"

"No!" He folded his arms and had a smug look on his face.

Faith raised her eyebrows. "Well, you seem to be prepared to tell me what you're going to do about this situation."

"Damn right. And today I'm giving you *my* proposal. My wife and I had all weekend to figure this out. All life is a series of negotiations over who has what and who is deciding the terms. What is given in exchange for what. We figure you want to protect the academy's perfect reputation, and any scandal would cost you a lot of money, maybe millions, might even destroy the place. Now, my wife and I don't want to see the academy hurt, and we have a plan to protect it. I can promise to leave Canterbury, removing the danger of scandal. You can help my wife and me—hey, call it a 'startup' gift, like for transitioning residents. We need more than seven hundred dollars. To buy a house we have to come up with fifty thousand. And that's a drop in the bucket, considering the millions the academy has."

Jim stopped, a smirk on his face.

Faith sat behind the desk, half shocked at this brazen proposal, half amazed at the transmogrification of a meek mouse into a roaring lion.

He leaned toward her with a defiant, "Well?"

Faith reached back into her hotel experience of negotiating, and said softly, "I'm sorry you didn't accept our good faith offer. You know it's only good through today."

He grunted. "Hah! I'll *never* sign that."

"Uh, what you proposed, would you put that in writing?"

"Oh, no, don't play 'gotcha' games with me."

"You know I can't act on your proposal alone."

"You relay my proposal to your muckety mucks, and get back to me. I'm going home now, but will be back in the office tomorrow."

Faith sat at her desk for a few minutes, gathering her thoughts. It was early, just before nine. She might as well call Bill, hoping to reach him before he met his first client.

Talking to Bill's secretary, Faith told her, "I don't often say something is urgent. If he can get back to me right away, fine. If not, I'll send him an email." She hurried to the kitchen to get a cup of tea to calm her nerves. Coming back from the kitchen, she told Jackie, "Hold all calls except Bill Ludwig."

At twenty minutes past nine, Bill called. "Honey, this better be good, and it's gotta be quick. I have an important client waiting in the outer office."

"Quick and dirty. Jim won't sign Brad's paper. He counters with a proposal that he keeps silent and preserves the reputation of the academy for fifty grand."

"Well I'll be damned to hell and back. That little mouse has turned into a big rat. Uh, what did you tell him?"

"That I couldn't give him an answer, all of us would have to respond to his proposal."

"Good girl. I've got to get to my client now. Phone Brad and let him in on this. Oh, and one more thing. Don't you let this worry you. We've seen lots worse."

"Thanks so much, Bill."

She called Brad Ashford, and gave him the same basic information she had relayed to Bill.

"But why the change of mind?"

"He said he and his wife talked about it all weekend, and they came up with this counter proposal."

"His *wife*? I think you understand as well as I do that fifty grand is a much more significant sum than six hundred dollars, and if they cooked up this blackmail scheme together, they might receive matching jail suits."

"I thought about that, but all I said was I'd relay his proposal."

"That's smart. Bill and I will go over this and get back to you. We're both busy, but we'll try to contact you by tomorrow or the day after."

Faith looked at the clock, half past nine, and already she was tired. She managed to get Agnes and Felicia on a conference call. Both of them had some choice names for Jim.

Faith left the office as kids lined up for playtime. A volunteer was doing a takeoff on Faith's skit, using chairs for trains, planes, and trucks. This leader announced that the chairs were taxis, and each child had to say where he was going, and what he was going to do when he got there. Leonard grabbed the first chair and yelled out that he was going to go to a Cubs ball game, sit in a front row, and catch a foul ball. Faith pulled a chair up after the last kid. When she moved to the head of the line, she told everyone she wanted to go to the lake, watch the waves, and feed the seagulls.

Faith somehow made it through the morning, taking care of letters and phone calls and casual conversations with residents. After lunch, Julia Kaminski dropped by her office.

"You're doing a great job holding the place together while Jeremy's away."

Faith chuckled. "Well, we'll see. Agnes and Felicia are great helpmates. Without them I couldn't do it. I've been wanting to talk to you, and this is as good a time as any. What I tell you now is in strict confidence."

"Sure. Sounds serious."

"We have a major problem, a potential crisis. I wouldn't tell you about it, except for the fact that it involves Brigitte, and you're the one closest to her. In a nutshell, Jim Anderson stole hundreds of dollars from the academy by overpaying the meat man in order to get a kickback. Jim also transferred six hundred dollars to Brigitte for start-up money, when we've had a cap of five hundred for start-up money. Apparently, Jim blackmailed her, threatened to tell her employer about Brigitte's juvie record if she didn't go along with his scam and give him the extra hundred."

"Holy Toledo! He'd do that?"

"He did it. Now we have a tricky ongoing negotiation with Jim that I can't discuss. And I'm so tied up with so many different people, I don't have time to talk directly with Brigitte. I'd like you to go speak with her, and first just ask her to explain the extra hundred dollars, and if she forked it over to Jim. Let me be perfectly clear. We don't want to punish her. We think she was forced into this deal, to save her job and protect her daughter. All we need now is to find out her version of the story."

"I know Brigitte pretty well. I think she'll level with me."

Faith wanted to talk over this new development with Scott, but didn't like bothering him at the newspaper. She forced herself to take care of busy work as the hands of the clock slowly moved toward four o'clock. At a quarter past four, Brad called.

"Bill and I had a few minutes at lunch and here's what we came up with. This issue has to be settled quickly. So, we'll squeeze you in at half past four tomorrow—you and your two colleagues. Come with ideas on how you want to handle Jim. Depending on what we all agree to, we may shoot for a longer meeting to finalize a deal on Thursday."

"I really appreciate your taking care of us so quickly. I'll call Agnes and Felicia. If there's a snag, I'll send an email. Otherwise, we're on for half past four in your office tomorrow."

Faith made a conference call to her buddies, relaying Brad's plan. "Why don't you two think about it tonight, and we can schedule a conference call at nine tomorrow morning, exchanging ideas on what to say to the lawyers."

By five o'clock Faith headed out of the office. Scott beat her home.

"Extra busy this afternoon?"

"A tough day, and tougher times ahead."

She quickly summed up Jim's blackmail proposal and Brad's plan to meet late tomorrow afternoon. "What do you think we ought to do? I have to get my head together so that we three women have consensus on what we want from the lawyers."

"Hell, you wouldn't even consider giving Jim any money, would you?"

"No way. All of us agree on that. The question is how do we handle Jim, and what do we expect the lawyers to follow through on."

"Dear, you tried the nice guy approach. From here on, you should be hardnosed. I guess that means outright rejection of his blackmail. Why don't you just turn him over to the authorities and have them file charges."

"You think we should do that?"

"It's your most obvious option."

"But Scott, if this goes public, we'd risk a stain on the academy's reputation."

"If you don't act quickly and honestly, you have a greater risk of losing credibility."

All evening they mulled over the mess, not reaching any clear solution to the dilemma.

12

Faith and Scott went to bed at eleven, Scott soon descending into a snoring slumber.

Faith couldn't go to sleep. At midnight she got up and retrieved her journal from her drawer, taking it with her to the lounger. She turned to the first blank page, yet couldn't focus her thoughts about Doug and Jim. When she first met them, they seemed nice, but later became selfish and self-centered.

Instead of writing, she closed her eyes and prayed to Saint Harriet and Mary for help. These prayers reminded her of the times she had made the trip to the south side and paid a visit to the stained-glass window before seeing Father Whitmore.

Several times he had told her to follow her conscience and just do what was right. That recollection soothed her mind. She didn't need to write out in the journal the advice she would take to the conference call with her girlfriends.

TUESDAY MORNING FAITH CALLED MAISIE, asking her to hold a breakfast for her. She rushed in to the kitchen about half past eight and gobbled down a meal so that she could place the nine o'clock call to her ladies.

She told Jackie she'd be busy with a telephone conference, and dialed her Winnetka friends.

"Ladies, let me know what you think about how to deal with Jim."

Felicia volunteered, "I think the process is the first matter to consider. My idea is that we can't go any further with this until we involve Father Murphy, because he's chairman of the board. I know him well and can contact him. And a decision we need to run by him is whether to designate Brad as the lawyer representing the academy. You know, Bill said because he's on the board, he can't do it. So that's what I came up while brainstorming."

Agnes chimed in, "Good idea to contact Father Murphy. You're probably right that we should focus on process, but I'm looking at the end result. As far as Jim is concerned—that scumbag—we were too easy on him last time. Now we need to show him that we mean business. I'd like to see him thrown in jail. Well, your turn, Faith."

"Here's a biggie that we'll have to dance around later today. Will we go so far as turning Jim over to the authorities and have them file charges? We might as well think about this, because Bill can't make that decision for us."

At that moment Jackie opened the door and told her, "Jim is here, would like to talk to you."

"Have him wait until I finish this conference call."

She returned to Felicia and Agnes. "Jim came to my office, wants to talk to me. I'll play it cool with him. He's probably impatient, but he can't expect an immediate answer from us."

When she hung up, she waited a few minutes. She placed her pen and legal pad on the desk to take notes. Then she went to the door.

"You wanted to see me?"

He walked in and plopped into a chair with a thud.

"Yes. Actually, I wanted to hear from you, if you accepted my proposal."

"We haven't had time to meet and consider it."

"You should meet as soon as possible. The other day I said I'd protect the academy's reputation for fifty thousand. If you keep me waiting too long, the price might go up."

Faith raised her eyebrows. "Really?"

"Could be seventy-five thousand. Or more."

"I'll tell that to the others."

"Be sure you do. And I expect a prompt answer."

"We'll get back to you as soon as we can meet and reach a decision."

"I won't waste your time or mine. I'll be taking annual leave today. You can reach me at home."

FAITH PICKED up the phone to redial Agnes and Felicia, then put it back down and walked to the kitchen. The exchange with Jim upset her stomach, and she needed a cup of hot tea to settle her mind.

"Maisie, thanks for that great breakfast. Now I could use some tea."

Maisie looked at Faith, and walked toward her, arms outstretched. "You need more than tea. Hate to tell you this, but you look like shit." She enfolded Faith in a gentle embrace. "Hey, I'm just the stove tender and meal fixer, but I know somethin's goin' on. You don't have to tell me any secrets. I just want to let you know that I'm here in case you're looking for support."

Faith closed her eyes. "You're so right. Your Winnetka sidekicks and I have a real problem on our hands. I just finished a conference call with them and got interrupted, so I have to get back with them. After that, do you have a few minutes?"

"Sure. I've got lunch started, and Maria can take over for a while."

Faith sipped on tea as she walked back to the office. The warm liquid made her tummy feel better and helped her relax.

Calling Felicia and Agnes, she filled them in on Jim's threat to raise the price of his blackmail.

Agnes roared, "That skunk! We ought to tar and feather him."

Felicia added, "After we draw and quarter the jerk."

"Well, ladies, before we do that, we have more unfinished business. I asked Julia Kaminski to talk with Brigitte and listen to her story about the extra hundred dollars Jim transferred to her. And— I didn't plan this, but I just got a cup of tea from Maisie, and she knows something's wrong. If you agree, I'll fill her in, because she can help us with the other business—the meat man. I won't talk to him until clearing it with Bill and Brad this afternoon. For now, I just want to see what she knows about the meat man."

Felicia and Agnes agreed that Maisie should be brought into the inner circle.

Faith went to the kitchen for a refill of tea, and had Maisie come to the office.

"Maisie, we have a big problem."

"Yeah, and it's not just Jeremy. Tell me what you can, and if I can help, let me know."

"To get right to the point, Jim has been overpaying the meat man for six months, getting a kickback. He stole at least six hundred dollars from the academy."

"I'm not that surprised. Jim hides in his office, and is kind of sneaky. What're you gonna do?"

"That's what we're trying to figure out now."

"Can I do something?"

"Tell me what you know about this Otto guy, who sells us meat."

"Otto is a good man."

"How can you be so sure?"

Maisie laughed. "You only see me in the kitchen, cooking meals, but when I was a school superintendent, I worked in a much hotter place. I had to deal with everything—teachers molesting students, administrators cheating on expense accounts, parents trying to bribe me to raise their kids' grades and fake college recommendations. I've seen it all. The only time I got in trouble is when I went soft and didn't press charges on a guy who stole from an athletic fund. So don't feel sorry for Jim and go easy on him."

"What would you do?"

"Burn his ass! Fire him and turn him over to the cops."

"Hmm, that's what Agnes thinks, too. I'm worried more about the scandal than the money."

Maisie, hands on her hips, sighed. "Yeah, we can't always do what we'd like to. All of that hassle is the reason I left administration and retreated to the kitchen, getting my jollies cooking. I've seen a lot of shady characters, but Otto is not a crook. His meat is quality. His prices are fair. He helps us out. When he has a great buy, he lets me in on it, makes suggestions for what to purchase. Otto is honest and reliable. When you meet him, you'll see he's on the up and up."

"You don't know about the payments?"

"No. He hands me the bill, we check off the items, and I pass on his bill to Jim."

"When does he deliver?"

"He came this morning, and he'll be back Friday."

"I may ask you to meet with him and me Friday."

"Is Otto in trouble?"

"I don't think so. It looks like Jim demanded a kickback, probably with the threat to find another supplier if Otto didn't go along with him."

"I bet you're right."

Faith shuffled back to the office and slumped in her chair. She leaned forward, arms on the desk and laid her head down. Temples throbbing, a sharp pain shot through her brain. She replayed the scene with Jim, knowing the next encounter with him would be even more tense. She worried that Julia might be delivering bad news about Brigitte and Jim. Mixed in with all this bad news, she dreaded the conversation with the meat supplier. Also, she faced a more immediate difficulty: the threesome had a crunch meeting late afternoon with the lawyers. Her headache intensified.

Jackie knocked on the door and walked in. "Oh, sorry—are you okay?"

"I'll be fine."

"I didn't want to bother you, but the person in charge of playtime didn't show up. It's ten-fifteen and the kids are antsy. Could you—"

"Oh, dear, today I'm just not up to it."

"Well, if you can't take over, I'll have to tell the kids no playtime today."

Jackie closed the door. Faith jumped out of her chair and hurried after Jackie.

Faith smiled. "No. Don't tell them. I have an idea."

In her loudest voice she started singing, "I've been workin' on the railroad."

The kids laughed and clapped.

"Come on kids, join in, it's a singalong." She rounded the children up and repeated "I've been workin' on the railroad," making sure everyone tooted as loud as they could. "Okay, boys and girls, let's leave the railroad and get in our rowboat. She led them in "Row, row, row your boat," and made sure everyone used their arms to row the boat. For the next song, they belted out "My bonnie lies over the ocean." Some children didn't know it, so she repeated it.

Next, she took requests for songs. The first was "Small World," followed by a number of others.

"Okay, little ones, we're gonna finish with a goofy, funny song, called 'Inka Dinka Doo.'"

The kids cheered.

Faith sang it the way her mother sang the song, changing the words to several phrases of "I love you." She sang it and then the kids joined her, murdering the Inka Dinka Doo phrase, but belting out the "I love you."

Several moms joined in the singing, and asked Faith where she heard the song.

"Last night my husband and I watched an old black and white

film by Jimmy Durante, and listened to his original version. That reminded me of the way Mom sang it to me."

The kids and moms clapped.

Faith went back to the office, rejuvenated by the kids' energy. Yes! The welfare of the moms and kids came first. To hell with Jim. They'd deal with him, and handle the other problems, so the academy could continue and the children could enjoy playtime. Happiness was singing Inka Dinka Doo to a bunch of happy kids.

Faith spent some time in the office with busy work. When she went through the lunch line, Maisie took her aside. "Listen to me, young lady, you're stressed out and exhausted. You should go home after lunch."

"Can't. I have a late afternoon meeting with the Winnetka gals and the lawyers."

Maisie shook her head. "You may have been a vice president at Horton Hotels, ordering other people what to do, but you aren't using your head to take care of yourself."

As Faith was finishing lunch, Maisie brought Colette over to her. "Boss lady, we're in charge. Colette is taking her girl to the lounge, and you're under orders to take a nap on her bed. Otherwise, you'll never make it through the afternoon and the late meeting."

Faith didn't object. Going to Colette's room, she stretched out on the bed, and in spite of all the thoughts rambling through her mind, drifted off to sleep.

An hour later Faith woke with a start, finding herself in strange surroundings. She ambled down to the kitchen and thanked Maisie. "That shuteye will make it possible for me to survive the afternoon." Then she found Colette. "You don't know how you saved me."

Walking to the office, Jackie stopped her. "Julia tried to reach you. I told her you'd call as soon as you could."

Faith dreaded the news from Julia about Brigitte.

13

"Julia, sorry to keep you waiting. It's been a busy, hectic day."
"I wanted to contact you right after talking to Brigitte. She wants to speak to you, but I said I'd have to clear that with you first."

"Give it to me upfront—good news or bad news?"

"Mostly good news. I met her over lunch, and came right out with the problem of Jim overpaying her. Brigitte put her hands over her face and started crying. Through her tears, she confessed, 'I told him his trick would never work, that someone would find out. But he forced me into it, said he'd blab about my juvenile record to the store where I work.'"

"I suspected as much. How was the money handled?"

"Jim transferred six hundred to Brigitte, and she handed a hundred back to him. They met at a fast-food place."

"Jim, Jim, the flim-flam man."

"Brigitte's scared to death. She knows the academy enabled her to get on her feet and put her life in order. Losing this job would be disaster. She wants to tell you that she only went along with Jim because if she didn't, she'd lose her job. She's grateful to you and the academy, and regrets being caught up in Jim's theft."

"Julia, thanks so much for relaying this information. I'd call her now and try to straighten this out today if I wasn't under pressure, with a lawyer's meeting coming up soon. Call her and tell her we thought she had been maneuvered by Jim. I'll try to contact her in the next day or two and talk this over."

FAITH ONLY HAD a little while before heading in to the loop to see Bill and Brad. Needing moral support, she called Scott, and he picked up.

"What's going on?"

"Getting ready for the attorney palaver. I just wanted to hear your voice and be reassured."

"You got it. I've seen you operate in Bill's office. You and your two henchmen . . . henchwomen . . . will protect the academy. Anything new?"

"A lot new, too complicated to go into now. I may eat with Felicia and Agnes after the meeting. When we leave the law offices, I'll call home."

"Break a leg. And I hope it's Jim's leg."

FAITH ARRIVED at the law firm about a quarter past four. Felicia and Agnes were waiting for her. Faith quickly brought them up to date on Brigitte, and said she'd tell the lawyers.

Brad joined the ladies and sat with them while Bill finished with his last client of the day. As they filed into Bill's office, he joked, "If we're going to make this a regular thing, we'll have to bring a deck of cards and poker chips. Well, maybe next time. Let's hear from you three. Scott calls you the troika. Or maybe you're the triumvirate. Anyway, first tell us of any new developments, and then we'll try to help you sort out the alternatives."

Faith told Bill and Brad about Jim threatening to raise the blackmail to seventy-five thousand.

Bill turned toward Brad and guffawed. "Brad why don't you hold a training session for would-be criminals. You know, 'How to commit a crime 101.' One of the first rules surely is, when you commit a crime, don't make it worse and compound your problems."

Faith summed up her call with Brigitte. "We've worked hard to enable her to become independent, and don't want her to be punished for what Jim forced on her."

Brad nodded. "We can try to keep her out of this."

Bill looked at the three women. "What have you come up with?"

Faith gestured to Felicia. "First, we should let Father Murphy know what's going on. I've worked with him for years on various financial difficulties with the diocese and the old academy, and I could talk to him. Second, we wonder if this isn't the time to have the board ask Brad to represent the academy."

"Good suggestions," Bill agreed.

Agnes announced, "Just for the record, we're totally against giving Jim anything, and we're ready to play hardball with him." She glanced at Faith and Felicia. "If it was up to me, I'd have him locked up."

Faith frowned. "We don't know how this will work out. We'll need your advice if the board decides to notify the authorities and asks for charges to be filed against Jim."

Bill turned to Brad. "Didn't I tell you these were three smart cookies."

"Yeah, and I'm glad they're on our side."

Bill smiled. "Ladies, all we have to do now is plan a strategy session for a second meeting with Jim. Brad and I will have to drive out to the academy, maybe about two o'clock Thursday. We want to clear this up right away. Here's what Brad and I have pieced together. We tell him no way are we gonna give him a cent. That would make us co-conspirators in defrauding the academy, which none of us wants. Then I throw the book at him, letting him know the prison time and fines for grand larceny. Here's a piece of Illinois law I'll hit him with. The penalties for fraud are stiffer for crimes against a charity or religious organization."

Bill laughed. "Sorry, folks, but this is how we get our jollies. We have to scare him shitless. He says he and his wife concocted this scheme. She may or may not be involved in the theft, but can be charged for the blackmail. I'll ask him how old his kids are—"

Faith interrupted. "They're about eight and ten."

"Well, I'd let him know that he might get out of prison before his oldest goes to college. How do you three like that?"

"Well," Faith mused, "that may get him to take back the blackmail threat, but what about the money he stole, and filing charges?"

Bill turned to Brad. "Why don't you handle that?"

"That's where the negotiation becomes more tricky, and depends on how Jim responds. If he's stubborn and doesn't cooperate, we can always bring a complaint to the state attorney's office. That will be up to the board. If you want to avoid publicity and a scandal, you may not want to do that. If he repents and hands over the money, you can be generous and let him leave without charges."

Felicia agreed. "My dad, a prosecuting attorney, said it's always better to find a win-win solution."

Agnes frowned. "That scumbag shouldn't get off scot-free."

Brad turned to Agnes. "Hey, he's losing his job and his reputation. That counts for something."

Bill cleared his throat and surveyed the room. "I don't think any of you women have been in back room negotiations. They're not like the formal and polite settings of the courtroom. When we meet with Jim, my language will get salty, so I apologize to you ahead of time."

The session ended on that note. Faith suggested that, like after the last late afternoon session, the women go to the Loop Café and eat while waiting for traffic to thin out.

She left a message on the condo phone, telling Scott she'd eat with the girls.

Sitting in a booth at the cafe, Felicia told the waitress, "I don't need a menu. I'm going for a bowl of chili and a big dill pickle."

Agnes looked at Faith. "What about it?"

"Yeah, make it three of the same."

The waitress laughed. "That's usually the favorite of young women who have something in the oven, and I think you three are past that stage of life. But whatever pleases you."

The meeting had energized them. They talked with Felicia about approaching Father Murphy. Felicia said she'd email the priest, asking if he was free for a conference call between nine and ten the next morning. The three thought it would be better to place the call in Faith's office, so her speaker phone would let all of them participate in the call.

Felicia laughed. "Father Murphy and I go back a long way. We've had lengthy discussions—heated arguments—about finances for the diocese and the academy. In spite of that, or maybe because of it, we get along and trust each other. But I have to warn you, like Bill cautioned us that he'll get 'salty' in a meeting with Jim, Father Murphy will get preachy with us. After all, he's a priest. Tomorrow if he starts a sentence with 'That reminds me of a sermon I once gave,' then prepare to sit back in your chair like you're seated in a pew, and listen to him preach."

The threesome chit-chatted for a while before they left the cafe. Agnes and Felicia raved over the weird meal.

FAITH BARELY GOT in the door of the condo before Scott started peppering her with questions. He couldn't believe Jim's audacity to hike the fee for his blackmail.

"The only thing worse than a crook is a stupid crook."

After Faith had explained the busy day's events with Jim, Scott shook his head.

"You know, Jim should have taken blackmail lessons from Doug. The difference between those two cads is, Doug had leverage. He had what you wanted and couldn't get—the medical records. Jim thinks he can use the academy's reputation as leverage, but he doesn't have it in his back pocket. He doesn't control Canterbury's good name, so he's weak there. And if you call his bluff, the only way he can hurt the academy is admitting to grand larceny, which puts him in the slammer."

"Yeah, he's really a loser. The only one I really feel sorry for is Brigitte. I want to protect her, no matter how we handle Jim."

"She's an innocent bystander, compared to that conniving cad."

Scott sighed. "Faith, my dear, let's talk a little about your favorite subject, Jim. You seem to be preoccupied, obsessed with him. Most of the time I can just play along with you, and ignore him. But let's get real about this subject. I need to speak to you newspaper reporter style, like us guys do after we've had a few beers."

"Does that mean I have to guzzle a couple of brews?"

"No, just soak up what I have to say to you."

"Sounds like guy talk."

"Rough talk. And I might as well unload on you right now. The down and dirty truth is—Jim is an ASSHOLE!"

Faith cringed. "Do you have to use that kind of language?"

"Yes, it gets the point across. Here's what you need to know about assholes. First, there are lots of assholes in the world. Every human being has one. An asshole is quite useful, especially for elimination. But you use it, wipe it, and then forget about it. You don't show it off to people or make them look at it. Frankly, I've seen and heard too much of Jim."

"Uh, Scott, do you have to call him an . . . asshole?"

He laughed. "Oh, no, if this was for print in a newspaper, I could refer to him as a circular anal orifice."

She smiled. "That's nicer."

"Yes, but you know that a rose by any other name is just as sweet. And a bunghole by any other label is just as stinky."

"Scott, I get your point. It's not fair for me to rub your nose in the mess about Jim."

"Yeah, once in a while we can deal with him, but not all the time."

"Sorry, I didn't realize how much I was bugging you." She chuckled. "And you taught me something—a circular anal orifice."

Scott nodded. "I know you don't like coarse language, but you might try an occasional dirty word."

"Okay, I'll try. You said an . . . asshole is good for elimination. What would you call it if two assholes had a competition to see which one could crap the most?"

"Gee, I don't know."

"An elimination contest."

Scott and Faith had a good laugh.

14

The next morning Faith met the Winnetka duo for breakfast at the academy. Maisie joined them and caught up with Agnes and Felicia.

Maisie got back to her lunch prep and the other three went to the office. They brought chairs close to the desk so everyone could participate in the call to Father Murphy.

When Felicia phoned, she and the priest exchanged pleasantries before he announced, "Let's get down to business. I know we're all busy. Well, talk about busy, this fellow Jim is in the running for criminal of the month. When I read your email, I thought you were pulling my leg. He certainly combines audacity with stupidity."

"Father, Agnes and Faith are here with me, and you're on speaker phone. Mostly we want to hear what you think of the problem and our approach to resolve it. Then Agnes and Faith may add their comments."

"Right off the top, I think you ladies are negotiating effectively, right on target. I'm pleased that you didn't even entertain the proposal to join Jim in his criminal enterprise. We've all heard the old saw about robbing Peter to pay Paul. He wants you to join him in robbing Canterbury to pay Jim. You know, his escapade reminds me of a sermon I once preached. I called it 'The Highwayman.'"

Felicia stifled a laugh, holding her hand in front of her, palm up toward the phone, as if making way for a dignitary.

"Bear with me for a few minutes. You see, when I attended seminary, I stayed on for a master's degree, and wrote a thesis on Chaucer and the *Canterbury Tales*. You're probably familiar with this medieval English story, but let me fill you in on a few little-known facts. In those days, the medieval word 'highway' meant a simple road, really a path, for people and horses. The highway was a dangerous place, and frequently robbers would deprive travelers of their valuables. They called a robber a highwayman—he usually had a horse for a quick getaway.

"Chaucer was robbed—twice—by highwaymen. He was carrying gold for the king, and lost all of it. Apparently, he admitted to the king that he was robbed, and didn't get blamed for it. He didn't try to steal other people's money to make up for it. And even after he was robbed, the government appointed him to important positions.

"The moral of this story is: if a highwayman robs you, stay on the highway to reach your destination, but don't become a high-wayman. That's how I ended the sermon.

"Even today there are highwaymen—like Jim—but we don't need to follow their example. I think you three women have done well to protect the name of Canterbury, and not follow in the foot-steps of Jim."

Felicia smiled. "That's a great sermon. I'm sure your parish-ioners profited from it."

"Well, one more thing before I get to my next appointment. Feli-cia, you and I have tangled in the past over the academy. It gives me pleasure to see it on sound financial footing and performing a valu-able service. I back you a hundred per cent. Hire this lawyer Brad if you think he's good. And if you have to file a complaint against Jim, you have my support."

Faith and Agnes thanked Father Murphy, ending the call.

The three women let out a collective sigh.

Faith motioned the others to come together for a three-in-one bear hug. "Felicia, you really came through for us with the good father."

"He's a great priest, a wonderful man."

Faith chuckled. "'The highwayman'. If we had the time and the artistic assistance, we could make that into a successful TV drama."

They joked about it until Faith got serious. "Ladies, I've got to contact Jim about the meeting tomorrow, and you might as well listen in. That way, I won't have to summarize it for you."

She sat at her desk and punched in Jim's number.

"Hello."

"Hello, Jim, it's Faith. I'll get right to the point. I'm calling to see if you're available for a meeting in my office tomorrow at two."

"Did you accept my proposal?"

"We'd like to discuss it with you."

"Nothing to discuss. Accept it or reject it."

"That's not what my people say. They want to hear your proposal directly from you before they make a decision."

"Yeah, you'd like to squash me under your gang, but I don't like that."

"If you want us to consider your offer, you need to present it to us."

"Who would be there?"

"Like before—me, Agnes, Felicia, Bill, and Brad. Brad will be representing the academy."

"Bringing out the legal guns, huh?"

"You can bring legal representation if you'd like."

"I don't need any lawyer. It's a clear yes or no, accept or reject the offer."

"Why don't you come and make that argument."

"Yeah. Maybe I will. Yeah. Sure. I'm not afraid of your loop lawyers."

"Fine. We'll see you tomorrow at two."

Felicia reached around Faith and patted her on the back. "You did great. Never committing us, and keeping him off balance."

"Okay, now I've got to notify Brad and Bill." She called and left a message with Bill's secretary that the meeting was on, and they had the backing of Father Murphy to hire Brad as academy lawyer, and do whatever they felt best.

Faith drummed her fingers on the desk. "I need to call Brigitte. Do you two want to listen in?"

"We might as well," Felicia said.

When Faith dialed Brigitte, she said gently, "This is Faith. If this isn't a good time to talk, let me know when you're free."

"Oh, I just have ten minutes before a sales meeting with my clerks."

"That's enough time for today. I wanted to let you know that Julia talked to me, and we understand that you were forced to go along with Jim in his scheme."

"Faith, I've been on pins and needles ever since he pressured me into that stinking deal. I'm very sorry to . . . have ever been involved with him. I'm relieved that you understand."

"We'll have to talk again. We're quite busy now in discussions with Jim, and I can't go into details about that. Let me ask if he has contacted you."

"No, thank heavens. That is, not since I met him at a fast-food restaurant and slipped him the hundred dollars."

"Good. My suggestion to you is not to accept calls from him, and not to meet with him. That will help us to keep you out of any legal proceedings the academy has against Jim."

"What will happen to him?"

"That's unclear now, and I can't say anything more about our actions. We may need to contact you in the near future. Let me just add that we're pleased with your transition and new job, and wish you well."

"Thank you so much. I better go to my meeting now."

Felicia and Agnes gave a thumbs up gesture to their leader.

Faith snickered.

Agnes said, "Let us in on the humor."

Faith held her hands up. "I surrender! Three heavy duty negotiations, and it's not even noon. I never knew that our plan to have the three of us run the academy during Jeremy's absence would result in major diplomatic discussions like this morning, and what lie ahead. I'd like to take you out to lunch. We need to have a break, and we should have a brain session for tomorrow's meeting."

15

F aith drove them to a nearby restaurant. After they ordered, Faith put on her serious face. "I'd like to hear what you two have in mind for tomorrow's meeting. Let me suggest that Bill and Brad come at half past one, to give us an idea what to expect, and let us know what Bill expects from us. When Scott and I had to go to court, Bill was always good with what he calls the 'hand-holding' session before the actual meeting."

"Great idea," Felicia said. "As for me, I think the more we stay out of the way of the two legal eagles, the better. They're the experts, and all we need to do is say, 'Uh-huh.'"

Agnes cocked her head. "I'd like to read the riot act to Jim—putting us through this nightmare. But if the rest of you want to play it cool, we can let Bill open the meeting, set the tone and direction for the discussion."

When they arrived back at the academy, Felicia urged Faith to take the afternoon off.

"Good idea. I'm just going to send an email asking Bill and Brad for a pre-meeting session, and then head for home."

At the condo she hurried into the bathroom and turned on the hot water, then took off her clothes and stepped into the tub, letting the liquid heat dissolve the morning's tension.

Relaxed and refreshed, she got out of the tub, dried off and dressed. It was still early afternoon, so she indulged in some chamomile tea and fetched her journal out of its resting place. She walked to her recliner, sipping tea for a few minutes. Setting down her tea, she opened the journal to a new page.

TROUBLE.

The trouble's name is Jim.

We will meet him and we will defeat him.

With the help of Saint Harriet and Mary.

And Jimmy Durante.

Inka Dinka Doo!

Faith had the wine glasses out when Scott came home, and filled them when he came in the door. They sat at the kitchen table.

"Well, how did the nation's top negotiator fare today?"

Faith summed up the meeting with Jim, and gave a quickie version of the priest's "Highwayman" sermon.

Scott roared with laughter. "I'd like to meet him."

Faith told him about her talk with Brigitte and the women's agreement to try to keep her out of the mess with Jim.

Scott walked around the table and kissed Faith. "Hey, with your new job, we don't need television. We have reality shows every day."

The next morning, as Scott left the condo, he called out to Faith, "Hey, dragon slayer, go get 'em."

Alone in the condo, Faith felt isolated. She wanted to be with people. She quickly showered, dressed, and drove in to the academy, arriving just after half past seven.

Maisie saw her and pulled her out of the food line. "Honey, you look like a frightened deer that just escaped from a pack of wild dogs."

"That's how I feel, too. Today's the showdown meeting with Jim. Even though the Winnetka women will be with me, I'm nervous."

Maisie bear-hugged her, chuckling. "Mousey Jim's no match for three clever cats like you women. Hmm. Hate to pile more junk on you, but tomorrow's Friday, and Otto the meat man will be here early in the morning."

"How early?"

"I don't get here until seven, and he usually shows up between seven and nine."

"If you ask him to be here at eight, I can make it. Well, I think. Depends on how tough the afternoon meeting is."

"I'll call him and see if he can come at eight or a little after."

"Great. Just leave a note with Jackie if he'll be here at eight. Then you and I can talk to him about the overpayments."

FAITH HELD her tray for the servers to dish out breakfast. Looking around, she saw Colette and her daughter. She winked at them, and Colette said, "We'll meet you at a table."

Faith sighed, thinking, *The academy is my home away from home.*

She had a good time schmoozing with Colette, and lingered after eating. Going back to the kitchen for a cup of tea, she returned to the dining table and chatted with several groups of mothers. Eventually she walked to the office, telling Jackie, "I'm too keyed up to do any serious work today. I'll take any calls you think are important."

Watching the hands of the clock slowly move toward ten o'clock, Faith knew the kids would be gathering for playtime. She left the office to see what the leader would do to entertain the children. The choice of the day was musical chairs. Every boy and girl sat on a chair and had to stand up and march around a line of chairs while the leader played music on a tape recorder. She removed one chair, then stopped the music, and everyone scrambled to find a seat. The rough and tumble kids like Leonard enjoyed the action, but the ones who didn't find seats and had to drop out, pouted. A little girl began to cry. Faith held her and comforted her.

Faith made a mental note never to lead that game, which meant that everyone turned into a loser except the last one to nab a seat.

The children, not too happy with this exercise, took advantage of Faith's presence.

"Miss Faith, can we singalong? Can we sing inky dinky?"

She gladly borrowed Jimmy Durante's tune and soon the whole room echoed with the song. The children cheered and clapped.

At that point, Felicia and Agnes entered the all-purpose room, insisting on having the tune repeated.

Then Faith led the Winnetkans to her office. "Playing with kids is my therapy, burning off nervous energy."

Agnes put her hand on Faith' shoulder. "We decided to come in early to have lunch with you, help ease the tension. God, if we're uptight, you must be higher than a kite."

They talked until lunch time and then lined up. They decided to split and chat with different groups of residents. After eating, they went to her office to wait for the lawyers to come at half past one. Faith told Jackie, "We'll wait for Bill and Brad. When Jim shows up, don't let him in until I open the door and ask him in."

At half past one, Bill and Brad made their appearance, dapper in dress, with smiling faces exuding cheerfulness and confidence.

16

They gathered in Faith's office, chairs in the same arrangement as the previous confab, with the hot seat for Jim in the middle. She asked Bill to sit at Jim's right, and Brad next to him. Felicia took the place to the left of the hot seat, with Agnes at her side.

Bill's mellow baritone voice set the stage for the pre-meeting. "Well, what are my three favorite investigators up to today?"

Faith looked at the two other women, then spoke up. "I told Felicia and Agnes that when Scott and I had to deal in court with the father of the twins, you did a good job preparing us for the proceedings. Why don't you give us an overview of how you'll handle the situation."

"Well, I can't give you an actual script, but I have in mind a three-act drama. The first act begins diplomatically and politely, when I thank Jim for coming, and ask him to explain his proposal. After he spits out his blackmail scheme, we begin dissecting it, spelling out why we can't allow Faith or the academy to become involved in his criminal scheme.

"From that point we segue into the second act, exploring the ramifications of his threat to expose the academy to a scandal, and how that would harm all the present residents and even future residents. Somewhere in this scenario, I get hot and say some nasty things to Jim. Now, ladies, this is where I would appreciate some expressions of anger. We want to show this perp that we're mad as hell, and won't let him get away with his scam. Once we've convinced him we're deadly serious, Brad and I will start threatening him with all the jail time that he—and his wife—are facing.

"Here we come to the unpredictable third part of the drama. I don't think Jim will be violent, but cornered rats are dangerous. We hope that by this point Jim gives up on his machinations. Please, don't go soft on him. Brad and I want Jim to return the seven hundred dollars before we discuss whether or not to bring charges against him."

Faith sat back in her chair, a half-smile spreading across her face. "See, ladies, I told you Bill would come through with a good pre-game pep talk."

Bill looked around the room. "Any questions?"

Faith piped up, "Oh, not a question, but you should know that Maisie and I plan to talk to the meat supplier tomorrow."

Bill's eyebrows raised. "Okay, but just get information from him, and don't give away any of our talk with Jim."

As the hour reached two o'clock, Jackie interrupted them. "Jim is here."

Faith shrugged. "We might as well go ahead and have him come in."

Bill held up his hand. "No, no. Let him stew for a few minutes."

Five minutes after two, Bill motioned to Faith. "Have Jackie bring him in."

Jim walked in, saw the one empty chair and sat in it.

Bill turned to Jim. "Good afternoon, Mr. Anderson. Thank you for coming. We'd like to settle this matter as quickly as possible, as I am sure you would, too."

Jim grunted. "Well, it's really simple. No need to talk. You accept my proposal, and we're done here."

Bill pursed his lips. "We'll see. We heard something about your proposal from Faith, but you could help us understand it better if you explained it to us."

"Uh, nothing to explain. It's simple. I have something you want, you have something I want. You give me what I want, you get what you want."

Bill forced a smile, looking at Brad. "Quid pro quo, this for that. You learned that in your first course in law school, right."

Brad nodded. "Yes, and everything depends on what defines this for that."

Bill looked at Jim. "Could you identify this and that?"

Jim shrugged. "You want to preserve the reputation of the academy and not scare away donors. I need a down payment for a house. Fifty grand."

Bill continued, "Where do you expect the money to come from?"

"Hah. I know the foundation has upwards of twenty million, so fifty thousand is just a drop in that financial bucket."

"You mean the academy should take fifty thousand dollars from its endowment and give it to you. And why would we—the academy and its board—be willing to do that?"

"Simple. You spend fifty grand to protect your investment, and keep donors contributing to a squeaky clean outfit."

"Jim, I'm always interested in the motivation of the people I deal with. What motivates you to press the academy for this money?"

"I figure—my wife and I figure—that if Moms and Kids didn't move to Chicago, I wouldn't be in this financial squeeze. We were doing okay in Springfield, with our own house, but real estate in Chicago and the suburbs priced us out of buying a house. We had to settle for a small apartment in a crummy neighborhood. We figure the foundation put us in this mess, so they should help us get out of it."

"Well, thank you for helping me understand your motivation. I don't agree with it, but now I see where you're coming from. Next, let me explain to you the motivation of the rest of us in the room. I represent Faith. Brad represents the academy and the foundation.

Felicia, Agnes, and I are board members concerned with the welfare of the academy, as is Faith, the acting head. We are unanimous in our rejection of your proposal. The main reason we would never agree to give you fifty thousand of the institution's money is because it's stealing. A criminal act subject to penalties such as incarceration and fines. You have chosen to steal money from the foundation. We choose not to follow your criminal path."

Bill paused. "Well, that's not the only reason, but it's an important, legal reason, and—"

Jim interrupted. "If we all keep quiet, no one will ever know. That's what I think."

Bill frowned. "What you *think*! Well, we're not in a court of law, so I don't have a judge cautioning me on my language, and I'll tell you how I look at it. Sooner or later an auditor would notice the missing fifty grand, and then everyone would be trying on prison clothes. I'd like to impress upon you that the others of us in this room are not just protecting our own hides. We are dedicated to improving the lives of women and their children. Your invitation to crime would jeopardize the wellbeing of the fifty current residents of Canterbury and their children, and future residents and kids.

"Now I'm going to tell you exactly what I think. I see you risking the future of Canterbury for fifty thousand dollars. That is selfish, it is criminal, and I'll be damned if I become a co-conspirator in this con." Bill took his Mont Blanc pen out of his shirt pocket, grasping it by the top, and raising it high above his shoulder. "What I would like to do is take a skewer and drive it through two small round parts of your anatomy." He swung his pen in an arc toward Jim's groin, narrowly missing the front of his pants. "And I'd roast those kebobs over an open fire."

Jim flinched, trying to scoot back, almost falling over backward.

Bill paid no attention to Jim, turning toward Felicia with a faint smile.

Felicia yelled, "And when those chestnuts got burnt to a crisp, I'd take a hammer and smash them." She pounded her fist on the desk, startling Faith.

Bill looked past Felicia toward Agnes. "Yeah, and I'd scoop up what's left and throw them into the fire and turn them into ashes."

Bill, Felicia, and Agnes fixed their gaze on Faith. Mouth agape, Faith caught her breath and then chimed in, "I'd gather up the ashes and take them in a boat and scatter them in the middle of Lake Michigan."

Jim's Adam's apple bobbed up and down as he struggled to catch his breath and speak. "You . . . you wouldn't do that."

Bill put on a saccharin smile, using his sweet voice. "No, Jim, of course we wouldn't. We just wanted you to know how mad we are. But I'll tell you what we would do, if we had to. We'd file a complaint with the Cook County State's Attorney. They would investigate and file charges. Honestly, Jim, I don't know what you had in mind when we didn't fork over the money. Were you going to turn yourself in to the state's attorney, and admit that you stole from the academy and blackmailed us?"

"I . . . uh . . . figured you'd give me the money rather than see the foundation go down the tubes."

"Let me spell out the stakes of your gamble. No, Brad should give you the basic facts, because he's a specialist in criminal law."

Brad looked directly at Jim. "To start with, because you upped the ante from seven hundred dollars to fifty thousand, the charge would certainly be grand larceny, and for that you could serve three to seven years and be fined up to twenty-five grand. The laws are stricter for defrauding a school or religious institution, so the judge might throw the book at you, considering Canterbury is affiliated with a church."

Brad asked Jim, "How old are your kids?"

Jim blanched.

Faith volunteered, "Eight and ten."

Bill said, "Well, you might get out before your oldest starts college. But of course, that doesn't include time for blackmail."

Brad added, "Yeah, could be another three to seven, as long as ten years, and up to a twenty-five-grand fine."

Bill smiled. "Jim, you wanted us to help you with a house.

Maybe we could do that, see that you are in a 'big house.' You know, that's what they call the penitentiary at Joliet, the big house. We hope you like those new accommodations, because you'd be confined there for years."

Bill rested his chin in his hand. "Let's see, you said the blackmail was a joint venture with your wife, so she'd at least be up for blackmail. If she helped plan the overpayment theft, you'd both do double time, although in separate facilities."

"Leave my wife out of this!" Jim yelled.

Brad shook his head. "No, afraid we can't. You said you and your wife planned the fifty thousand extortion con."

Jim forced a smile. "Well, you legal beagles aren't the only smart ones here. Faith tried to get me to write it down, but I refused. So, you don't have any evidence that my wife is involved."

"Don't you realize," Brad volunteered, "that you have five witnesses in this room who will swear under oath that you implicated your wife?"

"Maybe a jury would believe them, maybe not. You don't have any hard evidence."

Faith picked up her pen with one hand, holding out the other hand in a "stop" motion. She pressed several small buttons on her pen, and played back Jim's last statement, "You don't have any evidence that my wife is involved."

"Jim, I've recorded all of the times we talked about overpayments and the fifty thousand blackmail."

Jim closed his eyes, scowling, his face contorted in anger and pain. He raised his doubled right fist above his head and lunged toward Faith, screaming, "You lousy bitch, I'll kill you!"

Brad extended his leg in front of Bill and tripped Jim, who fell heavily against the front of the desk. Brad jumped to his feet and hovered over the stunned Jim. Slowly Jim picked himself up, a bad bruise on his forehead and a trickle of blood oozing from his nose.

Brad had his fist and arm poised for a blow. "Are you gonna behave, or do I have to punch you?"

Jim whined, "No, no, don't hit me," holding his hands in front of him. "Oh, I've gotta go."

Bill pushed him down in his chair, handing him a handkerchief.

Jim glared at him. "You . . . you're detaining me against my will. That's kidnapping."

"On the contrary. You made a threat of killing and an attempt at physical assault. We can tell the police this is a citizen's arrest. If you try to leave, we'll just dial 911 and have the cops arrest you."

"Okay, okay. You win. I give up. Just hand me the paper and I'll sign it."

"No, Mr. Anderson, that offer expired the other day. The terms are different now. And because of your bad conduct a few minutes ago, we have to take precautions. When you leave this room, you will go to your own office and remove all your personal belongings. You will never enter these premises again, and will not approach Faith. If you do, we'll arrange for a restraining order against you.

"You have stolen from the academy, and when we asked you about it, you lied, saying it was only six hundred, not mentioning the other hundred you squeezed from a transitioned resident. We can't trust you, so before we go any further with discussions, you have to make good on the money. By Monday you will deliver a certified check for seven hundred dollars to my office—here's my card. After you deliver the check, we'll arrange for a final meeting in my office."

"That's not fair!"

Bill snorted. "Huh. More than fair. Generous. We could have you perp-walked out of here in handcuffs."

Crying, Jim shuffled out of the office.

Bill and Brad shook hands, exchanging "Good work" comments.

Bill turned to the women. "Satisfied?"

Faith had a worried look on her face. "Bill, one more thing. Tell Jim he's not to visit or contact Jeremy. Soon I'll have to tell Jeremy about this mess, but right now he needs his rest."

Bill and Brad looked at each other. Brad suggested, "Why don't I tell him about Jeremy."

The women formed a threesome bear-hug and then brought Bill into their circle.

Felicia chuckled. "Bill, you were wonderful."

Bill glowed. "You three chimed in right on cue. If we had the time, I think we could do impromptu street theater."

Bill wagged his finger at Faith. "You naughty girl, using your recorder."

"I know you couldn't approve of it, so I didn't tell you. I considered it a way of protecting myself if it ever turned into a 'he said-she said' situation."

"You provided the spark that lit Jim's fuse and made him explode. I underestimated him."

Brad came back to the office. "Jim agrees he won't contact Jeremy."

Bill and Brad needed to get back to their loop office. Felicia and Agnes wanted to make it to Winnetka before rush hour.

Walking out the door, Felicia told Faith, "I'll be in tomorrow and start looking over bills. You asked me to be in charge of the budget, so for the moment that will fall to me. Right away we need to start looking for a new financial officer."

Faith grabbed her purse and rushed past Jackie, who stopped her. "Maisie said she'd see you about eight tomorrow morning."

17

D riving home, Faith tried to pay attention to the road and traffic. The tense scene with Jim rambled through her brain. She told herself to concentrate on the early morning meeting with Otto, but couldn't forget the monstrous look on Jim's face when he sprang out of his chair and said he would kill her.

She made it to the condo before Scott. He burst in, asking all about the encounter with Jim. Faith summed it up as quickly as possible, not eager to relive the drama.

Scott listened intently up to the point where Jim threatened her. "He actually said he was going to kill you?"

"Yes. Fortunately, Brad tripped him. He fell against the desk and hit the floor, stunned, with a bloody nose."

"Wow, your job has a lot more excitement than my humdrum reporter's life.

She wondered out loud, "How should I handle Otto?"

"Compared to what you went through with Jim today, talking to Otto will be a breeze." Scott rubbed his chin. "But if he walks in holding a meat cleaver, watch out."

THE NEXT MORNING Faith got up early, so she could arrive at the academy by eight. As she went out the door, Scott yelled after her, "Go get 'em, Dragon Lady."

On the drive to the academy, yesterday's drama still haunted her. She tried to focus on how to speak to Otto. At the same time, she thought about Felicia's review of the academy's finances, and interviewing a new financial officer.

When she arrived at the academy, Maisie enfolded her in a warm embrace.

"Honey, I know Jim is out of here. He came to the kitchen to get boxes to pack up his stuff. You don't need to tell me the details. I know you've been stressed out. Listen, if you don't want to talk to Otto today, we can put it off until Monday."

Raising her fist, Faith belted out, "Damn the torpedoes. Full speed ahead."

A few minutes later Otto walked in.

Maisie looked at Faith. "First we've got to check and put away the meat."

Faith noticed the meat neatly stacked in a clean container, arranged in the order of the bill, so that Maisie could take out each package and make a mark by that item on the bill. Faith appreciated neatness and efficiency. She also looked over his shoes. At the hotel when she interviewed men, she always observed how an applicant had laced his shoes and if they were tied in a nice bow. Proper care of shoes indicated propriety and courtesy in personal manner.

Otto had on work shoes, apparently with steel toes, which gave him good marks for safety. His shoestrings had been laced up right over left, in a symmetrical pattern with no twisted strands. The long laces circled the shoe tops for extra stability. Faith credited Otto with being neat, efficient, and careful. And he proved to be helpful to Maisie.

"You said you wanted hamburger for sloppy joes. This

hamburger is ninety percent beef to ten percent fat. Healthier for you than the fatty kind, but with just enough fat to give good flavor and allow you to crumble and brown it."

With the meat in the fridge, Faith ushered Otto and Maisie into her office.

Faith took a seat behind her desk, Otto and Maisie sat opposite her.

"Maisie tells me you provide quality meat, so we're not concerned with your product. I'd like to ask you about the academy's payment of your bills.

Otto sat up straight. "You've seen the bills and the checks?"

"Yes." She paused, waiting for him to speak.

Otto looked down at the floor. "Uh . . . if you saw the bills and checks, I think you can figure out what happened."

"I'd like to hear your side of the story."

He raised his head to meet her gaze. "Well, what you see is what Jim had me do. He said if I wanted to keep this account, he'd send me a check for a hundred dollars more than the bill, and I'd hand it over to him. I told him eventually someone would notice the difference, but he claimed he was the only one who looked at the books. And if I wanted to keep the academy account. I'd have to play ball."

"How did you handle your own books?"

"I could show you. I put down the extra hundred dollars as 'good customer rebate.' Not exactly the truth, not exactly an outright lie. Well, except for the fact that the money went to Jim, not to the academy."

"How did you get him the extra hundred?"

"He didn't want a paper trail, so at the end of the month we met at a burger joint and I gave him cash."

"A classic kickback scheme."

"Yeah, I hated it, but needed the account. I'm a small business-man. Most of my business is through personal contacts, like Maisie. I pride myself on providing quality meats at reasonable prices, with dependable service. I deal with some restaurants, but mostly insti-tutions, like old folks' homes and schools."

"Do you do this with other customers?"

"Occasionally the people I sell to ask for a couple of steaks, or a package of wieners, but I've never had someone operating an outright fraud like this. Maybe I should have walked away from Jim's scheme, but Canterbury is a major client." Otto squirmed in his seat. "Uh, how will you handle this?"

"This next month you won't receive an overpayment. Jim is no longer our financial officer."

"I'm glad to hear that. And if Jim isn't reimbursing you for the money he pocketed, I could make it up to the academy. Not all at once, but . . . say, a hundred dollars a month."

Suddenly the voice of Father Murphy resounded in her head, telling her that even in the modern world there are highwaymen. But if you are robbed by a highwayman, just stay on your highway and reach your destination—don't become a highwayman.

Faith smiled at Otto. "I'm glad you were honest with me, and appreciate your offer to make good for what Jim took. We'll expect him to reimburse us. All you need to think about is the future. Continue to provide us a good product at a reasonable price, and we can continue to do business."

They shook hands when he left.

A few minutes later Faith joined Maisie in the kitchen and ate the breakfast saved for her.

"My gawd, you handled that well. Now I know how you became a bigwig executive at a hotel."

Felicia walked in to the kitchen. "Hey, gals, did you save something for me?"

Maisie fixed Felicia something to eat as Felicia told Faith she would spend the morning and maybe part of the afternoon going over Jim's books.

Felicia hurried off to Jim's office while Faith lingered over a cup of tea. Her hand trembled as she picked up the teacup. Maisie walked behind Faith. "Put the cup down." She placed the back of her hand against Faith's forehead. "Well, you don't have a fever, but you're overstressed and about ready to collapse." She massaged

Faith's shoulders and moved up to her neck muscles. "You're tighter than a drum! Why don't you drive home while you're still up to it?"

"Oh, I've got to talk to Felicia after she scans the books."

Maisie shook her head and went back to her cooking.

Faith went to her office, telling Jackie, "Hold my calls for a while." She sat at her desk, resting her head on her folded arms. She dozed off, waking to Maisie's gentle touch on her arm.

"Boss lady, this is the Moms and Kids place. Today I'm the mom and you're the kid. You need some rest, more than a head on the desk nap. We have an open room from a resident who just transitioned. I'm going to take you there so you can get some Zees." She led Faith to the empty room, pulled the covers back and had Faith get in. "Sleep as long as you want."

18

Faith woke up in a strange room, disoriented, before she remembered Maisie had put her to bed in a resident's unit. She walked to the kitchen to find Maisie. "Thanks, Mom, for tucking me in. I needed that."

Maisie pointed to a chair. "Sit down. I've got a few minutes before lunch." She rubbed Faith's shoulders and neck. "You're still tense. You need more than a morning nap. You should get away from this place. It's not good for you to be under such stress."

"Yes, Mom, you're right, and I promise to consider a getaway."

Going to her office, Faith recognized a higher priority. She sat down and dialed Church of the Redeemer, asking the secretary if Father Whitmore had time to speak to her.

"He has an appointment in a few minutes. I'll see if he can talk to you."

"Hi, Faith, glad you called. I've only got a minute. What's on your mind?"

"I'll be quick. How about lunch Tuesday at Tropical Hut, eleven-thirty?"

"Uh, let me look at my calendar . . . yeah, I can do that. Before my next appointment shows up, how is Jeremy?"

"Better, but slow progress, and we don't know the long-term situation."

"Is that what you wanted to talk over?"

"Not really. It's problems at the Academy. Well, not problems in the plural, a problem. I've met another devil, and I'm trying to figure out how to handle him."

"Hmm. Until we can talk it over, let me repeat my best advice: follow your conscience. Okay, my appointment's here. Gotta go. See you Tuesday."

Faith felt a weight lift off her shoulders just making an appointment with her father-confessor.

A FEW MINUTES later Felicia knocked on her door. "Lunch?"

"Why not. First give me the preview. I'm not ready for any more bad news, so it had better be something positive."

Felicia chuckled. "I'll save the rundown for after lunch, but you don't have anything to worry about."

Felicia and Faith went to her office. "Well give me the good news. It's been a while since I've heard any."

"Jim may be an inept extortionist and a clumsy blackmailer, but he's a meticulous bean counter. The books are up to date, all bills are paid. I'll have to do a more thorough review, but from what I've seen, he's an efficient accountant."

"That *is* good news. I was afraid while he was pocketing academy money, he might have let our finances slide."

"No. It'll be easy for me to take over with the regular bills and stay on top of things until we can hire a new financial officer."

"You know, when Jeremy and I started considering a fundraiser, I told him that Jim might be good at taking care of the books, but 'he's not the sharpest knife in the drawer.' We agreed we ought to look for a professional fundraiser, and Jim should keep doing what he does best, pay bills. I never imagined he would turn to theft. Even a dull knife can inflict major damage. My best guess is that his wife put him up to it. And it's going to be hard on Jeremy to learn that his friend is a criminal."

Felicia leaned over the desk, putting her hand on Faith's. "Dear, you look very tired. Are you okay?"

"Handling the turmoil at the academy is more trying than any of the ordeals I faced at the hotel. Maybe it's because of my emotional investment here."

"It's time for me to beat the rush home, and I think you should take the rest of the day off. Get an early start for the weekend."

"Good idea."

ARRIVING AT THE CONDO, Faith felt relieved. She threw her coat on a chair and headed for the bedroom. Pulling back the comforter, she climbed in and let the warmth of the bed soothe her jangled nerves.

She woke up an hour later, not so tired, but still uneasy. She put on water for tea, and thought about penning a personal note. She went to the bedroom dresser and opened the drawer to take out her journal. Then she closed the drawer and took her tea to the lounger. Faith didn't want to write, she needed to think things out.

She wished Scott would come home and hold her. She leaned back in the lounger, realizing she couldn't nap. Getting up, she looked around the condo and surveyed the large bookcase. Her eyes rested on *Uncle Tom's Cabin*. It had been a long time since she had read that book. Or any book.

During her single years, books had been her best friends. After meeting Scott, she had slowly retreated from reading. And her joyous reunion with the twins gave her all the companionship she could ever want. She took Saint Harriet's book off the shelf, and had read a dozen pages when Scott opened the door.

"Hey, it's good to see you reading again. You've been more frazzled than I've seen you since . . . since your emotional meltdown in Peoria when we went to see Doug."

"You're right. My lady friends at the academy, especially Maisie and Felicia, told me to take some time off and get away from the academy for a while."

"Good for them. I've been thinking the same thing, but figured you'd be irritated if I mentioned it."

"Honestly, I'm more than frazzled. I'm like a can of soda left open all day that's lost its fizz."

"What are you going to do about it?"

"A start is an appointment with my priest-confessor on Tuesday."

"That's good. He can help you."

"Honestly, I'm burned out by the non-stop hassles at the academy. You know, the confrontations never bothered me so much at the hotel, because I could always walk away from them. The academy is different, it's like my second family. Any shadow over my brood throws me into an uninterrupted funk."

Scott laughed. "My wife, the mother hen."

When they went to bed, Scott told her, "Your academy ladies are right, you need a getaway. I know you want to see Jeremy Sunday, but tomorrow can be a Chicago getaway. Be ready to go out tomorrow when I come back from the paper, and I'll surprise you."

"That sounds good. I need a pleasant surprise."

THE NEXT MORNING, Faith pondered the events of the coming week, the ongoing negotiations with Jim, Father Whitmore's advice, and how Bill and Brad would handle Jim in the showdown meeting. She told herself to put the week ahead out of her mind, and be ready for Scott's surprises.

Scott called about eleven. "I'll be home soon. We're going out for lunch. Dress casual."

A little later he opened the door. "This is your getaway day. We won't be home until late."

Faith laughed. "You're in charge."

They took the elevator to the lobby and picked up a cab. "Loop Café."

Faith giggled.

At the café, they slid into a booth, as a waitress approached them with menus. Scott ordered. "We don't need a menu. Two bowls of chili and two dill pickles."

Scott eyed her. "I hear this is a specialty of the house."

The waitress just shook her head and went to the kitchen.

Faith beamed. "Very clever, Mr. Reporter, you listen to everything I tell you and don't forget. The Winnetka duo and I had fun at this place."

After their wacky meal, they grabbed a cab, and Scott called out, "The Aquarium."

"Now that's nice. I haven't been there in years."

They had a good time viewing all the marine life at the "fish house." Scott pointed out all the favorite specimens of the grandchildren when they toured the place. "Jeb especially liked this big octopus." He mimicked Jeb, holding his arms out, wrists dangling down, fingers waggling.

Faith tittered. "You're not only a good reporter, you're a pretty good mime. I haven't had such a fun time in ages."

After the Aquarium, they got in another cab and Scott announced, "The Art Institute."

"Yeah, dear, I haven't seen the impressionists in a long time."

"You can visit them if you want to, but I had in mind a special exhibition."

"I haven't kept up with the news. What is it?"

"A visiting collection of Japanese woodblock prints, Hiroshige and Hokusai."

They entered the museum and headed right for the Japanese prints. Faith gushed, "I never saw nature so natural, so supernatural, as in these images."

They only left the exhibition when the guards reminded them about closing time.

At the curb they found another taxi, and Scott asked the cabbie, "You know Happi Sushi?"

"Sure. Ten minutes tops."

Faith hugged Scott. "You know how to make my day. Japanese prints to tantalize my eyes, and then Japanese food to tickle my tongue."

They started with beer and edamame, later having sake with their sushi.

Leaving Happi Sushi, Faith sighed. "Oh, Scott, thank you so much for a wonderful day."

"Lady, it ain't over yet."

"There's more?"

"Yeah, it's a surprise."

The next taxi took them to Roosevelt University. They found their way inside to a movie club showing of Bogart and Bacall in *Casablanca* on a wide screen.

"You devil, you know that's one of my favorites."

He bought a box of popcorn as they walked in. They shared it, then held hands.

On the ride home, Faith whispered in his ear, "Scott, you're my favorite husband."

"And you're my favorite wife."

"A getaway can be anywhere, anytime, anything. But you know how to make it special."

When they went to bed, she made it special for him.

19

Sunday morning Scott surprised Faith again, announcing he'd go with her to church.

When they entered Church of the Redeemer, Faith steered him to the Madonna and child stained glass window she had commissioned.

Scott followed behind her. "So this is your Saint Harriet."

"Yes, but we don't let others know."

They settled in a pew, and as usual, Faith paid little attention to the sermon. She reverted to the time before she was a member of the church, and simply soaked up the divine ambiance, the sense of being at one with the Creator.

Breaking through this personal reverie came the authoritative voice of Father Whitmore, preaching. "Everyone knows a lost sheep, who has gone astray, and that's why the shepherd leaves the ninety-nine to go after the one lost sheep." Faith now paid attention to the sermon, recalling that she and the priest had once talked about Doug as a lost sheep.

Faith made a mental note that she and Father Whitmore would return to this theme at their Tuesday lunch.

On their way out of the church, the priest shook Scott's hand. "Glad to see you today. And Faith, I'll meet you Tuesday."

Leaving Church of the Redeemer, they headed directly for Oak Park. Scott drove, having Faith phone ahead to ask if they could bring fast food for lunch. She made the call and everything was set. They knew ahead of time that Jon and Rachel had another engagement and could not come.

Scott stopped at a restaurant in Oak Park near Jeremy and Melanie's house, loaded up with takeout sacks, and headed for Jeremy's house. Mark and Beth greeted them at the door. "Burgers and fries. Great!"

The kids attacked the food with gusto. While Melanie and Faith cleared up the meal, Scott retrieved the cardboard box theater and puppet socks, acting out Little Red Riding Hood. Then he had the younger set perform their favorite stories, with Jeremy as the appreciative audience.

The women made quick work of the cleanup. Faith sat at the kitchen table, a silent invitation to Melanie, who took a seat opposite her.

"Please tell me as much as you can about Jeremy's condition."

Melanie put her hands in front of her face, sniffling. "It's not that I don't want to tell you, I just can't. It's so uncertain. What we know is the infection is cleared up, and his kidney function is greatly improved. What we don't know is if there's any permanent damage done, any structural change. The doctors say, 'Time will tell.'"

"What about his return to the academy?"

"They'd like to have him rest for at least a few weeks, maybe a month or more."

"Thanks for letting me know. I think about him all the time."

"Yes, and I've seen the strain on you. Today you seem to be more upbeat."

"Scott treated me to a 'getaway' day yesterday, pampering me, which helped lift me from the doldrums. I hope you have a day away soon. You can't do 24-7 forever."

Melanie looked at the floor. "There's something you're not telling me. I sense something in the background. Let me in on what's bothering you."

"Here's all I can and should tell you now. The academy is rock solid, thanks to Felicia, Agnes, Bill, and Father Murphy. We have had a problem . . . .." She paused.

"A major problem?"

"Yes, and we're handling it. I hope it's cleared up this week. Eventually we'll have to tell Jeremy, but I wanted to wait until we had this issue taken care of. Why don't you call me next Friday and let me know how Jeremy is doing. If he's up to it, on the weekend I can give him an update on the academy and how we handled the difficulty."

Beth came into the kitchen. "Grandpa says he thinks they should go soon. C'n we have a prayer circle before they leave?"

The women laughed. Melanie said, "Sure thing."

Their prayers gave thanks for their family, with petitions for Jeremy's recovery.

ON THE WAY HOME, Scott glanced at Faith. "It's so good to see you back in a happy mood. We'll have to plan more getaway days."

"Second the motion!"

"Uh, you and Melanie had a heart to heart in the kitchen?"

"Yes. She needs a getaway day as much as I did. She's been under terrible stress, and the doctors can't tell her if there's permanent damage to the kidneys. I told her to call me next Friday, and if she thinks Jeremy is strong enough, I'll level with him about Jim and the academy."

"Yeah, you need to stay in touch with Melanie and help her ease Jeremy back into the situation at the academy."

MONDAY MORNING, Faith got up when Scott did, and made him a nice breakfast.

"Hey, I'll have to treat you nice every Saturday if you're going to fix breakfast. You're not eating anything?"

"No, it's good for me to eat at Canterbury with the residents."

"Mama hen and her chicks."

FAITH ARRIVED at the academy by a quarter after seven. She saw Otto in the kitchen with Maisie. "I had a sloppy joe from your hamburger, very good."

"Faith, let me say again I'm very sorry for the mess with Jim, and hope we can have a fresh start. I know you said you didn't expect me to reimburse the academy, but as a gesture of good will, I brought fifteen pounds of wieners. The kids love hot dogs. A quick and easy prep."

"Thanks, Otto. We appreciate your thoughtfulness. By the way, I can't talk about Jim, but if he gets in touch with you, just tell him that he should contact us."

"I understand."

Maisie smiled.

Faith joined the line and ate with a new resident.

After breakfast, Maisie came out and sat with Faith. "You're a different person today. I worried about you Friday, but over the weekend you seem to have recharged your batteries."

"Hah. Thanks to my husband."

She gave Maisie a quick summary of her getaway.

"You're lucky to have such a thoughtful guy."

"And lucky to have friends like you. Friday I almost collapsed, and you came to my rescue."

They hugged.

"Maisie, I won't be in tomorrow. You gave me good advice, to take some time off. I can serve Canterbury better if I'm rested and fresh."

"Good girl!"

GOING TO HER OFFICE, Faith began answering a backlog of correspondence, then went to playtime. A volunteer had brought a bean bag game, more suitable for older children, but the kids enjoyed something more active.

Jackie walked up to Faith. "Bill Ludwig is on the phone. I told him you'd be there in a minute. Do you want to talk to him, or—"

"I'll take it."

She ran to the office, breathlessly saying, "Hello, Bill."

"We have movement. A courier just brought us a certified check for $700 from Jim. Now the ball's in our court. I suggest a meeting with him in our law office Thursday at two. Can you be here?"

"Yes, and I'll make sure Felicia and Agnes can come."

"We should wrap this up quickly. I'll draft a new statement for Jim to sign. This one will have more teeth in it, and he'll scream bloody murder, but to hell with him. We want an airtight statement. I'll have Brad review it and email it to you later today. If you like it, send it around to the Winnetka gals and Father Murphy. We need a united front."

"Great. Oh, Bill, I should tell you that Friday I had a good meeting with the meat man, Otto. I told him we'd expect Jim to pay us back for what he stole, and if Jim contacted Otto, not to talk to him, just refer Jim to me."

"Good thinking. As usual, you're with me or a step ahead of me. Either Brad or I will get back to you by this afternoon."

Faith told Jackie to hold all her calls. She left messages for Felicia and Agnes about the Thursday meeting in Bill's office.

The call to Father Murphy, fielded by his secretary, resulted in Faith leaving a message. She summed up the situation, and asked if he couldn't attend, to give the other three board members his proxy.

At that moment Felicia knocked.

"You're just who I'm looking for." Faith brought her up to speed with Bill's suggestion for a Thursday meeting.

Felicia sighed. "Yeah, let's get it over with. All of us have used up a year's worth of adrenaline."

"I'm waiting to hear back from Father Murphy. I expect him to give us a green light to go ahead."

"Uh-huh. Say, girl, you look like superwoman today. What happened over the weekend?"

The story of her getaway got replayed again.

"Wonderful. You need to have more days like that."

"I'm taking tomorrow off. I have a lunch with my father-confessor. He's better than a shrink at seeing inside my mixed-up psyche."

They talked until lunch, then lined up and got their trays, and sat with different groups. Felicia excused herself early, wanting to have several hours to go through Jim's books more thoroughly.

Faith returned to her office, too nervous to work. A few minutes later Father Murphy returned her call.

"I listened to your message. I'm glad you're going ahead with this Jim character. He's a contemporary highwayman, for sure. You seem to be handling him very well. The academy is fortunate to have you three ladies looking after its best interests. Unfortunately, I'm booked solid Thursday, and can't attend the meeting. So you have my proxy to go ahead."

"This afternoon Bill Ludwig will be emailing a draft of the paper he'll ask the financial officer to sign. Do you want to see it before you give us your proxy?"

"That's not necessary. I mean, forward me the email, but it's more important for the rest of you to move ahead and reach closure on a difficult situation. I trust your judgment."

"Thanks, Father, I'll send you the email."

She hung up and checked her computer, finding an email from Bill.

20

I t only took Faith a minute to read Bill's succinct letter of agreement.

I, James Anderson, of sound mind and of my own free will, make the following statement. As the financial officer for Canterbury Moms and Kids Academy, I misappropriated at least $700.00 of academy funds. I will reimburse the academy for this $700.00 (and any additional funds that may be discovered to have been misappropriated).

My wife and I attempted to blackmail the academy, asking for $50,000 in exchange for not making public the financial improprieties. I have consulted my wife, and we agree not to pursue any blackmail in the future.

The academy, pending a complete financial audit, will not file charges against me or my wife at this time.

Signed,

James Anderson, Financial Officer, Canterbury Moms and Kids Academy Date

Janine Anderson, wife of James Anderson Date

Faith Armstrong, Interim Head, Canterbury Moms and Kids Academy Date

FAITH RECOGNIZED the outline of the original paper Bill had prepared, and Jim refused to sign. And she noticed the "teeth" in the new document. This paper omitted the two-month time frame for discovery of other misappropriations, and only promised the academy would not file charges "at this time." He added a new provision, mention of the blackmail scheme, including Jim's wife.

The emailed document seemed so harsh, Faith wondered if Jim would sign it. And what about his wife?

Wanting a second opinion, she rang Felicia, who was working in Jim's old office. "Could you drop by my office for a few minutes?"

When Felicia came, Faith handed her a printout of Bill's email. "What do you think of it?"

She read it. "Looks good to me. Boy, he thinks of everything, even named Jim's wife."

"It's tough."

Felicia nodded. "Tough as nails."

"Too tough?"

"I don't think anything's too severe for that jerk. Do you?"

"I just wonder, if our terms are too demanding, he may refuse to sign."

Felicia clenched her jaw. "Then we'll haul his ass into court. Excuse my French, but we already made that decision, right?"

"Yes, I suppose so. Well, I'll send the email on to Agnes and Father Murphy to see if they have any comments. I already talked to the good father, and he said he agrees to anything we decide on."

Felicia went back to her books. Faith re-read Bill's document several times, mulling over the language. Finally, she phoned Bill's office, asking the secretary to have Bill return her call today if at all possible.

FELICIA AND FAITH went to lunch together.

"Well, Faith, I'll keep looking, but don't find a single item out of place. Jim is so squeaky clean he'd pass any audit with flying colors."

Daydreaming, Faith didn't respond.

"Hey, wake up. Are you still worrying about Bill's email?"

"Uh, yeah, thinking about it."

"You're too kind-hearted. Us women and Bill have to hang together and really put the screws to Jim. For the good of the academy."

"I guess you're right."

When they finished lunch, Felicia went back to the financial records. Jackie told Faith that Ludwig's office had phoned saying Bill would give her a call about half past four.

Too keyed up to work, Faith pulled the copy of *Uncle Tom's Cabin* out of her purse and picked up the story. A phone call made her jump.

"Hi, it's Agnes. I read Bill's letter of agreement. It looks fine to me. This document is better than the first one, because it doesn't let Jim and his wife get away with anything."

"It's not too severe?"

"Are you kidding? Nothing's too severe for what they tried to pull. By the way, I'm on for the session in Bill's office at two on Thursday."

"Good. See you there."

Harriet's novel kept Faith busy until Bill's call, just after four-thirty.

"How are things with Moms and Kids?"

"Going as well as can be expected. Good news of a sort is that Felicia has been fine-tooth combing the financial records, and claims the accounts are perfect, so no new problems there."

"That's good. We don't have much time, so give me your take on the letter of agreement."

"Felicia and Agnes like it, and I . . .."

"You have some reservations?"

"Kind of."

Bill chuckled. "I expected as much. I anticipated your reservations. Felicia and Agnes are tough cookies, you're more like a soft
pretzel, and think I'm too nasty with Jim."

"Uh, well, I wonder if you had to be so hard on him."

"Yes, that was my intention, to be hard on him."

"In the first letter you didn't mention his wife, but in the second
letter you make her sign."

"Faith, I'll cut to the chase. I've been too gentle and easy on you,
not wanting to scare you. In my decades of lawyering I've had some
sleazy specimens, but this is my first experience with the threat of
killing."

"I don't think he meant it."

"You don't *think* he meant it. But you don't know, and neither do
I. Let me play bogey man and deliberately scare you with a few
examples of 'going postal.' In a number of post offices, a disgruntled worker walks in with a pistol and shoots his supervisor and
other co-workers. A few years ago, a man mad at the IRS crashed
his private plane into the local IRS office. Recently, a man with a
grudge against his wife's heart surgeon for letting her die on the
operating table, shot the surgeon while he was riding his bicycle to
the hospital. Look at all the shootings in schools and churches."

Bill waited for Faith to respond. Then he continued. "Jim
Anderson is a likely candidate for going postal. He's practically
ruined his life, and he's desperate. I can't rule out the possibility
that he would come in with a weapon and kill some of us before
turning it on himself. Yes, I deliberately put his wife in the agreement, because he wanted us to keep her out. That's an insurance
policy that he won't do something to any of us that would
boomerang and harm her."

"Well, Bill, your guided tour through the house of horrors gave
me a scare. And it helps me understand why you wrote up the
agreement the way you did."

"Have to go soon, but several other safeguards. We don't know if
Jim has skimmed other accounts, so that's why we say we're not
filing charges at this time, reserving the possibility of filing later.

And—you may not like this, but when Jim comes to my office, our security guard will frisk him, making sure he's not packing a weapon."

"You think that's necessary?"

"Absolutely. Now you and I don't *think* he'll bring a weapon. But I want to be sure. Damned sure. Double damned sure. The last time we met, I underestimated him, thought he was a meek mouse. Then he turned into a cornered rat and was going to kill you."

"Uh, I guess we're as ready for the meeting as we'll ever be."

"One other thing I should mention, another trick. Jim may not threaten us with a gun. He may whine and wheedle us with tears. Now I don't give a good goddamn if he falls on his knees, sobs and begs, we can't give in. So, do me a favor and don't go soft on him if Jim turns into a whimpering cry-baby."

"Okay, Bill, I'll do my best to support you. Maybe keeping quiet will be my best strategy."

21

Bill's call made Faith a little late getting to the condo. Scott beat her home, and had the wine glasses out.

"Are you ready for a little vino?"

"Yeah, if not something stronger."

"Rough day?"

"Bill just read me the riot act. But I'm getting ahead of the story." She pulled Bill's letter out of her purse and handed it to Scott. "Here, read this while we sip some wine."

He speed-read it as he walked to the lounger. "Bill's good. He's covered all the bases." Scott raised his eyebrows. "You go along with it, don't you?"

"I don't know, Bill's very thorough, and right on target. I just wonder if it's overkill, totally demolishing Jim."

"Babe, that's what you hired Bill to do, annihilate him. You don't want Bill to ease up, do you?"

"No, not really. I just wish there was some way we could let Jim go his way and we would go our way."

"Faith, my dear, I don't think you've ever gone to a boxing match. I have. When one fighter is winning, and has his opponent on the ropes, he doesn't give the guy a chance to catch his breath and regain his balance. He moves in and knocks him out. Let's face it, Faith, you need to go for a knockout."

I don't like to think of myself as scoring a knockout on Jim."

Scott cocked his head. "Okay, think of the fight between Jim and the Academy. One side wins, the other side loses. Rework your priorities. You want to protect the academy and the foundation. You'd like to settle this so Jeremy can come back to work with no loose ends. If you soft pedal the complaint against Jim, the whole case could fall apart, and put the academy in jeopardy. You shouldn't risk the future of Moms and Kids by going easy on a lowdown crook."

"I guess you're right."

They sat sipping their wine for a few minutes.

"Scott, remember on Sunday Father Whitmore in his sermon talked about the lost sheep?"

"Sure. We've talked about that before."

"When we dealt with Doug, I looked at him as a lost sheep, and thought we should somehow help him. You know, like the shepherd who left his ninety-nine sheep to find the lost sheep."

Scott guffawed. "Don't tell me you see Jim as a lost sheep, and the rest of us should rescue him."

"I don't know how to view Jim."

"Hah! I'll tell you how. Not as a lost sheep, but as a wolf in sheep's clothing. I recall a biblical passage that warns about false prophets who approach you in sheep's clothing but are actually hungry wolves ready to devour you. You can't let Jim eat you alive."

"For a preacher's kid, you're a good devil's advocate."

When they went to bed, Faith sighed. "Thanks for helping me think through the academy situation. I'm still so flummoxed and mixed up, it's good I have a session with Father Whitmore tomorrow."

～

Tuesday morning Faith felt like pampering herself on her planned day away from the academy. After a leisurely bath she took a cup of tea to the lounger and followed the tale of little Liza in *Uncle Tom's Cabin* until it was time to meet Father Whitmore. The scenic drive to the south side along Lake Michigan pleased her. She arrived at Tropical Hut before eleven-thirty and asked for a nice table.

Her priest rushed in, apologizing for being late.

"No problem. I'm just glad you had time for lunch."

"Well, even before we order, tell me how Jeremy is coming along."

"Much better, thank you. The infection's gone, and now he's regaining his strength."

When the waiter arrived, they ordered, and then the Father asked, "What's on the agenda today? Something about the academy? A problem?"

"I want to assure you first that the academy is on solid footing, thanks to the help of Felicia and Agnes. But while Jeremy was recuperating, Felicia discovered that our financial officer has been stealing money from Canterbury."

She quickly went over the story of Jim. "Thursday we have a crunch meeting of the board and Bill Ludwig to confront the finance man, make him admit his crime and leave the academy."

"Sounds like you have things under control."

"Bill is a highly skilled lawyer and the board members are great. Actually, the problem is with me. Remember when I told you about Doug, and when we totally defeated him, I began to feel sorry for him, like a lost sheep. I started to feel that way about our finance officer, Jim. In your sermon last Sunday, you mentioned the lost sheep, and how the shepherd left his large flock to find the lost sheep. I don't know if I'm trying to be the shepherd, but it seems like we should do something for Jim."

"What does Bill say?"

"He warns me not to go soft on Jim, insisting that the academy and its board have to be hard-nosed in this situation."

"Does Scott agree with Bill?"

Faith chuckled. "You know he was a pk, a preacher's kid, so he can trade one Bible verse for another. When I brought up the lost sheep passage, he reminded me that the Good Book also says to beware of false prophets, like wolves in sheep's clothing."

Father Whitmore slapped his thigh. "That's good!"

"But it doesn't help me with my conscience."

They kicked around the topic and the Bible verses for a while. As they finished their meal and the priest looked at his watch, he gave his parting shots. "Remember, my child, that the shepherd only left his flock because he wanted to restore the one missing sheep. Scott has a point; Jim is really a wolf preying on the flock. The shepherd wouldn't sacrifice his ninety-nine just to save one. Especially if that single animal is a pseudo-sheep. You don't want to jeopardize the future of the academy to try to save a predator."

The priest stood up to leave, and started for the door, then turned to look at Faith. "Remember the twenty-third Psalm, 'The Lord is my shepherd'?"

Faith mumbled, "Sure."

Father Whitmore smiled. "Well, the *Lord* is the shepherd, so don't try to take on all His work. The Lord can take care of His flock."

Faith laughed. "Thank you, Father."

RETURNING TO THE CONDO, Faith reentered the world of little Liza in Harriet's novel. She spent the rest of the afternoon reading.

She was ready to put the book down when Scott came home.

"Well, dear, did your priest give you absolution at your blessed lunch?"

"He surprised me, giving advice almost the same as yours. He liked how you countered the lost sheep verse with the wolf in sheep's clothing passage."

"Really?"

"Yeah, and he added the twenty-third psalm, reminding me that it's the Lord who is the shepherd."

"Touche! Now that's good."

"Honey, let's go out. I'm in the mood for a high-carb, high-cholesterol splurge ahead of my crunch meeting tomorrow."

"Where do you want to go?"

"The Loop Café."

"Not another chili and dill pickle binge."

"No. They have a deluxe burger and fries that might as well be called the heart attack special."

"Why don't we walk over and back, to give our arteries a cleansing in preparation for all that junk."

When they entered the Loop Café, the waitress recognized Faith. "Sorry, Miss, we're out of dill pickles."

"Oh, tonight I want your deluxe burger with fries."

Scott said, "Make that two."

The waitress grinned, bellowing out to the kitchen, "Two deluxe and fries."

Waiting for their order, Faith wondered out loud, "Being a preacher's kid, you must have heard a ton of sermons."

"You're right."

"And being a reporter-in-the-making, I bet you remember most of them."

"Right again."

"Okay, here's the test. Give me a sermon based on the Bible verses about a sheep in wolf's clothing."

"One of dad's best. Here's the setup. Dad's Congregational Church was a kind of middle of the road Protestant group. Some of the members leaned toward Fundamentalism, and had been watching television preachers. You know their story line—heaven or hell, salvation or damnation. These members got in touch with a fire-breathing televangelist, and, to make a long story short, wanted to pull our local church out of the Congregational orbit and move into a Fundamentalist organization. Dad had to be careful not to alienate any parishioners. That's when he preached his sermon on the wolf in sheep's clothing.

"He quoted several versions of the translations, which warn us to beware of false prophets, who come to us in sheep's clothing, but really are wolves. One translation says these wolves are 'ferocious,' another translation calls them 'ravening.' The point is that a false prophet will eat you alive. Dad didn't have to name names, he just let the members figure it out. Some hardcore fundamentalists left the church, but he saved it from being devoured by an aggressive televangelist type."

"Your dad must have been quite a minister."

They enjoyed their fancy burgers and gobbled up every one of their fries, then walked back to the condo and spent the rest of the evening reminiscing about Faith's upbringing in the Lutheran church, and Scott's experiences in his dad's congregation.

When she went to bed, she felt a little nervous about tomorrow's meeting with Jim and couldn't get to sleep. Scott soon began snoring.

Faith slipped out of bed and went to her drawer, pulling out her journal. She tiptoed to the lounger and opened the notebook to the first blank page.

A problem.

The problem is Jim.

He's a lost sheep.

Is he a sheep in wolf's clothing?

The Lord is my shepherd.

The Lord will take care of his flock.

I don't have to take care of all lost sheep.

Saint Harriet and Mary, help me find my way among the sheep and protect my flock.

SHE CLOSED the journal and returned it to its place before slipping into bed.

22

I n the morning, Faith told Scott, "I'm a little nervous, and don't want to be alone. I'll drive to the academy and eat breakfast with the residents. Watching playtime with the kids will help pass time, and I'll have lunch with Moms before heading to Bill's office."

He kissed her when he left. "Don't worry, you'll be fine." He thought a moment. "Baa, baa, black sheep, have you any wool? Just watch out for that black sheep and don't let him pull any wool over your eyes."

"Thank you, mister court reporter jester."

When she got to the academy at half past seven, Maisie pulled her out of line. "You're looking perky. Is today showdown time?"

"Yes, at two in the lawyer's office."

"You need a good breakfast."

"You can fortify me with lunch before I head out."

After breakfast she went to the office and read more of *Uncle Tom's Cabin* until playtime, and had fun listening to the singalong. The kids spied Faith and insisted she lead an Inky Dinky song. Afterward she schmoozed with residents and went to lunch with them.

Faith arrived at Bill's office at one-thirty. As she expected, the Winnetka women were waiting for her in the outer office. They had their own pre-meeting session. Faith told the other two, "Bill's going to play hardball today, even have Jim frisked to make sure he has no weapons."

Felicia gasped. "No."

Faith managed a weak smile. "Quoting Bill, he wants to be sure, damned sure, and double-damned sure Jim doesn't 'go postal' on us."

Agnes groaned. "I wouldn't put it past him, that slimy bastard."

Faith continued, "Bill's playing hardball. The letter is a take it or leave it agreement. I think he'll give Jim until tomorrow to say if he and his wife accept it, and until Monday to return the signed paper."

Felicia and Agnes nodded.

They chatted for a while, kidding each other about the Loop Café's signature chili and dill pickle meal. Faith joked, "Their heart attack special of deluxe burger and fries is wonderful for a once a year splurge."

Bill walked in as the women were laughing uproariously. He flashed them a wide grin. "Hey, can I join the party? But let's move it to the conference room. I don't want you to bump into Jim before the meeting."

Bill took the seat opposite the door, with Brad and Faith on his right and the two others on his left. "Ladies, today Brad and I can handle everything, and we'll make this as quick as possible. All I need from you three is your silent support."

Just after two, Bill's secretary told them Jim had arrived.

Bill looked around. "Any final questions before we begin?"

The women shook their heads.

Bill left the room, reentering a few minutes later with an armed security guard, stationing him inside the door. Then he brought Jim in from the waiting room.

Faith tried not to gasp at the hunched over figure of Jim. He looked haggard, the skin on his face drooping down like a wet dishrag hanging over a kitchen faucet. A two-day stubble on his cheeks gave him the appearance of a homeless person. His eyes seemed to be staring at a fixed point outside the room.

Bill told Jim, "This is Reggie, he'll be our backup security. Just a formality precaution, but because you made a threat at our last meeting, Reggie will frisk you to make sure you have no weapon."

Jim's eyes widened. "That won't be necessary, I don't have anything. Hell, I had to walk through a metal detector to get into your office."

Reggie grunted, "A knife can be plastic, won't show up on a metal detector."

Bill nodded. "Just a formality. Reggie, go ahead."

Reggie stood behind Jim, using both hands to pat him down, mumbling, "He's clean."

Bill motioned the security guard toward the door. "Fine. You can stay here in case we need you."

Jim grumbled, "Do you manhandle everyone who comes here?"

A smile spread across Bill's face. "No, just those who threaten violence. Take a seat. I need to inform you that these proceedings are being recorded on our surveillance cameras."

Jim shook his head. "You Chicago lawyers are worse than a hangin' judge."

Bill ignored him, announcing, "Let's begin. For the record, I represent my client, Faith. Brad represents Canterbury Academy. Jim comes without legal counsel, representing himself. Because we had a previous meeting, I won't sum up the situation here. Jim, we received your certified check for seven hundred, which we understand is what you misappropriated from the academy."

Jim said nothing.

"Jim, is the seven hundred all you misappropriated from the academy?"

"Yeah."

"We haven't conducted a complete audit, but trust that no other discrepancies will appear. We have drawn up an agreement for you and your wife to sign. Here is—"

"My wife?"

"Yes, according to what you told us, she helped frame the blackmail proposal. Jim, read the proposal first, and then we can discuss it."

The women looked back and forth at each other while Jim read. Quickly scanning the document, he demanded, "What is this paper? I came here to sign the agreement you showed me last time."

Brad answered, "You had a chance to sign that agreement, and rejected it."

Jim mumbled, "Well, give me the original paper, and I'll sign it."

"That offer is no longer on the table."

"Well, maybe I won't sign this one, either. You changed the language. I mean, look, 'no charges filed at this time.' That leaves it open-ended."

Brad nodded. "Yes, until we can complete an audit of all books."

"Why do you have to do that?"

Bill jumped in. "At first you said you only took six hundred dollars, overpayment to the meat man. Then we found out you had pulled a similar overpayment scheme with a resident. You lied to us once, so we have to make sure you aren't lying about the seven hundred being all you took."

"And you didn't need to bring my wife into it. I'll take all responsibility for everything."

Brad shook his head. "Not according to what you told us. You claimed you and your wife worked together on the proposal for the fifty thousand you figured the academy owed you when your family moved from Springfield to Chicago."

"Hey, I paid back the seven hundred and never saw any of the fifty thousand, so you can eliminate the blackmail language."

Bill held his hand up. "Jim, I should have made it clear at the beginning of this meeting, we have an agreement for you to sign. You can sign it or reject it, but we didn't come to negotiate. It's strictly a take it or leave it deal."

"You really want to stick it to me, don't you? And I only got away with seven hundred dollars. Peanuts to this rich foundation. It wouldn't hurt you any to just close this account and say 'no charges will be filed.' Not the open-ended phrase of 'at this time.' You have no reason to be so nasty."

Bill gritted his teeth, speaking slowly and forcefully. "Alright, Mr. Anderson, let's you and me do some arithmetic. You're the accountant and I'm just an amateur mathematician, but I looked at some figures, and they don't add up. You were taking in a hundred dollars a month with the meat supplier scam. That's twelve hundred dollars a year. And you say you need—at this point in time—fifty thousand for a house down payment. If you put that hundred dollars a month in a mattress, at the end of forty years you'd only have forty-eight thousand. I don't believe you and your wife are that patient."

The women locked their eyes on Bill as he did his math, then noticed Jim squirming in his chair.

Bill continued. "I have to think that you and your wife are impatient, not willing to wait forty years for that down payment. I would guess that you only tried out the scam with the meat man and the transfer of an overpayment to a resident as your warmup practice. On one point—only one point—I agree with you, seven hundred bucks is small potatoes to the foundation. But I think it's quite likely you have been planning, or may already have started, to pocket larger sums, not just from operating funds, but from the foundation's endowment."

Bill leaned back in his chair waiting for Jim to speak.

Jim said nothing, looking down at the table, avoiding eye contact. Then he twisted in his chair and stared at the wide-angle surveillance camera in the corner of the room. "Can't you turn that thing off? It gives me the creeps."

Brad asked, "Is it because of what you've already told us, or what you're about to tell us? More than the seven hundred bucks you already confessed to?"

Bill stared directly at Jim, asking slowly and deliberately, "What about it, Jim, was seven hundred all you misappropriated, or did you take other money?"

Jim raised his head, glaring at Bill. "You ambushed me, ganged up on me again. I should have brought a lawyer with me."

Brad jumped in. "A lawyer won't help you with the facts. Is it a fact that you took more than seven hundred?"

"This isn't a court. I don't have to answer that."

Brad snorted. "Hah! No, you're lucky it's not a court, because the judge would order you, 'Answer the question.'"

Bill softened his tone. "Jim, you got caught with your hand in the cookie jar. And you want to get by with a slap on the wrist. As I told you the last time, defrauding a charity, and a fifty thousand blackmail scheme, could put you in the slammer for a long time. Make it easy on yourself. If you have something else to tell us, now is the time. If this goes to court, the judge might throw the book at you."

Jim closed his eyes tightly, tears rolling down his cheeks. "I told Janine this would never work out. Someone would notice."

Brad said firmly, "Tell us when, how much, to whom."

"I've already got my wife in this. I don't want to involve anyone else."

"If you don't tell us, we'll find out, and it'll be worse.

"Okay, but the one who got the money is completely innocent. It's my wife's sister."

"Name?"

"Annie Bledsoe."

"Where?"

"Springfield."

"When?"

"Last month."

"Let me guess. Bank transfer."

Brad was writing everything down.

"So, you had the foundation put money in your operating fund, and then transferred a thousand to your sister-in-law's bank account?"

"Yes, I told the foundation we needed a thousand dollars for a computer consulting job, and created a fake invoice from her. She runs a small firm of her own."

Felicia jumped up out of her chair, leaning forward, hands on the table. "You slimy bastard. I remember that invoice to a Springfield consulting firm, so I thought it was legit. If you forged your sister-in-law's name to the invoice, that's another count of fraud against you. I hope you rot in jail."

Brad and Bill both held their hands out in a stop motion. Bill said, "We can settle the details later."

Felicia held her head high, nose in the air. "Damn right, we'll settle the details later. If I have to, I'll double check and verify every invoice back to the source. So, if you have any more fake accounting tricks to fess up for, you'd better do it now. Otherwise we'll throw your sorry ass in jail."

Bill nodded. "Yes, Felicia, the board will have to reconsider the matter. Jim, you were clever. By having the foundation make the deposit to the operating fund, you avoided the foundation's auditor —not like you trying to take it directly out of the foundation's coffers. Let's see. A thousand a month, twelve thou a year. Four years nets you forty-eight grand. But let's get something straight, Jim. First it was six hundred, then seven hundred, and now this evolving confession has advanced the theft to seventeen hundred. Is there another chapter in this misappropriation tale?"

"No. That's all. I swear."

Felicia yelled at Jim, "If you're lying, again—"

Bill interrupted her. "Felicia, we'll have time to check that later." Facing Jim, he asked, "Do you have a checkbook with you?"

"No."

"A credit card? One good for a thousand bucks?"

"Uh, yeah."

"You could authorize us to have my secretary run it through for a thousand, which we would send on to the academy."

Jim sat stiffly in his chair.

Brad asked, "Do you authorize our firm to charge your card for a thousand dollars, to be sent to the academy?"

Jim mumbled, "Yes," stood up, pulled his wallet out of his back pocket and removed a credit card, handing it to Brad, who took it to the secretary.

Bill announced, "If anyone needs water, we have some in the mini-fridge in the outer office. Let's wait to begin the discussion of the agreement until Brad returns.

23

B rad came back with the credit card and a slip for Jim to sign.

Bill announced, "It's good you admitted the extra thousand, which we would have found eventually, when it would have presented greater problems. I assume you're prepared to sign the agreement. Of course, it calls for your wife's signature, too, so the agreement can't be completed today. I suggest you take the paper home and let us know tomorrow if you will both sign it, and then have it in our office by Monday."

Jim's face twisted into a contorted frown. "My wife . . . my wife's leaving me."

The women's mouths dropped open, and Faith started to say something.

Bill held up his hand to silence her. "We regret any marital problems, but the misappropriation and blackmail matters remain a problem of the past that must be settled, regardless of any future separation of you and your wife."

Brad turned to Jim. "Is your wife still in the Chicago area?"

"She will be until Monday. She's renting a trailer and taking household belongings to Springfield."

"You have an address for her?"

"I can give it to you, her sister's place."

"Are you prepared to sign the agreement?"

Jim closed his eyes. "You leave me no choice."

Bill looked at Faith. "Are you prepared to sign the agreement?"

"Yes, and I—"

Bill held his hand out. "That's all we need to know now, that two of the three people have consented to sign the paper. Now, Jim, do you think your wife will sign?"

"Huh. She's on a tear now, mad at me, furious with the academy, angry at the world. She's likely to tell all of us to go to hell."

"Well, it's my duty as legal counsel to Faith—and Brad's duty to the academy—to advise you it's in your best interests, and your wife's best interests, to sign the paper and be done with this. I'd hate to think that we had to draw up a different agreement just for you, Jim, and then to file charges against your wife. She'd have to go on trial in Chicago. A criminal lawyer would be very expensive, and we have overwhelming evidence against her. She'd likely spend years in prison away from her children."

Bill glanced at the women, who twisted and turned in their seats, cringing at Bill's prediction.

He continued. "Now why do I tell you this? To scare you? No, to motivate you to persuade your wife to sign the paper."

Jim covered his face with his hands, sobbing. "I never thought it would come to this."

The women exchanged glances. Bill gave them a stern stare, moving his head back and forth in an unvoiced negative.

Bill switched to his smooth baritone voice. "I think that concludes our meeting. Jim, we look forward to hearing from you and your wife tomorrow. We won't intrude into your personal situation, but we hope the best for you and your wife."

The women eased back in their chairs.

Head down, Jim shuffled out of the room without any comment.

Bill breathed a sigh of relief. "Ladies, that went as well as could be expected. I apologize for not letting you speak, but we were heading for a successful conclusion, and I didn't want us to detour into any side concerns."

Faith stared at Bill. "I'm glad you're on my side. I'd hate to be on the other side."

"That's one of the best compliments you could give me. Thank you."

"I have to admit, Bill, you were right to keep us women from talking. Jim got so pathetic that I started feeling sorry for him." Faith turned toward Felicia and Agnes. "I forgot to tell you. Bill warned me not only of Jim bringing a knife or gun, but one of his most powerful weapons—tears." Faith looked at Bill. "Your man Reggie is skilled at frisking people with his metal detector, but he doesn't have a tear-detector."

Agnes spoke up, "My tongue must be bleeding, I bit it so many times, stopping myself from swearing at the creep."

Felicia frowned. "I was furious that he tricked me with that phony invoice. And then he pulled the 'poor me' maneuver."

Bill chuckled. "Brad and I are used to defendants trying every trick in the book. They don't always shout and threaten. Sometimes they'll resort to what we call the 'soft approach' of crying and tears to wrangle a better deal. Brad and I are familiar with this ploy and better prepared not to give in. The two of us took turns pressuring him from each side like trapping him in a vise, and I didn't want any expressions of sympathy from the three of you to help him wiggle out of our squeeze play."

"What will happen now?" Felicia wondered.

Bill shrugged. "It's up to them. We have to wait. Hopefully Jim's wife will come to her senses."

Agnes wagged her finger in the direction of Jim's empty seat. "The threat of being separated from her young children—that's what made us women uncomfortable. And even if Janine hates the agreement, she won't risk losing her children."

"I know about losing children," Faith volunteered. "There's nothing worse."

Agnes snorted, "Hah! I've never met Janine, and shouldn't badmouth her, but from what we heard today, she seems to be a real shrew. She put her husband up to this devious scheme, and let him do all the dirty work."

Bill cocked his head. "I don't like to pay compliments to my adversary, but I'll share my candid thoughts. He's a criminal, a stupid criminal. Even so, as Agnes pointed out, Janine played the role of the evil genius behind this misguided venture. Often in cases like this, a defendant will heap blame on a partner. Jim could have said, 'My wife made me do it.' Instead, he tried to keep his wife out of the picture, taking full responsibility for the caper. And he does this even after she leaves him. We have to give Jim some credit for that."

Faith added, "Maybe we should consider him a good man gone wrong."

Felicia nodded. "A good man led astray by a not so good woman."

Bill stood up. "We could talk all afternoon about the dynamics of this case. Let's just hope that Jim gives us a call tomorrow saying the deal is on. I'll let Faith know as soon as I hear. Congratulations, ladies. Brad will type out notes of our meeting, in case we need a written record. Uh, Faith, I assume you didn't tape this session?"

"No, you've scolded me for that, and I didn't want to get in the way of your negotiations. Anyway, your surveillance camera will provide both video and sound."

"Well, members of the Chicago Triumvirate, a good job. A successful meeting like this depends on all the preliminary planning behind the scenes, that you handled very well. Meeting adjourned."

The three women chatted in the elevator.

Felicia volunteered, "It's a little early to eat. Why don't we take off for home and get ahead of the rush hour?"

A three-way bearhug ended the afternoon.

Faith called after the Winnetkans, "I may tell Jeremy about Jim this weekend if Melanie thinks he's up to getting the news."

HOME AT THE CONDO, a hot bath enabled her to decompress from the tense negotiations. After dressing, she called Scott. "Pick up a pizza on your way home."

"Can't you get the pizza? I've been slaving away here all day, I'll have to fight traffic home, and I don't feel like stopping. You could have it delivered. Are you trying to tell me there's bad news?"

"No, it's almost all good news. It's just that I'm so tired I don't want to go out. You can hear a rerun of the meeting as we eat."

"Okay, okay, I'll make the pizza run."

Scott arrived home a little early, carrying a pizza. Faith got two sodas out of the fridge and started summing up the conference at Bill's firm. Scott liked especially the part about security frisking Jim, and marveled at how skillfully Bill finessed Jim into admitting the thousand-dollar transfer to his wife's sister.

"I'm not surprised at all that he and his wife had their sights on more money."

Faith mentioned the trio's dim view of Jim's wife, staying behind the scenes to goad her husband into criminal activity.

Scott laughed out loud. "Your priest and I missed the point of this story. It wasn't so much about a lost sheep or a wolf in sheep's clothing. We should develop a new saying: Behind every sheep that goes astray, there's a ewe that led him astray."

That prompted a laugh from Faith.

Scott finished the last piece of pizza. "So where does that leave you and the academy?"

"We're all in limbo, waiting to see if Jim persuades his wife to sign the paper."

"She doesn't have much choice, does she?"

"Maybe not, but I expect some kind of resistance or objection from her."

"You know, dear, I don't wish you any trouble, but you lead a much more exciting life than me. Every night is a new episode of reality theater, hearing the latest machinations at the academy."

"Scott, you remind me of that ancient Chinese curse: 'May you live in interesting times.' It's entertaining for you, but I hope we can look forward to receiving our daily dose of reality theater from television shows."

THE NEXT DAY Faith took her time going to the academy, and went right to her office, checking for mail and messages with Jackie. Sitting at her desk, she wrote a note to herself to phone Father Murphy after hearing from Bill about the agreement. Then she'd place a conference call with Felicia and Agnes. Next on the to-do list came brainstorming with Felicia about hiring a new finance officer.

Faith answered a few letters and returned some phone messages, but couldn't concentrate while waiting for Bill's call. She watched playtime, then chatted with moms until lunch, and ate with two new residents.

Julia, the social worker, saw Faith at a lunch table and asked to talk to her. They went to the office.

"I know you've been too busy with personnel matters—Jim—but soon we need to go through the backlog of applicants and decide on who to admit as new residents."

"Thanks for reminding me. I hope we can take care of the finance matters by next week, and then return to a normal routine."

After talking to Julia, Faith wondered,

WHAT IS A NORMAL ROUTINE?

Jeremy's sickness and absence threw everything out of synch.

The problem of Jim presented the academy with another headache.

If we can survive Jim's exit, at least we'll be able to focus on Jeremy's condition.

A CALL from Bill interrupted her daydreams.

"Faith, I have clients waiting, will have to give it to you quick. Jim called, he and Janine will sign the papers."

"Good!"

"It wasn't easy. Janine wanted to negotiate the terms to say no charges filed, period—not open-ended. And she tried to plea-bargain to just the misappropriation, no mention of blackmail. I repeated the hard line of no negotiation, accept or reject the agreement. Jim talked to his wife, and called back, insisting we were mean, but they would sign. The papers should be delivered Monday. Can't talk more now."

"Great work, Bill."

FAITH SHIFTED to her efficient hotel executive mode, quickly making phone calls.

She left a message with Father Murphy's secretary, just saying that their difficulties were on their way to being favorably resolved.

Next, she called the *Trib* and left a voice mail for Scott, telling him, "All sheep accounted for. Sorry about the other night—I didn't think about you first when I asked you to get pizza."

Then she dialed Father Whitmore. She expected he'd be busy, so she left a message thanking him for helping her handle a difficult issue, which had been taken care of.

She phoned Felicia and Agnes last, knowing they'd gab for a while.

Both of the Winnetkans were happy that the paper would be signed.

Felicia sniped, "I misspoke yesterday. I called Janine a shrew. She's a full-fledged witch."

Agnes sputtered, "You won't say it, but I will. She's a *bitch!* A bitch on wheels."

They laughed.

"What bothers me," Faith said, "is the kids. It's always the youngsters who suffer from family breakups."

They agreed to get together sometime at the Loop Café for chili and a dill pickle.

Faith decided to take off early for home, when Jackie said Melanie was on the line.

"Hi, Melanie, how are things with you and your patient?"

"Much better. Jeremy's taking a nap now, so this is a good time to talk. Uh . . . you said to call today."

"I know you don't want to stay on the line long. Is Jeremy strong enough for me to give him an update on the academy this Sunday?"

"I think so. The doctor says in another week or two he can start back half days. You sound mysterious. Difficulties?"

"Here's the quick and dirty. Jim Anderson, believe it or not, was stealing from the academy, and we had to let him go. That's the heavy load I've been carrying around and couldn't tell you about."

"What? I can't believe it. Jim was with us at One Way."

"Yeah, it'll be a shock to Jeremy, which is why I didn't want to tell him earlier. We've got the situation under control now, so that Jeremy won't have to deal with it when he comes back to work."

"Oh, the kids need me. We'll see you Sunday."

"I'll check with Scott to find out what he has in mind, so that he can take the kids, and I can talk to you and Jeremy."

24

W hen Scott came home, Faith provided him with a
rehash of Canterbury Days, the name they had given
to the reality show at the academy.

Scott laughed out loud at Agnes calling Janine a bitch on
wheels. When Faith told him about Janine trying to renegotiate the
agreement, he joked, "She'd haggle with Saint Peter for larger angel
wings and a pair of golden slippers."

"Oh, Scott, I'm so tired of all these confrontations. I'd like my
time with Moms and Kids to be more constructive and creative. The
other day I wondered what a normal routine would be at
Canterbury."

"Hang in there, you've paid your dues, and things will settle
down."

"Oh, I didn't tell you that Melanie called, and she had good
news. Jeremy's better, soon may be able to return to the academy
half days. I told her about Jim, and Sunday I'll update Jeremy on
the academy. Could you plan something to take the kids out of the
house? That way I could have some time with Melanie and Jeremy."

"Sure, we'll go to a fast-food place with an indoor play area.

After burgers they can run off the calories climbing around the play equipment."

"Great. I'll fix sandwiches for the three of us so Melanie doesn't have to cook."

SUNDAY SCOTT WENT to church with Faith so they could go directly to Oak Park after the service. As they left the church, Father Whitmore said, "Glad to see you again, Scott."

Faith leaned close to the priest. "Father, everything's fine, thanks to you. I'll tell you about it."

ARRIVING AT JEREMY'S PLACE, Faith took a picnic basket to the kitchen while Scott loaded up the kids and headed for a burger joint.

As Faith unpacked the basket at the kitchen table, she turned to Jeremy. "It's great that soon the doctors will let you start back half days."

"Seems like a year since I was at the academy. I've really missed it."

"We all missed you. Thanks to Felicia and Agnes, we've held the place together. While the kids are out with Scott, I want to bring you up to date on Canterbury. You know the program, and we haven't changed it. Agnes still does some tutoring, and as soon as you get back, we'd like to expand the instruction and training programs. Agnes and Felicia will handle that. Jon and Rachel plan to help us, especially with beginning and advanced computer training. Felicia has been busy assisting me, so we haven't been as active in fundraising as we'd like. Because a few residents transitioned, we have some empty rooms. Julia and I need to screen applicants for new residents."

Jeremy put his sandwich down. "I can't thank you ladies enough for filling in. Sounds like you've done a terrific job. It's good to hear that things are going well."

Faith sighed. "Yes, the academy is doing fine, and we only had one major problem while you've been away." She quickly summed up the discovery of Jim's theft and the legal maneuvering to handle it. This news stunned Jeremy.

He frowned, squinting at Faith. "I can't believe that Jim Anderson—"

She gave him the details of the blackmail scheme, and the fact that he had even threatened to kill her. Jeremy groaned. "I want to talk to Jim and hear him say he took the money."

Faith shook her head, almost yelling at Jeremy. "No! We have solid evidence in receipts that he cheated the foundation, and we've got it under control. There's no point in you second-guessing us."

Jeremy stuttered, "Well, it just doesn't seem right to me. What . . . what will happen to Jim?"

"He's going back to Springfield. Felicia and I are beginning to look for a new financial officer. We can wait until you return to decide on the new appointment. Felicia is taking care of the bills and day to day expenses. Don't worry, we made him agree not to contact you, me, or anyone at the academy. He cleaned out his office and will never return to Canterbury."

Jeremy started to get up, and stumbled, almost falling.

Melanie yelled, "Jeremy, watch out."

He sat back down. "Mother, I had no idea. It wasn't fair to expect you to put up with that. I'll ask the doctor if I can come back right away."

Faith forced a smile. "We put out the fire, so there's no need to call the fire department."

Melanie looked at Jeremy. "Dear, I don't think you're up to handling the stress. I—"

Faith interrupted. "That's why I didn't tell you two earlier. I wanted to wait until we took care of the situation."

Melanie turned to Faith. "How in the world did you survive all that?"

"With the able help of Felicia, Agnes, Bill Ludwig, his able colleague Brad, my priest—and even our head cook Maisie. Without them I couldn't have done it. Oh, don't forget my main support, Scott. He's been a sounding board as well as a pillar of strength."

Melanie and Jeremy stared at each other. Faith read the silence, suggesting, "We've handled some difficult matters today. Maybe we should let it rest."

Melanie nodded. "That's enough for one day."

"Sorry to spoil your meal."

They finished eating and Melanie made tea while Faith and Jeremy moved to the living room.

"Hey, son, let me give you some good news. The mothers and children are doing great. When it's playtime, if I'm not busy, I watch or participate.

Jeremy sniffled. "Thank you, Mom. Thanks for everything."

Scott and the kids came busting into the room, full of chatter about the fun they had at the burger joint.

Faith put an arm around each grandchild. "I brought some cookies, but don't suppose you're hungry after hamburgers."

Mark and Beth yelled, "Yay, cookies!"

After the cookies, Scott and Faith traded glances. He told Melanie, "Well, we don't want to tire your patient too much, we'd better be heading back to the city."

Pulling out of the driveway at Jeremy's, Scott asked, "How did it go?"

"Rough on both of them. Jim has been their friend since One Way in Springfield, and they couldn't believe he'd steal from the academy."

"You know that old saying, with a friend like him, you don't need enemies."

"Yeah. Hey, I want to change the subject. We don't know when Jeremy will be coming back, but on the day he returns I'd like to have a welcome party. Hopefully you'll be able to attend, and maybe Jon and Rachel can swing it."

"Let me know a few days in advance so I can clear it with the paper."

For a few minutes they sat in silence. Faith spoke up, "I hope Jim and Janine sign the agreement and deliver it tomorrow. That should mark the end of the turmoil of Canterbury Days, and we can return to a ho-hum uneventful life."

Scott snickered. "What planet do you think you're living on? There's always something."

MONDAY MORNING FAITH woke up feeling like she was beginning a new life. She had a cup of tea with Scott while he ate, then hurried off to the academy, with plans for a full day.

Maisie found her in the breakfast line. "After you eat, I want to see you."

Faith enjoyed sharing a meal with the early birds, then excused herself to meet Maisie in the kitchen.

"Honey, I've been thinking, Jeremy will be coming back some time."

"Maybe in a week or two he'll start with half days."

"That's good. Begin with a light schedule. And I hope you and the Winnetka team will keep up the good work. It's too much for Jeremy to handle all by himself."

"You're absolutely right."

They had been standing in the kitchen. Maisie led her to a large room behind the kitchen. "We converted this storage room into overflow for our pantry, and put in a lot of shelves, but we really don't need it. Why don't we turn this into an office for you?"

Faith looked around, sizing up the room. "Yeah, that would work."

"Take out the shelving, and you could easily fit a desk and chair, file cabinet, and other office furniture, and have space left over."

Faith nodded. "A place to keep papers, with the privacy to inter- view residents. My dear Maisie, you have a good recipe for everything, even a mini-office. I have some ideas about how to make the best use of this space."

FAITH HURRIED TO HER OFFICE. Julia had left a stack of resident applications for her. She read through several dozen before going to the kitchen for tea. Taking the cup back to her desk, she ranked the applicants by referring to the notes she had jotted down on a legal pad.

Faith wanted to take a break and watch playtime, but did several quick searches of headhunting sites, and looked over some bios of people seeking financial officer positions. She heard scraping of chairs, a sign someone was organizing playtime. The leader for the day had the children playing bus driver. Faith grabbed a chair and took the last place in line. When it came her turn, she said she was driving a school bus, and sang out "The wheels on the bus go round and round." The kids loved it as much as Faith.

Playtime energized Faith to get back to work. She called Felicia to discuss the search for a finance officer. Felicia volunteered, "Let me handle it. I know a guy in an employment agency, and I'll see if he has someone to recommend. Hey, I was just getting ready to join you at the academy. See you at lunch."

Next, she phoned Julia. "I've read through the stack of applications you left on my desk. When can we meet to discuss them?"

"How about three tomorrow afternoon?"

"Fine."

Jackie told Faith she had a call from Bill Ludwig.

"Good morning, Bill. And I hope you have good news."

"How's this for good news: the signed agreement just arrived in our office."

"That's great, but you're holding something back—bad news?"

"Let me put it this way. It's unexpected news."

25

"I'm almost afraid to ask—what's the unexpected news?"

"Along with the agreement, Jim sent a letter."

"He did?"

"Addressed to you."

"Oh, no."

"Uh-huh. I could sum it up for you, but it's better that you read it. I just put it in the fax machine. You'll have it in a minute. Read it, and then we can kick it around for a while."

Faith heard the fax machine chattering, and hovered over it until it spat out a single sheet. She grabbed it and scanned it.

DEAR FAITH,

Let me begin by apologizing. I did some things I am ashamed of. I said some things I regret. I wish I could change the last year, but that's not possible.

It was a mistake for Janine and me to move to Chicago. We got in over our heads and made bad choices. Now it's not clear how we can make a fresh start back in Springfield. I don't know if she and I will be together, or will go our separate ways.

Whatever happens, my next priority is finding a job in Springfield. Which is why I'm writing this letter, to ask you for a letter of reference. I hope you can look past the mistakes of the past year to the good work I did for One Way and for Moms and Kids.

Bill Ludwig has my address and can forward a letter to me in Springfield.

Good luck with Moms and Kids.

Sincerely,

Jim Anderson

FAITH SIGHED. "Well, that was, as you said, unexpected."

"What's your take on it?"

"It's unbelievable. How could he have the . . . I don't know what. Guts? Gumption?"

"Maybe the word you're looking for is gall."

"After stealing from the academy, lying to all of us, blackmailing. On top of that, threatening to kill me. And he wants a recommendation. What do you think I should do?"

"I have one solid piece of advice. As with Doug, don't contact him directly. Everything goes through my office."

"Well, I can't in good conscience recommend him to someone else. I wouldn't want anyone to recommend him to me."

"You don't have to reply at all if you don't want to."

"Let me think about it and see if I can come up with an answer. Sheesh. I assumed we were through with him."

"I've got to get back to work. Let me know what you want to do."

Faith sipped another cup of hot tea to soothe her troubled innards, while considering a diplomatic reply. She repeated to herself Father Whitmore's frequent advice to follow her conscience and do the right thing. She forced herself to sit down at the computer and type out a draft.

Dear Jim,

Your unexpected letter surprised me. After all the recent events, I didn't think you would ask for a recommendation. You will understand why I can't in good conscience provide a reference letter.

The best I can do is encourage you to make a new start in your life. You are going back to Springfield, which may be a good place to begin again. My suggestion is that you ask for letters from people who know you there, maybe the One Way people.

I hope that you and your wife can reunite and hold your family together.

Good luck.

Sincerely,

Faith

FAITH SAVED THE DRAFT, then went to lunch, finding Felicia and Agnes in line. The sight of these two friends lifted Faith's spirits.

"Come with me to the kitchen, gals, I've got something to show you." She led them into the storage room. "Maisie has a great idea. We could convert this space into an office for the three of us. We could line up three desks and a few chairs against this wall. That way, when Jeremy comes back, he can have his office, and each of us will have some of our own space. What do you think?"

Felicia smiled. "Sounds good to me."

"Why not," Agnes added.

Faith laughed out loud. "We can have fun, too. I came up with a name for this cubby hole—the Canterbury Henhouse." They howled with glee.

Maisie stuck her head in the room. "Let me in on the joke."

Felicia said, "Welcome to our new office, the Canterbury Henhouse."

Maisie's chortle made her jowls and belly fat bounce like jello. "You gals are too much!"

~

A<small>FTER LUNCH</small> with the other members of the troika, Faith went back to her office. She reread the letter to Jim and emailed it to Bill.

Sitting at her desk, trying to erase Jim's letter from her mind, she thought about Maisie's clever idea for office space. Faith knew she should clear this idea with Jeremy. At that moment, Jackie interrupted her with a call from Melanie.

"Good news. The doctor says this week and next, Jeremy should go out for long walks and do some driving in the neighborhood, and if he does well, he can return to work half days, two weeks from now."

"That's great news. We look forward to his return. I was just going to call you—is he up to talking for a few minutes?"

"Sure, here he is."

Faith quickly described the plan for converting the storage room into an office for her and the Winnetkans. She told him, "It would be an outlay of five thousand or so, but it would mean the three of us would have some space and our own phone lines. Felicia should be able to field phone calls on her own line. If she only lands one donor by having her own phone, it would more than repay the remodeling costs."

"Gee, Mom, don't you think I can handle the academy alone?"

"No! You've been doing fine, but the operation has gotten too big and complicated for just one person. It's no wonder you got sick, with all the stress you had to put up with."

"I guess you're right. Go for it."

Faith began planning the renovation of the storeroom, complete with honey-colored laminate wood flooring and robin egg blue paint. She bought three light oak desks and chairs to match the floor. Henry, the maintenance man, tore out the shelving and handled the contractors.

J<small>ACKIE ANNOUNCED A CALL FROM</small> B<small>ILL</small>.

"My dear Faith, you were nice with Jim. Almost too nice. You did the right thing, not giving Jim a recommendation. But you let him down easy and even offered him sound advice. That was generous. If all people were as thoughtful as you, we'd have a lot less law suits. I'll forward your letter to Jim, and remind him that all correspondence to you goes through our office."

"Bill, I just want to be done with this!"

"Hang in there, we've traveled a long way on this road, and should be about at the end."

FELICIA DROPPED by on her way home. "Have a few minutes?"

"Sure."

"I talked with a finance guy I know, asking him what we should do about a financial officer at Canterbury. He said since most of the money is handled by the foundation and their auditor, we don't need a high-powered finance expert. He says we're really talking about a bookkeeper, and any young person with an associate's degree in business administration will be adequate. We should be able to find such a candidate at the junior college where the residents are taking courses."

"Thanks. I'd like to have a few names for Jeremy to consider when he comes back."

"Good. Let's go home before traffic gets bad."

"See you tomorrow—if you're coming in."

"Sure. I want to take care of bills. And I need to double check Jim's bank transfers. It ticks me off that I missed the transfer to Jim's sister-in-law. He fooled me—the invoice he faked for her consulting firm looked legit."

FAITH ENJOYED her time in the condo before Scott got there. She had not yet digested the day's events. Elation at the prospect of having an office for the Canterbury trio. Deflation at the specter of dealing with Jim. The good and the bad. The sweet and the sour.

Scott breezed in, gave her a kiss, and asked, "Well, how did your first normal day at the academy go?"

"Very abnormal. First a real picker-upper. Maisie came up with the idea of turning an extra room into an office for me. I looked it over, and figured it could be a triple office, with a desk for me as well as desks for Felicia and Agnes. I'm going to call it the Canterbury Henhouse."

A wide grin spread across Scott's face. "Terrific."

"Well, you know we've called this daily rehash 'Canterbury Days.' Today it could be labeled Canterbury Daze—spelled d-a-z-e.' You won't believe it, but Jim asked me for a letter of recommendation."

"What! You didn't give him one, did you?"

"No. I told him to go back to Springfield and try to find someone there to vouch for him. Maybe we should call what happened today Canterbury Craze, because of Jim's crazy request."

"I warned you this morning, it's an insane planet we live on, and we shouldn't be surprised to have weird events popping up every once in a while."

"I've had my share."

"Yeah, more like Canterbury Maze, trying to figure out how to negotiate the hazards and emerge in one piece, still sane."

"Let me change the subject. I've felt awful guilty spending so much time at the academy and with Jeremy and Melanie, in the process neglecting Jon and Rachel and their kids. Let's try to get together with them this weekend."

"Sure. Set it up."

She called and reached Rachel. "Can we invite ourselves over next Sunday? I wanted to call early to make sure you weren't busy."

"Sure. We've wanted to get together with the rest of you, but realized you were overwhelmed with managing the academy, and Jeremy's been sick. If you're going to church Sunday, come over after church. I'll check with Melanie to see how Jeremy's doing, and if they can come."

Faith hung up and turned to Scott. "We're on for next Sunday. Now I hope the rest of the week can be more normal!"

26

F aith had missed talking to Father Whitmore, and knew it would be hard for her to make a special weekday trip to see him. She remembered he was off Monday, and sometimes went in early on Tuesdays. Taking a chance that he might be in, she dialed.

"Church of the Redeemer, Father Whitmore speaking."

"Hello, Father, it's Faith, your prodigal parishioner."

"Good to see you and your husband in church Sunday. I've wondered about you, and appreciated you whispering when you left last week that everything's fine."

"Yes, thanks to you. I wanted to come talk to you, but it's been hectic with Jeremy's kidney problem, and then the hassle with the finance man. Since I couldn't come to you for advice, I relied on the suggestions you've given me: 'Follow your conscience.' It's been very difficult, but Scott and the Winnetka duo have been great support. We managed to retrieve the stolen money, got rid of the finance director, and avoided any scandal. The academy is in good shape. Oh, yes, Bill Ludwig and Father Murphy helped us resolve issues."

"That's wonderful. But you skipped past Jeremy. How's he

doing?"

"He should be back to work half days soon. Felicia, Agnes, and I will keep volunteering, taking some of the load off Jeremy."

"You helped me start my week with good news!"

"I wanted to call and thank you for all your help in the past. Your advice has a long shelf life. During the past month when I was trying to make difficult decisions, I came back to your principle of following your conscience and doing the right thing."

"Your moral compass is in good working order."

"Saint Harriet and Mary help me stay on the straight and narrow path."

"Well, here's my first appointment. Good to hear from you, and before too long, let's meet."

Faith smiled after talking to her priest. He didn't give the Latin blessing, pax vobiscum, peace be with you. He didn't need to. Just schmoozing with him spread a mantle of serenity over her.

Faith drove back to the academy and scanned the morning mail. At ten she took a break to watch playtime. The leader for the day was very clever, doing imitations of animals and asking the children to guess the animals. She barked and meowed, and hooted like an owl. The kids loved the game. The leader asked Faith to participate. She hopped to the front of the room, arms outstretched and flapping, then did a cock-a-doodle-doo and clucked like a hen.

The kids yelled out "chicken" and "rooster."

At that point Felicia and Agnes entered. They clapped at Faith's inspired poultry performance. Agnes announced to the kids, "That's a mother hen, a Canterbury hen."

Faith led Felicia and Agnes to the storage room. "What do you think about a color for the walls? In my office I have a sample of a light blue called robin egg blue."

Felicia pumped her fist. "Great! That would be a pleasant relief from institutional off-white drab."

"We'll have them put in a new ceiling fixture to brighten up the room."

The women loved this classy combination of light blue and oak furniture and flooring.

Felicia joked, "Honey, the next time I'm redecorating, you're my first choice. But right now, I'd better get back to doing the final check of Jim's books. I'm sure glad we're through with him."

Faith sighed. "I hope so."

Felicia did a double take. "What do you mean?"

"When he returned the signed agreement for him and his wife, he included a request for a reference letter."

Agnes wailed, "That skunk. I'd give him a recommendation to the Devil."

Felicia shook her head. "Even the Mafia would reject him as being a second-rate thief."

They ate lunch together, then Felicia went back to checking Jim's books, and Agnes had a tutoring session.

Faith looked through the stack of applications for new residents. Two candidates stood out: Carole, who had experienced mental problems, and Cynthia, who was physically handicapped. She put them at the top of her list. After these two priorities, she ranked the next twenty applicants.

Canterbury had five vacancies. Faith made the decision to fill only four, leaving one room open for Jeremy to use if he needed a nap. She remembered that Maisie had Colette give up her room to Faith one day when she was frazzled.

Julia showed up at three with her sheaf of applications. "How do you want to do this?"

"First, let me mention that we have five open rooms, but I want to set aside one for Jeremy to use if he needs rest. So, let's start with our top four candidates. My first two are Carole and Cynthia. After them, I have a half dozen who are very close."

Julia put the top of her pen against her lips. "Uh, you have Carole and Cynthia as your top picks?"

"Yes, how did you rank these two?"

"Last."

"That's a big difference. Why did you put them last?"

"My social work training taught me to help as many people as you can, but always to tailor the help to your capabilities, and not promise assistance if you can't make good on it."

"You don't think we can help Carole and Cynthia?"

"We could, but it would take extra effort, and that would mean less attention to other residents. My recommendation would be to refer these two to social agencies that deal more effectively with mental challenges and physical disabilities."

Faith sat with her mouth open. "Hmm, I never looked at it that way. You know I was a hotel executive for decades before coming to the academy. I always told staff, 'When you don't know, ask someone who knows. And listen to what they say.' So I hear you loud and clear."

"I have to give you my best judgment."

"I value that. You may have saved us some trouble down the line." Faith chuckled.

"That's funny?"

"Oh, don't mind me. I was laughing at myself. I often talk to my priest, and he tells me it's good to look after lost sheep, but don't endanger the whole herd of sheep by focusing just on one. Your advice made me think we're in a similar situation. I'm concerned with two women in need of help, but you point out that trying to help them might keep us from attending to our other residents."

"Well, yes, that's one way of putting it."

They turned to the rest of their two lists, which overlapped, and they easily came up with six likely candidates.

"Julia, why don't you start tomorrow calling the first four, setting up interviews. And thanks again for your insight and advice."

Because of rush hour, Faith was even later getting home. Scott had stopped by a deli for sub sandwiches and German potato salad.

Faith began wolfing hers down. "A good choice, dear."

"Well, how were Canterbury Days today?"

She summed up the academy news, telling him that Father Whitmore and Julia would make a good team, reigning in her soft-hearted, do-gooder tendencies.

27

The rest of the week played out as an uneventful time at the academy. Scott joked that if she couldn't come up with more exciting news from Canterbury, he'd have to start watching reality shows on TV. For the next few days Faith had to peek into the remodeling project and visualize the new Canterbury Henhouse.

ON SUNDAY SCOTT agreed to go to church with Faith so they could drive afterward to Jon and Rachel's.

Jeremy's family had already arrived. The kids erupted with excitement when Faith and Scott drove up. They pestered him with questions about what he had planned to do with them. He had the kids get the cardboard theater and gloves out to play "What I want to be when I grow up." He had his video camera and recorded the performances.

Faith motioned Jon to follow her to the kitchen. "It's great to be back with the whole family. I said it before and want to mention it again, I apologize for spending the past few months almost entirely with Jeremy and the academy, neglecting your family."

"Don't worry about it, Mom, we understand. We just wish there had been something we could do to help out."

"In another week or so, when Jeremy returns half days, we're going to have a Welcome Back Party. I hope you and Rachel, and maybe even the kids, can help us celebrate."

"If our schedules are free, we'll be there."

"It'll be informal, no¹ major speeches, just a time to recognize that, without him, there'd be no Moms and Kids Foundation."

"Well, I want you to know that Rachel and I haven't been sitting on our hands. We've been eager to get involved in the academy, and the only reason we didn't come by earlier is we knew you were just keeping the boat afloat and couldn't handle any new issues. Rachel and I checked out the online computer courses at several junior colleges, and have recommendations for your young mothers, both beginner courses and more advanced programming courses. We've made a decision to spend a half day each week at the academy tutoring students with their course work."

"That's wonderful. Agnes will be thrilled to hear that."

"Uh, one more thing I'm a little hesitant to mention, kind of out of my field, more in the domain of Scott, but if you two aren't offended, I have an idea for you to think about."

"How could you offend us?"

"Well, here's what I have in mind, an online newsletter for the academy. I'm hesitant, because Scott is the newspaper man. Well, I have some ideas roughed out, and if the two of you go over it and find the ideas useful, I could move forward with it. My notion is that it would be something to recognize the residents, and also to promote the academy to a wider audience."

"Sounds wonderful."

"Tell you what I'll do. Later today I'll email you a sketch of what the newsletter would look like, and you and Scott can critique it. Now, we better get back to the other room, or we'll both end up in the doghouse."

Jon and Faith caught the last of the live performances in the cardboard theater, and then watched the replay over the television. As usual, the kids loved the drama.

Rachel had fixed a nice lunch. Before they sat down, Faith assembled the family for a prayer circle. In addition to thanks for the meal, they offered prayers for Jeremy's health.

After they ate, Faith looked at Scott, raising her shoulders a little. He caught the signal. "Well, folks, it's been great getting together with you, but I think we should be heading back to the city."

They left, making it easier for Jeremy and Melanie to leave early.

ON THE WAY back to the condo, Faith wondered out loud, "Can a computer jockey like Jon do a newsletter for the academy? He quickly mentioned something about it in the kitchen, and said he'd email me his ideas."

Scott shrugged. "He's good at digital and electronic manipulation, but I doubt if he can put together a journalistic project."

"Well, he asked us to look at it, so we should at least give it a once-over."

Arriving at the condo, Scott confessed, "I had an ulterior motive in leaving Oak Park early. You've been tired and stressed out. Why don't you take a nap?"

"You're right. My batteries need recharging."

She slept for more than an hour, then joined Scott in the lounger.

"My fair lady, I have a mini-surprise for you. We don't have time for a full weekend getaway, but we have a few good hours left of Sunday. Let's go out for an early dinner."

He led her to the elevator, and they caught a cab outside the building. "Boccacio's."

"Scott, you devil, you."

At the restaurant he ordered. "A bottle of your house chianti. We don't need a menu. Lasagna for both of us, and salad with your house dressing."

Faith grinned. "You know how to make my day."

At the end of the meal, the waiter asked if they wanted dessert. Scott shook his head. "No, we'll get dessert on the way home."

They took a cab to Roosevelt University.

Entering the lobby, Faith read the signboard for the film society's showing of a Charlie Chaplin movie. "Oh, now my weekend is complete." They held hands during the movie.

In the taxi on the way back to the condo, Faith thanked Scott for a delightful time. Tired from a full day, they went to bed as soon as they reached the condo. They made love and fell asleep in each other's arms.

THE NEXT MORNING Faith beat Jon out of bed, and was out the door before him. "Double surprise today—the henhouse should be painted, and Jon should have the draft of his newsletter in my inbox."

When she arrived at the academy, she made a beeline for the old storage room. Maisie followed her in. "Faith, I couldn't wait, had to take a look." Maisie flipped the switch, making the robin egg blue come to life and light up the room. "You gals can call this the henhouse. I think it should be the blue room."

Faith stood still, mouth open, scanning the room. "It looks so spacious and cozy. Thanks for thinking of this remodel."

She ate a quick breakfast with the early birds, then hurried to her office to read Jon's email about a newsletter.

MOM, here's my quick and dirty for the newsletter. The title could be Canterbury Canticle, the subtitle, "an occasional newsletter from the

Canterbury Moms and Kids Academy." By "occasional" I mean at least once a month. The purposes of the letter would be both internal, giving recognition and support to residents, and external, providing feedback and promotion to friends and donors.

The publication online would make it cost-free and available to anyone with computer and internet access. My notion is to recognize people, but keep the communication anonymous, only using first names.

The newsletter would maintain consistency by featuring a number of columns in every issue. Here are some examples:

Newbies: a brief paragraph about a new resident—first name and age, name and age of child, and personal goal while staying at the academy.

Birthdays: names, ages, and birthdates of those with birthdays in the past month or since the last issue.

Transitions: names and ages of residents who have returned to mainline society, including how they happened to come to the academy, and what they achieved there. (This might be the main feature of each issue, about 250-300 words.)

Red Badge Club: names of residents who took a writing course, and the book/novel they read to earn their red badge. (Maybe including a brief tease about the book/novel to encourage others to read the work.)

Academy news: announcement of online classes and instructional opportunities.

Canterbury Companions: brief comments from friends, donors, and supporters. (This would provide an opportunity for "outside" readers to provide input or make suggestions.)

Canterbury Bits and Pieces: Trivia such as an unusual meal, an interesting playtime, or a special visitor.

Well, these are some of my ideas, and no doubt you and Scott can judge if they will work, and how they might be improved. The newsletter could be printed out and posted on a bulletin board for those in the academy without a computer. A first issue could be printed and mailed to your donors and friends list, and relevant organizations. Readers then could access it at Moms and Kids.com or sign up to be on an email list.

JON'S PROPOSAL thrilled Faith so much that she blurted out, "Bravo!"

Jackie came running in to the office. "Are you okay?"

"Yeah, just higher than a kite. Scrape me off the ceiling and bring me back down to earth."

28

Trying to hold back her enthusiasm for Jon's project so Scott could make his own appraisal, Faith forwarded the newsletter proposal to him, with the simple message, "Look this over, and we can talk about it this evening." She printed out a copy to take home with her.

A call to Melanie confirmed that Jeremy would come to the office the following Monday. The doctors said it would be better for him to spend mornings at the office, while he was fresh.

Faith had Maisie come to her desk to plan the Welcome Back Party. Felicia and Agnes joined them. Faith hurried the women to the henhouse where the Winnetkans oohed and aahed over the paint job. "The flooring is scheduled for Wednesday and Thursday, and furniture will be delivered Friday. Hey, gals, I have a funky idea. Let me know if you think it's too kooky—three signs to go above corkboards in front of our desks: Faith's nest, Felicia's nest, Agnes's nest."

The Winnetkans gave their stamp of approval with cackles and chicken wing motions.

They had lunch and then split, Felicia taking care of bills, Agnes tending to tutoring. Faith reviewed the applications for two new residents, before Julia came for appointments at two and three. The interviews went well, and they agreed Julia should call the women and invite them to enter Canterbury.

Faith left early, eager to return to the condo and hear Scott's evaluation of the newsletter.

～

ABOUT SIX THIRTY, Scott came home. "Long day. A very tedious city council meeting, and I had to pound out a short summary for tomorrow's paper."

"Did you read Scott's proposal?"

"I noticed your email, but haven't had time to look at it."

She placed her printout on the table. "You can read it while I fix sandwiches. A little wine?"

"That would help lubricate my brain. Let me relax in the lounger while you get us something to eat. I'm bushed."

After they finished their meal in the loungers, she gave him a shoulder and neck massage.

"Thanks, babe, now I'm up to looking at Jon's proposal."

Scott read for a few minutes, saying nothing. Then he exploded. "This is Jon's writing? Behind those transistors and electrical circuits, he has some clever concepts. He didn't put it this way, but I think a major contribution is the underlying narrative of the mission of Moms and Kids, reinforcing individual residents, unifying them as a community, and linking them to donors."

"You like it?"

"Love it. This is powerful. It costs nothing and the benefit is tremendous. You'll get supporters across the state and the country. Of course, it has to be written well, but he seems to have a handle on the message. He should be listed as the editor, so he can control the content."

"I think he and Agnes will be co-editors."

"That works."

Faith stopped to call Jon. "We both love your newsletter

proposal. Scott says he thinks it's good for you and Agnes to be co-editors."

"Yeah, I didn't put it in the proposal, but if it's okay with Agnes, we'll use some of her writing students as reporters, sniffing out stories for the Bits and Pieces column."

"We can't wait to see the first issue."

Scott was watching the news on television. Faith walked up to him, plopped in his lap, and gave him a hug.

"What's that all about?"

"I'm just so happy. My family's together, we're all dedicated to Moms and Kids, and the academy is doing well. What else could I want for?"

Scott rubbed his chin. "Uh, I don't know. You gave up a corner office at Horton Hotels for Canterbury. I don't think the academy has any corner offices."

"Wait til you see the Canterbury Henhouse. Maisie calls it the blue room. I wouldn't trade it for any high-rise executive perch."

TUESDAY MORNING FAITH was still running on the adrenaline of the excitement over the henhouse. She arrived at Canterbury for an early breakfast and lingered afterward for a cup of tea with Maisie. Faith gushed, "I never imagined this storage space could be spiffed up into a neat and cozy office."

Faith dialed Church of the Redeemer, hoping to reach her father-confessor before his first appointment.

When he answered, she jumped ahead to say, "I know you don't have much time, but want to let you know that the academy is doing very well, and we've planned a welcome back celebration for Jeremy next Monday. You and your wife are invited, if you don't have something else planned for your day off."

"I'll check with my wife. We've both heard so much about Moms and Kids, we'd like to have a firsthand look. Oh—here comes a parishioner, have to hang up. I hope to see you Sunday, and maybe at the academy on Monday."

THE REST OF TUESDAY, Faith spent her time at the academy, just keeping busy. Wednesday morning, she asked the playtime leader to have the children sing Inky Dinky. She added, after every "I love you" phrase, a shouted "JEREMY." The kids ate it up. She explained that would be their own way of welcoming Jeremy back.

She stayed until after five, waiting for the flooring man to bring the laminate flooring. She held up one piece of the honey-colored plank next to the blue wall, and loved the way they complemented each other.

She phoned Scott and said she would call in pizza.

Faith arrived at the condo right after the delivery man.

"Honestly, dear, I've never seen you so animated about any decorating project as you are with your new office."

"It's not just an office, honey, it's my henhouse, and I have my own nest in it. You'll see when you come Monday."

THE NEXT MORNING, she rushed to the academy. Maisie went with her to inspect the floor. "The lightyellow boards really lighten up the room." She had breakfast with Colette and other early birds.

Mid-morning the Winnetkans showed up. Faith led them to the new office.

Felicia oohed and awed. "Oh, honey, this is lovely. Now all we need is the furniture, and we'll have a perfect henhouse."

Faith shook her head. "Gals, I have a surprise for you, something nobody else has seen. This blank wall opposite our desks will become a photo gallery, with the title The Story of the Moms and Kids Foundation. I'd like you two to help me install the pictures."

29

T he three hens went to Jeremy's office, where Faith showed them a stack of neatly wrapped square and rectangular containers. "You're looking at the ingredients of a visual history. Let's take them to the henhouse and unwrap them."

Faith started with the smallest ones, which contained two baby pictures in black frames. She had swung the door open, and leaned the two baby pictures against the wall, just beyond the door. "For thirty years, these were the only baby pictures I had of Jeremy and Jon. I kept them in my billfold. The title of these two pictures, hung close to each other, will be 'Birth of Twins.'"

Felicia smiled. "I think I see where you're going with this, but why do you need to title them?"

"This way, if I'm not here, someone else can lead them past the pictures for a show and tell narrative of Moms and Kids and the academy."

Felicia held two thumbs up. "Great idea."

"Ever since I got back together with my guys, I've been squirreling away pictures for a day like this. I had professionals prepare the duplications and do the framing. Now let's see what comes next." She unwrapped two larger packages, high school pictures of

Jon and Jeremy. "The title for these two, spaced a few inches apart, is 'Twins Separated.'" She leaned them against the wall about two feet from the baby pictures.

Then she picked up one of the largest packets, containing the *Tribune* story about Jonathan Rockwell and Jeremy Goodman. "You know this episode, how Scott stumbled onto these two guys as identical twins. This one will have the title 'Twins Reunited.'" She placed it against the wall in line with the others.

Agnes laughed. "I love it, I love it!"

"Well, you'll really adore this next one. It's the first picture of me and my boys after we found each other. This title will be 'Mom and Kids Reunited.'"

Felicia had unwrapped another package, asking, "What's this? Looks like an old department store."

Faith smiled. "That's Jeremy when he was running his religion campaign, One Way, in a former Montgomery Ward store, and began to head up Moms and Kids. See the little 'Moms and Kids Foundation' sign on the desk? This picture will have the title 'Birth of Moms and Kids Foundation.'"

Agnes tore the paper off another parcel. "This looks almost the same as the last one. It has the same 'Moms and Kids Foundation' sign on the desk."

Faith nodded. "Yes, but that's after Jeremy left Springfield and began running the foundation in Chicago. This image I call 'Moms and Kids Moves to Chicago'. You know, this is when the foundation was just helping young women financially, before we had a building."

"Yeah," Felicia agreed, "and I can anticipate the next picture."

"Right," Felicia said, opening a package with a photo of the old hotel where Moms and Kids had operated. "Our first residential building. This one we'll call 'Moms and Kids Find a Home.'"

Agnes tore the paper off a large photo of the present building. "So what will you call this?"

"It'll be 'Canterbury Moms and Kids Academy.'"

Felicia looked at the two remaining packages. "You've lined up a whole wall of pictures, a regular panorama. What about the last two?"

Agnes and Felicia each opened one, a picture of moms and kids eating in the dining hall, and a photo of mothers watching their children at playtime.

Faith announced, "These two are the climax, which I'll label 'Moms and Kids in Action,' and place them one above the other on the wall opposite the door."

Felicia shouted out, "My gawd, you have the whole story of you, your twins, and the growth of this project."

"Bingo! You just won the grand prize. Go into my office and bring a long narrow packet here."

In a few minutes Felicia was back with the slim item. "Open it," Faith told her.

Doing as instructed, Felicia read the framed message: "The Story of the Moms and Kids Foundation."

"That will be the heading above all the pictures on the side wall. I'm going to ask the maintenance man to hang the pictures, so we don't ruin his nice paint job."

This made the women late for lunch, but they had a great time gabbing about the photo gallery.

"I like the narrow black frames, which contrast with the light blue wall, and don't take away from the images," Agnes said.

Felicia agreed. "They really do tell a story."

Faith turned to Felicia. "See, when you have a potential donor, you can bring them into the henhouse, and they can see at a glance what we're up to. Although people may forget the words you tell them, they'll remember the pictures you show them."

After lunch they had Maisie view the pictures. She closed her eyes, and babbled, "Love it, love it, love it!"

Agnes had to run to a tutoring session, and Felicia had bills to take care of. Faith called the office supply store, confirming that the furniture would arrive Friday morning before noon.

Too antsy to concentrate on work, Faith went to the kitchen and double-checked the plans for the Monday Welcome Back Party.

Maisie patted her on the shoulder. "Don't worry, I'll come in early Monday and bake enough sheet cakes. How about a banner that says 'Welcome Back, Jeremy'?"

"You're a dear. You think of everything." Faith called the office supply store, asking them to make a banner and deliver it Friday with the furniture.

THE NEXT MORNING as Faith rushed out the condo door, Jon kibitzed, "The early bird gets what? If not the worm, the world?"

"I'm on top of the world right now, with the completion of the henhouse."

Faith arrived at the academy even before the early crowd. She made it a point of eating with some residents she hadn't talked to for a while, got a cup of tea from the kitchen and schmoozed with other women. When the breakfast crowd thinned out, reluctantly she went to her office, taking care of a few letters and phone calls.

The sound of children gathering for playtime pleased her. She watched until the leader ended the session, and then asked for the kids to sing Inky Dinky, with the shouted 'JEREMY.' The hands of the clock moved past eleven, and finally she heard the rumble of a large truck announcing the arrival of furniture. It only took two men a half hour to unload the order. As the men placed each desk and chair in the room, Faith's dream of a triple office gradually changed to reality. The men placed the cork bulletin boards on top of each desk.

She had the maintenance man secure the corkboards to the wall and place the three hen signs above the boards. She asked him to fasten to the wall the labels for each picture of the panorama. The final touch was attaching the Canterbury Henhouse sign above the door outside their new office.

Felicia and Agnes arrived and rushed to their chairs, swiveling in them like two schoolkids. Felicia closed her eyes. "If I died and went to heaven, don't wake me."

Agnes sighed, "Never . . . never in all my days teaching, did I have anything close to this. So cozy. So homey. So friendly."

Faith agreed. "Scott teased me about settling for a made-over storeroom after having a corner executive office at Horton Hotels, but I'm much happier here. This is my home, where I belong."

They went to lunch, almost too excited to eat.

Faith told Agnes and Felicia that after a little "housekeeping," she was taking the afternoon off. "Getting the henhouse ready has kept me so agitated that I'm worn out."

To make Jeremy comfortable in his office on Monday, she removed all of her photos and personal items from his desk. Then she went to the storeroom and gathered up a box of office supplies for the three hens and put them in the new desks. The sight of the empty desks made her realize what she had forgotten. Back in Jeremy's office she looked up the office supply website and made a quick decision on three basic laptops and an all-purpose printer.

She drove home, and drew a hot bath, letting the water drain her pent-up feelings. After a leisurely soak, she called Scott. "Hi, hubby, I'll pick up deluxe subs and champagne at the deli. The henhouse office is finished, and I feel like celebrating."

When Scott got home, they toasted each other and enjoyed the unusual combination.

Faith chuckled. "I've been saving a surprise for you. Wait til you see the henhouse."

"I've cleared it with my boss to take a couple of hours off Monday to be at the welcoming of Jeremy."

THEY SPENT A QUIET WEEKEND. Monday morning Faith bounded out of bed and hurriedly got ready for the day, giving Scott a peck on the cheek as she teased, "You'll never guess what the surprise is."

The smell of cakes baking greeted Faith as she entered the academy. After breakfast, she turned toward Jeremy's office, and then remembered the henhouse, pivoting and walking into her new digs. A flip of the wall switch, and the ceiling fixture flooded the room with light. Slowly stepping by the display of images, Faith relived her life, from an unintended pregnancy to a destiny of separation from her twins, followed by a glorious reunion. The two pictures on the back wall, of Canterbury Moms and Kids in Action, made her take a deep breath and sigh. She announced to herself, *I have so much to be thankful for.*

She left the henhouse and sat with residents eating late breakfast. She wanted to be there when Jeremy arrived.

30

A t eight-thirty Jeremy sauntered into the academy, stopping just inside the entrance, surveying the place he had not seen for so long.

Faith walked toward him and began clapping, joined by all the residents and their offspring. She hugged him. "Welcome back, son."

Women and their children crowded around Jeremy, shaking his hand and greeting him.

Jeremy's gaunt face blossomed with a wide grin. "It's great to be back."

"Before you get to work, I have a surprise for you." She led him into the kitchen and pointed to the Canterbury Henhouse sign.

"Mother, are you raising chickens?"

"Well, you could say that all these young children are our little chicks, and we have them under our wings."

She swung the door open to the henhouse and motioned for him to enter.

Looking at the pictures, he took a deep breath, and said "Holy Toledo. You've been busy."

"Yes, and we'll keep at it. Felicia, Agnes, and I will keep volunteering, taking some of the load off you. We needed a place to hang out, and Maisie came up with this idea."

Jeremy read aloud the sign on the wall, "The Story of the Moms and Kids Foundation." He squinted, a tear dribbling down his cheek. "This tells the story. Who we are. What the academy does. It's wonderful. Thanks for this lovely display." He cried as he hugged Faith.

WHEN JON ARRIVED with his family, Faith ushered him into the henhouse.

Looking at the gallery of pictures, he let out a lengthy "Ohhhh."

"Is that a sign of approval?"

"An expression of awe. You've summed up our family and the foundation in one pictorial scene. It's truly awesome."

"Glad you like it."

"Mom, if you don't mind, I'll steal this as the lead story for the first issue of Canterbury Canticle."

"Steal away."

Melanie and Rachel entered the henhouse and walked slowly past the line of pictures. At the end, standing in front of Canterbury Moms and Kids in Action, they turned with tears in their eyes. Rachel cried openly. "Mom, how could you do it, all those dark years? And yet you came back and devoted your life to helping other women so they don't have to live apart from their children."

"Well, it was hard, and I lived through some difficult times, but it's worth it now, to see the family united and the academy thriving."

Melanie added, "Jeremy and I are so grateful to you for holding the academy together while he recuperated."

Agnes and Felicia peeked in. Faith introduced them. "Here are my two main supporters. Without them, I couldn't have done it."

Playtime started, a singalong ending with a version of Inky Dinky with a shouted "JEREMY" after every phrase of "I love you."

Father Whitmore and his wife joined the party, enjoying the tour of the henhouse and the picture gallery.

Scott showed up late, delayed by a breaking story. After he ate, Faith showed him the henhouse.

Scott gushed, "Wow! When you said you had a surprise, you weren't kidding. Nobody knows the drama of your life story better than me, but these images help me relive it with you."

"Jon's making this story the main feature of the first issue of the newsletter."

"He has a nose for news."

"How do you like the henhouse?"

"Very tasteful. Could you come to the *Trib* and redecorate the newsroom?"

They talked for a while until Scott excused himself to get back to the newspaper. "Sorry, I've got to fly the coop."

Faith gave him a playful slap.

The Welcome Back Party and all the socializing with family and friends left Faith with a pleasant high. Tuesday morning, she drove to the academy early, ate breakfast with residents, and then retreated into the henhouse. She sat at her desk and reveled in the afterglow of "The Story of the Moms and Kids Foundation." She swiveled in the chair, glancing down the line of pictures. Reliving the drama of that personal journey, she enjoyed the climax of the last two pictures showing the moms and kids at Canterbury eating and playing.

She remembered that once, while juggling the anxieties of Jeremy's illness and Jim's financial shenanigans, she had wondered out loud to Scott what it would be like to have a normal routine at the academy. Now she looked forward to an unexciting, boring pattern for life at Canterbury. It pleased her that everyone seemed to settle down into a regular schedule.

With Jeremy back, she could relax more. When she had time, she drove in early and ate breakfast with residents. The main event of every day at the academy was watching the children during playtime. She made a point of visiting every resident, to become more familiar with these young mothers. As they opened up to her, their tales ranged from heart-rending to heart-warming.

Faith and Jeremy hired a young man with an associate's degree in business administration as their financial manager, which freed up Felicia to be more active in fundraising. She and Faith developed a protocol for handling donors. Felicia invited their guests to a morning brunch with residents and a personal tour of the facility and its activities, ending with a private session in the henhouse where their donations were graciously accepted.

Agnes continued recruiting volunteers, especially people with business backgrounds who could provide mini courses on business, and sessions on the job application and interviewing process.

The rest of Faith's family became active participants in the academy. Jon and Rachel had arranged with Agnes to do their computer class tutoring on Thursday afternoon, so it didn't conflict with the tutoring Agnes scheduled on Tuesdays. Until residents signed up and began classes, Jon and Rachel divided the interested residents into beginner and advanced sections, and had question and answer sessions. Mark and Beth had such a good time at Jeremy's Welcome Back Party that they asked to come along. Leonard and Mark became good buddies. Beth took on the role of big sis to a group of youngsters who colored with her and listened to her read stories.

Even Scott got into the act. "Agnes, if you set aside an hour between nine and ten Wednesday morning, I can read stories and send pictures over Skype and have them displayed on the television in the lounge."

JON BROUGHT out the trial issue of Canterbury Canticle, first explaining the purpose of the newsletter to keep everyone informed of the academy's activities, and then using Faith's photo gallery to illustrate the mission of the institution. He summed up Faith's separation from her own sons as the motivation to establish a foundation that helped young mothers raise their children. The first issue they mailed out to all of the academy's contacts, inviting people to send their email addresses to Canterbury for subsequent issues. The enthusiastic response persuaded him to plan the initial regular issue, to be transmitted electronically.

Working with Agnes, Jon explained to her the Transitions column he wanted to use as the main article. They knew the first Transitions account would be the pattern that other residents would use to describe their experience at Canterbury. Agnes suggested, "Why not ask Amelia. She was the first woman to transition, and her writing is good." Amelia wrote these paragraphs about her experiences for the second issue of Canterbury Canticle:

Amelia's story

Hi. My name is Amelia, my son's name is Robbie. I'm nineteen, he's eight months. I came to Canterbury when Robbie was a few months old. The editors of Canterbury Canticle asked me to tell my story, and here it is.

The summer after I graduated from high school, I was excited about going to college, and had been accepted to a four-year school. Then I got pregnant, and my world turned upside down. Being a teenager is difficult. Being a teenager and pregnant is a lot tougher. My parents wanted me to have an abortion and continue my plans to get a college degree, but I couldn't bring myself to go along with that option. We had heated arguments about it, which continued until I delivered.

Being a teenager and a mother was even more difficult, and the relations between me and my parents got worse. I heard through church about Moms and Kids, and figured it would be best for me to leave home and stay at Canterbury until I got my life straightened out.

At first when I came to the academy, I was a loner, totally wrapped up with little Robbie and my own inner struggles. Then Faith befriended me and Robbie. She's the first person Robbie really allowed to hold him. As we talked, she heard about my college plans, and helped me take the plunge of enrolling for an online course. It was a writing course, and I read Red Badge of Courage for my first essay. It was hard, but also very rewarding. That renewed my commitment to get a degree. It also showed my parents that I wasn't a loser, a dropout.

To make a long story short, my parents and I settled our differences, and Robbie is the light of their life. I'm back in their home now, completing my associate's degree, and plan to transfer to a four-year college.

I am grateful to Faith and Jeremy and the people at Canterbury Academy for helping me restart my life.

THE FIRST REGULAR issue of Canterbury Canticle featured Amelia's story as the main article. Jon included short pieces in the other columns. For the Canterbury Companions column, he asked Bill Ludwig to contribute a paragraph. Bill began with, "In three decades of lawyering and being involved in various charitable organizations, I have never seen a social service as worthy of support as Canterbury Academy."

In the Newbies column, Jon introduced the two new residents Faith and Julia had admitted.

He listed the first names of women and children with birthdays during the past month.

For the Bits and Pieces section, he gave an overview of the Welcome Back Party for Jeremy, mentioning his sick leave and return to half-time status.

Agnes wrote a brief explanation of the Red Badge Club—for those who had taken a writing course, read a book, and written a paper. She listed the first names of the women who had received their red badges.

Under the title of Announcements, Jon summed up the new business courses Agnes was preparing, and the computer instruction Jon and Rachel had in the works.

SCOTT LOVED CANTERBURY CANTICLE, telling Faith, "It's a nifty newsletter. Succinct, yet chock-full of items that will keep the residents happy and inspire donors."

For Faith, the newsletter put the cherry on top of her Canterbury banana split. The residents and youngsters were happy. The trio got along famously, taking care of their own responsibilities, and retreating into the blue room for cluck-cluck gabfests. From time to time Maisie joined them in the henhouse and they had spirited arguments about which of Maisie's meals was best. The academy hummed along.

FOLLOWING a tiring week and a lazy Sunday, Faith and Scott sat in their loungers sharing an after-dinner glass of wine. Scott beamed. "I've never seen you happier. Leaving Horton Hotels for Canterbury Academy was the best decision you ever made."

"You're right. Hotel work satisfied me, but didn't make me happy."

They talked the evening away, reviewing the low and high points of their life together. Scott went to bed early and Faith joined him, yet couldn't turn off her reminiscences and get to sleep. She recalled, all too vividly, the many coincidences that led to her present blessed situation. Change just one happenstance, and her entire life would have been quite different.

She traveled back to the beginning of her journey in Canton and Pappy's Pizza Parlor. What if she had not been stubborn about working in the pizza joint, and instead had volunteered at church camp? She would never have met the twins' father.

What if she had never gone to Riverfront Park with Doug? What if she had never flirted with him and let him kiss her, and . . .? She would not have gotten pregnant and never experienced her twin destiny.

What if her parents had not been so piously self-righteous and not forced her to give up her boys? She would never have been separated from her twins, and somehow she would have been able to bring them up and see them grow into young men.

Aaron and Sarah Armstrong blocked all those possibilities, forcing Faith to go through with adoption, making her a childless mother, spending decades wondering about her twins.

What if Scott had not been assigned to write the news article about Jon and Jeremy? She would never have been reunited with her boys, instead advancing into senior citizen status as a lonely old maid.

What if the meeting with the twins after three decades of separation had not gone well? She would have turned into a bitter spinster.

Even after her reunion with the twins, what if her meeting with the devil Doug had torn apart the family?

And after the move of Moms and Kids to Canterbury, what if Jim had created a scandal that destroyed the academy?

THESE RUMINATIONS KEPT her wide awake, so she got out of bed. Faith went to her drawer and pulled out her journal, holding it for a while, then sighing and sticking it back into its resting place.

She strolled to the lounger, leaving the lights off and taking in the panorama of a sky speckled with glimmers of light. The scene reminded her of Van Gogh's painting "Starry Night," and this in turn called up the sounds of Dan McClean's musical rendition of "Starry, Starry Night." She played McLean's video on her cell phone and viewed again the Dutch painter's perceptive insight into the frailty of human life. In spite of, or maybe because of, Van Gogh's journey into the hearts and minds of others, his own tortured soul struggled with sanity, and eventually he took his life. Faith shuddered at the memory of her own flirtation with suicide when she was pregnant and depressed. Only the lives of her unborn twins prevented her from taking that fatal step.

Faith looked into the darkness of the night and the sparkling points of light. She longed to gaze into the lake to see if it had a sign for her, but its black surface revealed nothing. She wondered what next event might shape her twin destiny.

32

F aith always remembered the exact time of the call, 3:30 A.M., because she glanced at the bedside clock when the phone rang. She fumbled for the receiver, hoping it was a wrong number, and she could return the receiver to its cradle.

A deep bass voice boomed into her ear. "Hello, this is Captain Moskowicz of the Cook County Fire Department. I'm calling for Faith Armstrong."

She bolted upright in bed, throwing off the covers and swinging her feet onto the floor. "Yes, this is Faith Armstrong."

"I'm calling because you are listed as the emergency contact for Canterbury Academy. We—"

"There's a fire?"

"Was."

"Oh, no, anyone—?"

"Let me give you a quick overview, and then you can ask questions. A half hour ago we responded to a fire call at the academy, and arrived within a few minutes. Don't worry, no fatalities, no injuries. The fire was limited to an outbuilding. It suffered considerable damage, but we put out the fire and there's no more danger.

Just as a precaution, we had all the people in the main building evacuate their rooms and assemble in a large hall."

"The all-purpose room."

"I guess so."

"Anyway, department procedure is to notify the emergency contact as soon as we contain the fire. You have nothing to worry about. The people living there can return to their rooms."

"The fire—how did it start?"

"All I can tell you now is the origin of the fire was outside this small structure. We'll return later in the day with a team investigating the cause of the fire."

"I live about a half hour from the academy. I'll get there as soon as I can."

"No need to hurry. No need to come."

"I've got to be there for the moms and their youngsters." She hung up.

Scott propped himself up on his elbow. "A fire? At Canterbury?"

"Yes. An outbuilding. Must be the maintenance shed. I've got to go, be there for the residents."

"I'll go with you."

"It's the middle of the night."

"That's why I'm going to drive. You're in no condition to be behind the wheel."

WHEN THEY ARRIVED at the academy, shortly after four, the fire trucks had left, but several cars with flashing lights remained. Yellow tape surrounded the maintenance shed. Scott and Faith parked and walked around the burn site, then hurried into the main building. Some mothers and their kids still sprawled on the floor with blankets. She hugged the moms, some cradling their youngsters.

Colette blurted out, "Oh, it was scary. The alarm went off, and the emergency lights came on, and we all went down to the all-purpose room. The firemen told us to stay put until they gave the all-clear, which was only about fifteen minutes."

Faith waited until all the moms had taken their children back to their rooms, then turned to Scott. "Let's look at the burnt building."

A fireman waved them off. "No admittance, folks, we're still investigating."

"I'm Faith Armstrong, interim director for the Canterbury Academy. Captain Moskowicz contacted me."

"Good. Tell me one thing. The sign says Moms and Kids. How old are the kids?"

"Mostly infants and toddlers, all preschool."

"No teenagers or preteens?"

"No, why does that matter?"

"Prime age for playing with matches. Wrong time, though. Kids are usually daytime or early evening firebugs."

"So it was deliberately set?"

"Definitely arson, but I can't release any information until the investigation is complete. Will you be available later for the investigation team?"

"I plan to be here all day."

Scott and Faith went back to the academy. She heated some water for tea and they sat in the henhouse with their cups. Scott shook his head. "What a way to start the day."

"Uh-huh. The beginning of a long day. I'll have to call Bill and Father Murphy, to let them know what's going on. I'll wait until Jeremy comes to fill him in."

Maisie arrived to prepare breakfast, and had to hear about the excitement.

Scott told Faith, "Listen, you're already stressed out, and it's only going to get worse. You need to go to that extra room and catch some rest while you can. I'll drive directly to the office, and give you a call this afternoon to let you know when I can come by for you."

"I probably won't be able to sleep, but should probably relax for a while." She went to the spare room, pulled the covers back on the bed, and climbed in. She fell into a fitful sleep, her dreams flitting from Canton to Chicago and Horton Hotels, and then Canterbury.

A loud, rapid knocking on the door wakened her. Jackie called out, "Sorry, but the fire department investigator insisted you would be available to talk to him."

"Sure. Be a dear, and bring me a cup of tea to the henhouse. Oh, and ask the fireman if he wants something."

Faith felt more comfortable sitting at her desk in the henhouse, sipping tea. The investigator took a seat by the side of her desk, clipboard in one hand, pen in the other.

"The preliminary investigator established that you don't have any preteen or teenage kids here."

"Yes, just preschoolers."

"Okay, I'll make this as quick as possible. We're looking at arson, and we can rule out kids playing with matches. You don't have homeless people around here, right?"

"I've never seen any homeless in this area."

"Okay, any known enemies?"

"You mean me?"

"You, the academy."

"We're a social service, taking care of single women with young children."

"I wouldn't suspect anyone living here would set fire to the place. But maybe you kicked someone out, who had a grudge against you and the place."

"We've never turned anyone out."

"Okay, next come employees. Any disgruntled employees?"

"Disgruntled?'"

"Yeah, pay dispute, work assignment, failed promotion, demotion, that kind of thing."

"Well, there was one man, we had to . . . let go."

"Fired?"

"We let him resign."

"Problems? What kind?"

"Financial."

"Major?"

"He was skimming money, a kickback scheme."

"How much?"

"Several thousand."

"What happened?"

"We had him pay back the money he misappropriated, and let him resign."

"Misappropriated. You mean stole."

"Uh, yes."

"You have a copy of the police report?"

"We never filed charges."

He shook his head. "Is that all he did?"

"No, he tried to blackmail us, to keep it quiet, so we could avoid an embarrassing scandal for the academy."

"You have proof?"

"I . . . uh, have a recording of the blackmail proposal."

"I'll need a copy of it."

"I don't think this has anything to do with the fire. Jim would never do anything like that."

"Jim. Jim who?" He was writing on his pad.

"Jim Anderson."

"Okay, we have a name. Tell me about him."

"He left Chicago and went back to Springfield, so I don't think he could have anything to do with the fire."

"Let us figure that out. He stole from you and blackmailed you. Did he ever threaten you?"

"Uh, yes."

"What was the threat?"

"Once when he was mad, he said he'd kill me, but I don't think he meant it."

"You say you have this on tape?"

"Yes."

"He was on staff, so you must have his social security number."

"Yes, but we don't usually give out personal information.

"Getting straight answers out of you is like pulling teeth. I'm not a dentist, and this isn't a game. Ms. Armstrong, I'll tell you like it is. Last night we were all lucky. A woman in the academy was up with her baby, and saw the fire right after it started. If she had not called 911, the outbuilding might have burned to the ground, and with any breeze, might have set the main building on fire. Many people could have died. Now I need your cooperation to find the jerk who started the fire."

"I'll get you Jim's information."

Faith left the henhouse for the main office, and ran into Jeremy, who asked, "Mom, how did the fire happen? Was it an accident, or do they think someone might have started it?"

"Son, I'll talk to you soon, but now I have to give Jim's information to the fire investigator."

Jeremy shook his head. "It was arson?"

"Yes, it was deliberately set, with gasoline, and they're trying to figure out who might have done it."

"You're giving them Jim's social security number, but surely you don't suspect him. Jim's in Springfield. He couldn't start the fire. He's in enough trouble without any false accusations."

"What do you mean about Jim being in enough trouble?"

Jeremy looked at the floor. "After Jim resigned and went to Springfield, he asked around for references, and they called me to find out why he left Canterbury. I told them about the financial problems, and the word got around pretty quick. Now he can't find a decent job, and because he wasn't laid off, can't get unemployment. The last I heard from the One Way people, he settled for some flunky security job.

Faith frowned, shaking her head.

Jeremy opened his eyes wide. "Uh, you don't think I should have talked to them?"

"Well, that wasn't such a good idea. Jim asked me for a reference, and after all he had done, and even threatened me, I couldn't recommend him. I told him to go back to Springfield and have the One Way people help him. You probably made it hard for him to get a decent position.

"Mom, I had to tell people the truth. Was that wrong?"

"Maybe not wrong, but not the best thing to do."

"Have you talked to Jim?"

"No, and I don't think you should, either. That's what our lawyer Bill has advised us to do. All contacts with Jim come through the lawyer's office."

Jeremy scratched his head. "Hmm."

"What's the matter?"

"Mom, I don't get it. You think I shouldn't have talked to the One Way people, because that hurt Jim's chances at landing a job. But now you're ready to hand over his social security number to the police. I don't think that's good."

"Why not?"

"You said Jim has enough problems without me making it worse, but you're throwing suspicion on him, going to the police."

"Jeremy! I didn't go to the police. The fire investigator came to me. And he told me to give him the names of any residents or employees who had conflicts with the academy."

"Are you accusing Jim of starting the fire?"

"No! All I'm doing is giving the fire department the information they request, and letting them investigate."

"But you don't have to give them that information, do you?"

Faith exhaled sharply, closing her eyes. "I—"

Looking directly at her, Jeremy said slowly, "Mother, all the years we've worked together at Moms and Kids we've never had a serious disagreement. Now . . .."

"You feel strongly that I shouldn't give the fire department Jim's social security information? After all he's done?"

"Think about it. For the theft of money, you had the accounting records. That's evidence. And he admitted, you know, confessed that he took it. But when it comes to the fire, you don't have any evidence linking him to the fire, and he didn't say he did it. You didn't even ask him. For all we know, he's been working in Springfield. That's why I don't feel it's fair to dump on him an unsubstantiated accusation."

"Son, I see your point. And let me make it clear that I'm not—
no one is—accusing Jim of setting the fire."

Jeremy hung his head. "It sure sounds like an accusation."

"Well . . . I have to get back to the investigator. How about this.
You come with me, and when I give Jim's information to the him,
we can both say that we're not accusing Jim of anything, and after
all, a person is presumed innocent until presumed guilty."

Jeremy stared at the ceiling a few moments. "I don't really like it,
but maybe it's the best you can do."

They walked back to the henhouse. The fire investigator was
looking at Faith's wall of photos. "Have trouble digging up the
number?"

Faith nodded. "It took a while. Here's Jim Anderson's social
security number and the contact address for him at his sister-in-
law's house in Springfield." She turned to Jeremy. "This is my son
Jeremy, head of Canterbury Academy. We don't usually give out
personal information, and would like to repeat what I told you
earlier. We suppose Jim is in Springfield and has nothing to do with
the fire. By giving you his information, we're not accusing him of
anything."

The detective looked back and forth at Faith and Jeremy. "Sure.
Whatever you say, Faith, and Mr.—or is it Reverend—Goodman."

Faith volunteered, "Yes, Reverend Goodman."

"Well, Rev, in law enforcement we always say innocent until
proven guilty. I guess in the church you have your own way of
dealing with guilt."

Jeremy flinched. "In the church, we deal with guilt—"

The detective broke in, "Yeah, in religion, the innocent pray for
the guilty. But in crime, the guilty prey on the innocent. You know,
p-r-e-y."

Jeremy flinched. "Right now, we don't know who's guilty."

"Righto. What we're doing now is investigating, not prosecuting.
Thanks for the information, which will help us look into the case.
I've got to get back to headquarters and write a report."

Shoulders slumping, Jeremy shuffled to his office.

Faith placed calls to Bill Ludwig and Father Murphy, in each case leaving barebones messages that there had been a minor fire, no one was injured, and everything is under control. She waited for Felicia and Agnes to show up to talk to them in person.

The Winnetkans rushed into the henhouse, enfolding Faith in a clamshell hug. They chatted for a while until Faith went to the financial office and found out the details of the security service they had continued when Moms and Kids took over the facility. She told Felicia and Agnes, "It's a lightweight operation. They check the doors and do a walkaround at nine, midnight, three, and six. Let's see if Jeremy's free. We need to discuss a night watchman, say ten to six."

The threesome was seated in the henhouse talking about better security, when Jackie, breathless, interrupted them. "Sorry to disturb you, but you need to look at a text message right away."

33

They walked to the office and had Jeremy join them around Jackie's desk. "Sorry, it's been so hectic I didn't check the phone until just now. The message came in a little after three this morning."

They read the terse note:

GLAD NOBODY HURT IN FIRE. *For insurance policy to make sure no more fires, put hundred thousand dollars in small bills in a bag. Wait for phone call to this number next Sunday night at nine thirty. Delivery instructions by text message. For your safety, no police.*

THEY STOOD in silence rereading the demand. Jeremy looked at Faith. "Mom, what should we do?"

"First, call Bill. He'll give us the best advice." She turned to the Felicia and Agnes. "Why don't you wait for me in the henhouse. The fewer who know the details, the better."

She and Jeremy went back into his office and she phoned Bill

Ludwig, telling the secretary, "This is an emergency. Have Bill call me as soon as possible."

A half hour later he returned the call. "I know you wouldn't say 'emergency' if it wasn't serious. Is this related to the fire?"

"Yeah. A text message to the academy demands a hundred thousand dollars to make sure there are no more fires."

"Think it's legit?"

"The text was sent a little after three this morning, so it must be from the one who started the fire."

"Faith, I'm getting ahead of the story, but are we watching a remake of Jim's blackmail scheme?"

"I can't help but suspect him. Still, I don't want to accuse him of anything."

"Faith, this is not the time for feel-good sentiment. Having a bead on the perp helps us plan strategy. And we have to act fast. Let's assume it's Jim. In that case, he's working alone, and most likely unarmed. We've underestimated him before, so let's keep in mind he can be clever. He says no police, but they're smarter at this game than he is. You have to let the fire department and the police know what we're facing."

She told Jeremy what Bill advised. He agreed that the new threat and demand for money changed the situation. She called Captain Moskowicz and explained what she and Bill had discussed.

"Your lawyer's right. Our department looks into fires, but the demand for money is extortion, the bailiwick of the police." Moskowicz gave her the number of Frank Middleton, a police detective. She reached Middleton, who was busy all afternoon, and made an appointment for nine the next morning at the academy. He added, "I want to see the scene of the fire and get the lay of the land."

Jeremy and Faith agreed to meet at the academy the next morning at eight thirty to wait for Middleton.

Faith left the office and retreated to the henhouse, glad to have the support of the Winnetkans. Agnes put her hand on Faith's. "You're trembling!"

"Jitters. A policeman will come tomorrow morning. Better if I don't tell you any details. No need to get you two involved."

They ate lunch, then Agnes insisted Faith go to the spare room and get some rest. Faith didn't argue. She let Jackie know where she was in case Scott called.

After an hour nap she phoned Scott, who told her he'd pick her up at five and they could stop for something to eat on the way to the condo.

"I just want to get home."

WHEN SCOTT CAME FOR HER, Faith brought him up to date on the day's events.

Sliding his fingers through his hair, Scott said, "If it wasn't so serious, it'd be a joke. Twice Jim got away with his tricks, but this is his third strike, and I imagine this time he'll do time."

"Dear, we don't know that it's Jim. Jeremy and I had a disagreement, like we've never had. He says I'm rushing ahead to accuse Jim without any evidence, without even talking to him."

Scott snorted, "Hah! Evidence and proof may come later, but let's consider the circumstances. Jim has a beef with the academy, a history of threats, and he knows the lay of the land. Jeremy has a soft heart, but Middleton has a hard head. He'll follow the circumstantial evidence until he has solid proof."

When they got home, Scott offered, "Let me fix you something. What do you want?"

"Let's lie down. I just want you to hold me."

"Scared?"

"Uh-huh. Not afraid of Jim, but worried that something bad might happen to the academy."

"You checked with the security service?"

"Yes, and tomorrow I'll have them assign a night watchman, eleven to seven."

"At least until this blows over."

Scott fixed sandwiches and they ate while half watching news, then went to bed early.

THE NEXT DAY Faith went in to have breakfast with residents. Schmoozing with mothers and their children always put her in a good mood. She dreaded the session with the policeman.

She joined Jeremy in his office. They chewed over the past problems with Jim. Jeremy mumbled, "I still can't believe Jim would start a fire, and then threaten another fire if we didn't pay him off."

"Face it, dear. He knew the security schedule, and must have waited until they made the three o'clock round before he lit the fire."

Jeremy threw his hands above his head. "There you go again, accusing Jim!"

"My heart doesn't like it, but that's where my brain is leading me."

In the middle of this argument, Frank Middleton breezed in and got right down to business. "I've got a general picture of the situation, but have to verify all known facts. If we're going to try to catch this guy in the act, we'll have to deploy a number of detectives, and this needs to be authorized from the top. Here's what I have—correct me if I'm wrong. Monday morning about three the academy had a fire, and a few minutes later you got a phone text demand for a hundred thousand or you'd have another fire. The likely suspect is the finance officer who got canned for stealing and blackmailing. So far, so good?"

Faith nodded. "We can't accuse Jim without some evidence, but he's the most likely suspect."

"Sorry, but I have to see for myself the text message with the demand." They went to Jackie's phone so he could view the text.

"Okay, I'd like to eyeball the fire scene."

They walked to the maintenance building. "The fire inspector said it was a crude device, a rag in a can of gasoline. Strictly amateur, but still deadly."

Faith looked directly at Middleton. "What will you do about Sunday night?"

"All that has to be authorized from the top. Everything I tell you is strictly QT. Because of the verified threat against a large facility, probably they'll okay a team. They'll have to pull some strings to use Jim's social security number to learn his employment info. And we'll make sure he's not working Sunday night. No use forming a surveillance team if he won't show."

"What about the details?"

Middleton looked at Faith. "The first question is whether you're willing to be part of the payoff. It would be hard to plan it without you, because the perp would spook."

Jeremy shook his head. "Mom, I don't like you taking a risk like that. Let me go."

Middleton objected, "Ixnay. If it's who we think it is, he'll expect Faith to show up."

Faith put her hand on Jeremy's. "It has to be me. I'm willing to do anything. Well, anything within reason."

Middleton shrugged. "We'll do everything we can to keep you safe."

"What about the money?"

"That depends on what the higher-ups decide."

LATE IN THE AFTERNOON, Middleton called Faith at the academy. "We leaned on some connections and used Jim Anderson's social security number to squeeze his employment info—he's working for a sleazy security outfit in Springfield, Monday-Friday on the grave-yard shift. He was off the night of the fire, so he could have come here and started the fire. He'll be off Sunday night, so he could drive here and pick up the payoff. Because all signals seem to be green, we're putting together a surveillance team. You don't need to know the particulars. I'll be hunkered down in the back seat of your car, giving directions to the team. Any questions?"

"We'll meet at the academy Sunday night at nine or so?"

"Yep. We don't want to miss that call."

FAITH WENT HOME EARLY, too nervous to stay at Canterbury. She called Scott, asking him to order a pizza before he left work.

As they ate, Faith went over the rough plan for the Sunday rendezvous. Scott scowled.

"What's the matter?"

"I don't like it. Too sketchy. Too risky. Jim, or whoever it is, could be armed and hurt you."

"You don't think I can handle it?"

"Of course you can. The question is, can you bring it off without getting hurt. I just don't see how they'll coordinate everything."

"Trust them, they're experts at this, and do it all the time."

"Okay, if you're dead-set on playing detective, I'll do what I can to support you."

34

The week went by too slowly for Faith. She participated in every playtime, and gabbed with Agnes and Felicia in the henhouse. Saturday afternoon Scott took her to a special showing at the Art Institute, and then a leisurely dinner at Boccaccio's. Sunday he went to church with her. In the greeting line after church, Father Whitmore didn't let go of her hand. "Are you okay?"

She shrugged. "I'll give you a call next week."

SUNDAY EVENING SCOTT drove her to the academy. They waited in Jeremy's office with Detective Langston, who would ride with her to the drop off point. The police hid tracking devices in Faith's clothing, and also in her car, as well as in the payoff bag—which they stuffed with newspaper and zipped shut.

Promptly at half past nine, the text message came in on the academy land line.

Text me your cell phone number. Will call you right back.

She texted her cell number. A minute later her phone rang with new instructions.

Get in your car. Alone. No police. Drive to the north side of the loop and park on Michigan Avenue. Text me when you're there.

Scott hugged her. "You'll do fine, babe."

Langston got in the back seat, and phoned his team that they were on the way to the loop.

When they reached Michigan Avenue, they sent a text and got a reply.

Drive south down Michigan Avenue and turn right on Madison. Turn right on State. Text me when you're on State.

Langston kept an open line to the backup car. "He may be positioning the drop near a subway station so he can make a getaway on the subway. Be ready to intercept him between the drop and the closest station."

When Faith turned onto State, she pulled to the curb and texted her location.

Faith's phone rang with another text instruction.

Drive past the theater. Turn on your hazard lights and pull to the curb. If you have someone with you, no deal.

Faith did as instructed, and Langston relayed their move to the backup car.

The phone rang with another text.

Pull away from the curb. Make four right turns and come past the theater again.

Faith drove, the detective relayed to the backup.

As she made the fourth right turn, the theater doors opened and the sidewalk filled with people.

Langston yelled, "Shit!" and told his partners to be alert for the perp to sprint to the subway. He raised up from the back seat enough to look out the rear window, seeing a line of taxis.

Faith's phone rang, this time giving directions in a muffled voice. "I can see you. Turn on your hazard lights and pull to the curb. If anyone is with you, the deal is off. Drop the money in the garbage can by the curb. I'll wait a minute for you to drive away. If you stop, or if someone gets out, the deal is off."

Faith worked her way to the curb, pulling up next to a

garbage can. She turned on her hazard lights, picked up the money bag in the passenger seat and opened her door. "Here I go." She felt like a kindergartner making her first stage appearance, with all eyes glued on her. Behind her a booming command startled her. "Lady, you can't park there!" She turned around and almost ran into a blue uniform. He yelled, "Move it or I'm writing a ticket."

She tossed the bag into the garbage can and hurried back to the car.

Langston ordered, "Drive off, and make another four right turns. I'll get out after your first right turn. I'll be in touch by phone, but we'll plan to meet in front of the theater. Just keep circling."

As Faith drove around the corner, Langston yelled, "Stop!"

Langston opened the door and jumped out while the car was still moving.

Faith's heart had been racing, and now seemed ready to leap out of her chest. She drove slowly as taxis crowded her and gave her the horn. Crime scene images filled her head: Jim being thrown to the pavement and handcuffed, then dragged to his feet and shoved into a police car, a cop's hand forcing Jim's head down.

After the fourth right turn, she approached the theater again, expecting to see Langston and other cops manhandling Jim, shoving him into a police car.

Faith gasped, seeing an almost empty sidewalk in front of the theater. She pulled to the curb. A patrolman tapped his flashlight on her door window and yelled, "Move it!" The intersection ahead was half blocked by a car and taxi that had collided. She managed to steer around the wrecked cars and turned right.

She wanted to call Scott, to tell him the drop went off okay, but knew she had to keep the line free for Langston's call. Turning the first corner past the theater, she welcomed the phone ring.

"Bad move. No money, no insurance. You and the academy will pay for this."

Faith recognized the voice as Jim's and tried to object, but the line went dead.

The steely tone of this direct threat unnerved her more than anything since the fire.

She panicked, swerved to the right and hit the curb. A tailgating taxi tapped her bumper. The cabbie jumped out and screamed, "Crazy bitch. Watch where you're goin'. You ain't hurt none. Go home and sleep it off."

Faith gripped the wheel tightly, took several deep breaths, and slowly inched around the block. Still no sign of Langston. Rounding the corner by the theater again, she steered to the curb and called Langston.

"Yeah? Where are ya?"

"Just around the corner from the theater. I—"

"Just keep circlin', and I'll call you as soon as I can."

"Jim called a few minutes ago. I know it's Jim, I recognized his voice."

"What did he say?"

"Something like, bad idea, no money, no insurance, you and the academy will pay for this. I tried to talk to him, but he hung up."

"Okay. We're still tracking him. I'll try to be in front of the theater soon. Just keep circling."

The theater crowd had disappeared, along with the line of taxis.

The scenes playing out in her mind changed from manacled Jim to a vengeful demon, who might be watching her from the shadows of a doorway. Or he could be speeding to the academy to torch it.

Rounding the corner for the umpteenth time, Faith felt caught in a whirlpool. Langston stood on the curb in front of the theater, waving his arms frantically. She lurched to a stop as he ran in front of the car.

"Get out. I'll drive."

"Where are we going?"

"I've got to take you back to the academy to pick up my car and rejoin the team. We'll be pulling an all-nighter."

"You didn't catch Jim?"

"No. He grabbed the bag, and ran to the front of the taxi line, claimed an emergency, and took the first cab. We expected him to run for the subway. Our backup car sped after the taxi, ran a light, and got in an accident. You probably saw it."

"You don't know where Jim is?"

"No. We've contacted the taxi company. The driver said he got out a few blocks away, and told the cabbie to take the bag to Michael Reese Hospital. We were able to track the bag there, but of course that didn't do us any good. So far as we know, Jim is still in the Chicago area."

Faith gasped. "Oh, my God!"

Langston was driving faster than Faith ever did. She saw the speedometer pass eighty. "I haven't got much time, so let me give you some tips. Does Jim know where you live?"

"Yes. Downtown in a high-rise."

"Call your doorman, tell him not to let anyone up, no deliveries. Do you have any family or friends you can stay with until we locate Jim?"

"No."

"You may want to get a hotel room."

"Thanks for the tips. I'm not so worried about me as the academy."

"You did hire a night watchman, didn't you?"

"Uh-huh."

"Tell him to be very careful, and make frequent rounds of the buildings."

"I'll do that. Probably I'll sleep at the academy tonight. I feel responsible for all those women and children."

"Suit yourself."

"I'm calling my husband to let him know we're on our way."

She rang Scott. "Hi. Langston is driving me to the academy. We'll be there in a few minutes."

"How did it go?"

"The drop went smoothly, but Jim escaped, and he's made another threat. I'll tell you the whole story when I get there."

35

L angston drove into the academy parking lot and skidded to a stop next to his police car. He jumped into it and gunned the engine, then backed up and yelled at Faith. "Better move your car from the parking lot. Leave it on a side street where it won't be so obvious."

Scott was waiting for her at the door. She melted into his arms.

"Tough night, huh?"

"It's past midnight, but it's not over."

She gave him a quick rundown of the misadventure, ending with, "I've got to sleep here tonight. I couldn't leave, knowing that Jim's still on the loose."

"Then I'll stay with you."

"Maybe a cup of tea will settle my nerves."

They moved to the kitchen and got teacups, then went to the henhouse. They heard a mom in the kitchen warming a baby bottle.

Faith walked into the kitchen and volunteered, "Here, let me hold your daughter. We'll sit in the henhouse." Faith cradled the little girl, and gave her the bottle.

"You're always so good with the little ones."

"I missed out on this when my twins were young." Faith lulla-bied the baby to sleep and passed her back to her mother.

Faith went to the office and called the security company, asking them to make additional rounds, and to contact her in the morning.

Faith and Scott walked to the spare room and rested with their clothes on, on top of the bedspread. Faith snuggled next to Scott. "I don't think I can sleep. Just hold me."

Faith dozed off, dreaming about her endless circling of the theater, when she couldn't find Langston. Several times she woke with a start, and reached out for Scott. Eventually she fell into a deep sleep.

A loud knocking on the door startled her. "Sorry, ma'am, it's the night watchman. You insisted that I talk to you before I left. It's seven o'clock. I didn't see a thing all night."

"Thanks."

Faith had never been so happy to see daylight, knowing the academy was safe.

She and Scott greeted Maisie as she prepared breakfast. The women persuaded Scott to have breakfast before he hurried off to the paper. "I'll give you a ring when I can come by for you."

"Hon, I think I'll stick around for playtime, and then have a taxi take me to the condo. I need a hot bath and decompression."

When Scott left, Faith sat at her desk in the henhouse and forced herself to focus on the situation at hand. She called Bill Ludwig's office and left a message, summing up the night's escapade. She repeated the task for Father Murphy.

When Felicia and Agnes showed up at the henhouse, Faith welcomed a three-way embrace, giving them a quick recap.

Felicia wondered out loud, "An evening of cloak and dagger, an all-night vigil, and you're still standing!"

"I'm bailing out after playtime. That's my morning cocktail."

They chatted, mostly about Jim and what they'd like to do to him.

At playtime, the kids spotted Faith and insisted she lead them in Inky Dinky. Singing with them, she smiled for the first time in days.

Jackie came running to Faith. "It's the police. They insist on talking to you."

Faith ran into Jackie's outer office. "This is Faith Armstrong."

"Langston here. Well, we caught the bastard. We were right, it was Jim. We had a watch on the Chicago bus station, but a shift change left the station unwatched when the bus departed for Springfield. We had a patrolman meet the bus in Springfield and make the arrest. We're using a preliminary charge of a harassing phone call to hold him until we can forward the arson charges. We'll ask for at least a half million-dollar bail, considering he threatened the entire academy. Hey, I've been up all night, and can't talk longer, but you'll appreciate this about the stupid perp. Instead of throwing away that traceable phone, he kept it, and now we have solid evidence linking him to all the calls. Well, gotta go. Uh . . . I guess I should say you were a cool cucumber last night. Great to work with you."

Faith had been standing, but collapsed into a chair. The tears streaming down her face turned into a river as she sobbed and cried openly. Agnes and Felicia had stood outside Jackie's door, but walked to Faith and embraced her.

"Oh, I've got to call Scott." She went to the henhouse and rang him at the newspaper. "Hon, I know you're extra busy, but here's the latest news—they nabbed Jim getting off the bus at Springfield."

"They caught him! So it's over."

"Hah. Another way of looking at it is, it's just getting started. In downstate Illinois we say the exciting part about fishing is catching the fish. But after that, the cleaning—scaling, skinning, gutting, cutting off the head—is messy. And then cooking and serving— that's a lot of work. The cops caught Jim, which involved some high-tension excitement. What comes next—processing, charging, and prosecuting him, probably convicting and jailing him, is messy." She paused. "The courts will take care of the legal processing. Father Whitmore will help me with the emotional and spiritual processing."

Scott laughed. "Well, I've got to take care of cleaning up a couple of articles before I head home. Get some rest and we'll talk about it tonight."

Then she went to Jeremy's office. "Son, you might as well hear it from me now. It was Jim, they caught him getting off a bus in Springfield and have him in custody. The important thing is that the academy and the residents are safe."

Jeremy mumbled, "Jim . . . Jim."

"I know you didn't want to believe it, and I didn't, either, but he's the one. I realize you're upset about it, but we can talk more about it later."

"I always want to think the best of people, and can't get over Jim . . .. Uh, I didn't sleep much all night, and think I'll take the day off."

"Good idea. There's nothing that can't wait."

FAITH TRIED to gather her thoughts. She left messages about Jim's capture for Bill and Father Murphy, then called Church of the Redeemer, setting up a ten o'clock Tuesday morning meeting with her priest. She dozed in the taxi to the condo, then enjoyed a hot bath before jumping in bed. She was still asleep when Scott arrived.

They snacked and then talked all evening. Scott wanted detailed information on Jim, but Faith didn't know any more than him. Scott quipped, "He's a sorry jerk. He's ruined his life."

"Uh-huh, I can't help feeling sorry for him."

"What? After he threatened to kill you?"

"Think of his wife and children."

"Yeah. Feel sorry for *them*. Not for him."

Faith carried those words to bed with her.

TUESDAY MORNING FAITH arrived at Church of the Redeemer at nine-thirty, allowing time for a lengthy commune with Mary and Saint Harriet before her appointment at ten. Detective Langston had praised Faith for being a cool cucumber during the rendezvous. He didn't know that most of the credit should be directed upstairs. Faith gave fervent thanks to her benefactors for helping her brave the storm. She felt a serenity and calm pervade her soul, good preparation for meeting with her priest.

Father Whitmore looked up as Faith entered his office. "A long session with your saints."

"They helped me through some very difficult times." She summed up quickly the academy fire, Jim's threat, and his failed extortion.

"I could tell last Sunday you were under stress, but had no idea . . .. Well, now it's over, huh?"

"That's what Scott said, but for me it's almost like the battles I had with Doug. When I beat someone so badly, I feel sorry for the loser."

"Your conscience is working overtime."

"Right. And indirectly, I feel a twinge of guilt, a hint of responsibility for Jim's predicament. It's hard to explain, but lately I was thinking that minor events can lead to life-changing consequences. One tiny thing leads to a chain of sequences that inevitably lead to disaster. Jim and his family were happy when they lived in Springfield. He worked for One Way, they had their own home and a comfortable life. They looked forward to being part of Moms and Kids in Chicago, but didn't realize they couldn't afford a house, and were unhappy in a cramped apartment. They needed fifty thousand for a down payment, and made the wrong conclusion that our foundation owed it to them, because the move of Moms and Kids to Chicago was the root of their problem."

"Hmm, your conscience places you in his position?"

"It bothers me that I never talked to him about the down payment money. If he had told me about it, I would have been glad to take fifty thousand of my retirement money and give him a long-term loan, which he could pay back whenever he had the money. Then he wouldn't have started skimming money from the academy and got caught, which pushed him and his wife into the more daring caper of blackmail, and that led to his wife leaving him. Finally, in desperation, he risked everything with the arson and extortion attempt. Now his life is ruined. He's separated from his wife and kids, and will spend years in jail, and never have a respectable job again."

"You mean, because you could have prevented this chain reaction, you feel . . . indirectly . . . kind of responsible for it."

"What really hurts me is knowing it could have been prevented, but now there's no way, nothing, anybody can do to reverse the situation."

"I don't know what to say."

"My phrase is, 'Bless me, father for I have sinned.' I think your response is 'Go and sin no more.'"

He laughed. "Is that do-it-yourself confession and absolution?"

She sighed. "Well, it makes me feel better, just communing with my saints and confessing to my priest. I can't expect them or you to solve all of my problems."

Faith got a call on her cell phone. Frank Middleton from the police department wanted her to come in to sign some papers. She left Church of the Redeemer for her appointment.

36

Arriving at the police station, Faith was escorted to Middleton's office. "Langston said you served as a good stake out partner. We could use more gals like you who don't get flustered."

"Thanks. My husband and I are curious to hear what happened to Jim Anderson after the handoff."

"Well, he grabbed the bag and ran to the head of the taxi line, claiming an emergency, and ordered the cabbie to take him to Michael Reese Hospital. A block or two from the drop-off, he realized the bag had no money, so he told the driver to take the bag to his wife at Michael Reese ER. He got out and hoofed it to the bus station. He paid a homeless man for his shopping cart and hoodie, and blended into the vagrant scene. Then he purchased a ticket to Springfield with cash, and waited until early morning to board the bus just before it left."

"Clever, I guess."

"Yeah, but amateur criminals mix clever with stupid. Sure, he planned the dropoff carefully, timing it for the end of the theater performance. That was clever. And he wore rubber gloves, so he didn't leave any fingerprints. But he was stupid, keeping the throw-away phone that linked him to your calls. Maybe he was too cheap to get rid of a good phone."

"What happens now?"

"We're having Springfield hold him until we can transport him here. Because the arson and extortion took place in Chicago, we have jurisdiction."

"That means he'll be prosecuted here."

"Yeah. If you have to testify, that'll make it convenient for you."

"Will the court convict him?"

"Should be a slam dunk. We'll have phone records linking his calls to you, and they'll place him near the drop-off. If he gets smart, he'll plead guilty and cop a plea bargain."

"How much time will he do?"

"Depends on prosecuting attorney and the judge. Arson is serious, and threatening to burn down a residence for mothers and children—how much worse can you get?"

"I feel for his family."

"But not for *him*, surely."

"He's ruined his life."

"Lady, he could have killed—burned to death—a whole bunch of people. Don't waste any sympathy on him."

"He'll be separated from his wife and kids."

"His family can come visit him in prison."

"Just his family?"

Middleton gave her a stern look. "Ya don't mean you'd go see him?"

"Maybe. We knew him for years, before he turned bad."

Middleton leaned back and guffawed. "Oh, now I get it. You're the do-gooder who takes care of young women and their kids. Well, Jim is a do-badder. Don't tell me this do-gooder is going to try to turn a do-badder into a do-gooder."

Faith arched her eyebrows. "Well . . . I might."

"Just make sure you have no contact with the perp until he's convicted and doing time. If you talk to him before the trial, it would muddy the water for the prosecutor."

"I'll wait until he's in prison."

"Hell's bells. The department's gotta hire you. When you're not doin' stakeout, you can be a counselor and probation officer."

They segued into Middleton's agenda of signed statements and videotaped depositions, two hours of tedious detail. Middleton thanked her for her patience.

FAITH ARRIVED at the condo just before Scott. He asked, "Did your father-confessor soothe your soul?" before pumping her for information about Jim. Scott joked, "I love it, Middleton has Jim pegged, an amateur crook who mixes clever with stupid."

"Maybe Middleton has me pegged, too, a do-gooder wanting to turn do-badder Jim into a do-gooder."

"To convert Jim into a good guy, you'd have to be a miracle worker."

They chatted all evening, chewing over Jim's shenanigans.

When they went to bed, Faith asked Scott, "Can I ever settle down to a boring no-excitement life at the academy?"

He laughed. "You've had enough high energy, adrenalin-filled days to last for a while."

FAITH ARRIVED LATE for breakfast at Canterbury. Just as she finished, Colette hurried in. Faith held her baby so Colette could eat. Julia came looking for Faith. "Remember, we've got two interviews this morning, nine and ten." Faith had some time to catch up on email before meeting with Julia.

The interviews went well. They agreed to admit the two applicants.

After the interviews, Jeremy tapped on the henhouse door. "Have a few minutes?"

"Sure. We have a lot to talk over. Where do you want to start?"

"With an apology. I was wrong insisting on hard evidence before accusing Jim. I overlooked the circumstances that led the police to Jim."

"No apology needed. Your heart was in the right place."

"But that prevented me from seeing the danger of the academy going up in flames. I was so bummed out by my blindness, I even mentioned to Melanie resigning as head of Moms and Kids."

"Don't even think about it. You're the spark plug that keeps our institution running."

Jackie interrupted their discussion with a call for Jeremy.

FAITH WAS KILLING time at her desk in the henhouse when Bill Ludwig called. "Listen, young lady, I renew my offer of a position as an investigator in our research department. I understand you have job offers of undercover surveillance, and prisoner counseling and probation officer. Let us know what it takes to recruit you to our team."

"I'd be happy just to vegetate in my henhouse."

"Kidding aside, Faith, you're doin' a helluva job running Canterbury. More power to you."

"Bill, it's great to have your support. We really appreciated your nice note in the first issue of Canterbury Canticle."

"I'm glad you got rid of Jim and don't have to worry about more fires."

"While you're on the line, let me ask you as a board member if you support us hiring a full-time night watchman."

"Absolutely. You have my vote."

"Good. I'm sure the other board members are for that, but I want to make it official."

FAITH WAITED until Thursday when Jon and Rachel came to the academy to convene a meeting to discuss the fire. Felicia and Agnes joined the group. Faith opened the meeting. "I know everyone's busy, so let me mention two items and offer suggestions for them. One is a general meeting for all residents, giving them an overview of the fire investigation, and an assurance that we're committed to their safety and welfare. The other item is to have Jon provide the same overview and assurance in the Canticle."

Everyone agreed to Faith's ideas.

Jon volunteered, "Why don't I write out a draft and circulate it so that all of you can provide input?"

The next day Faith had Jackie post a notice of a three o'clock general meeting in the all-purpose room.

Jeremy opened the meeting and then turned it over to Faith.

Faith stood in front of a rather tense audience. "I've mentioned something to individual residents, but want to make a public statement. We regret very much the recent fire, and are glad no one was injured. The police have in custody the man they think started the fire, and no doubt will put him away for years.

"When Moms and Kids moved into this facility, we retained their security protection program. We will continue that service, and our board has approved adding a night watchman to protect the premises for an eight-hour shift. We will make periodic reviews of our security measures, and do our best to maintain the safety of the academy."

After Faith fielded some questions from the residents, she told them the next issue of the Canticle would inform donors and supporters about the fire and the new protective measures.

Jon praised Faith. "Mom, I'll steal your remarks for the article in the Canticle." By the next day he circulated a draft statement to the staff, summing up Faith's talk. Making a few minor revisions, Jon sent out electronic copies of the Canticle with the lead article about the fire.

The henhouse had become Faith's retreat and regrouping area. Felicia and Agnes spent a lot of time with Faith in their nests while waiting for feedback to the announcement of the fire. The troika had believed Jim's prediction that any kind of scandal might harm the academy's reputation and hurt the stream of donations. Much to their surprise, donors praised the academy for its honesty and pro-active steps to protect residents. One supporter wrote, "Here's my check, and I hope others will add their checks to fund the night watchman."

37

J eremy's condition improved enough that he shifted from only mornings at the academy to three mornings and all day on Tuesday and Thursday. His doctor said if he continued to gain strength and watched his diet, in another month he could return to full time.

Faith gravitated to a schedule of a four-day week, saving Wednesday for personal time. She loved Thursdays when Jon and Rachel put in their half days, the adults tutoring and Stephie and Jeb socializing with kids.

Being free on Wednesday enabled Faith to keep in more regular contact with her priest. Her next trip to the south side began with a silent session of devotion to Saint Harriet and Mary, then shifted to a heart-to-heart discussion with her confessor.

"Father, you know me better than I know myself. Tell me if I'm being too conscientious, feeling sorry for Jim. Everyone else— Scott, and the police officers, as well as Bill Ludwig, tell me not to waste any sympathy on Jim. Detective Langsford laughed at me, saying I was just a do-gooder trying to turn Jim into a good person."

"Well, I can't fault you for your conscience and compassion. Nor can I blame the others for doing what they have to do. Scott, bless his soul, wants to protect you, and he's done a great job of it. Bill Ludwig helped you preserve the academy, and he had to play some legal hardball to accomplish that. The police faced an arsonist and extortionist, and they were successful in capturing Jim and preventing him from burning down Canterbury."

"So where does that leave me?"

"My dear, this is not a case where one side is right and the other side is wrong. You're right in following your conscience, and the others are right in doing their duties."

"Well, that doesn't make me feel better. When Langsford and I were talking, I hinted that I might go see Jim. He thought I was crazy, and said if I insisted on visiting Jim, I'd have to wait until he was in prison, because contacting Jim before sentencing would mess up the state's case against him."

"He didn't think you should see him, even after he went to prison?"

"No, but I seem to recall that Jesus had a different view of that situation."

"Yes, I'm sure you're thinking of the words of Jesus in Matthew: 'I was hungry, and ye fed me. I was naked, and ye clothed me. I was in prison, and ye came to me.'"

"You quoted it better than I remember it."

"Yes, Jesus has his own priorities, taking care of people who need being taken care of."

"My feeling is that Jim needs someone to take care of him."

"Here's my tried and true advice—just follow your conscience."

"Let me ask you a somewhat different, kind of convoluted question. It's about two words, guilt and guilty. My conscience tells me I should have feelings of guilt for not doing something to help Jim with his home down payment, so he didn't fall into a moral tailspin that ended up putting him behind bars. But just because I have feelings of guilt, does that mean I'm guilty? In the courts, the American way is 'innocent until proven guilty.' I didn't commit any crime, so I can't be convicted and found guilty, but nevertheless I have feelings of guilt. Does that make me guilty?"

"Well, Faith, I have the standard answer for that. There are two forms of sin, errors of commission, and errors of omission. Errors of commission are when you do something bad, like stealing or killing. Errors of omission are when you fail to do something you should do. When you should help someone, but don't. In the case of Jim, you're talking about an error of omission, when you didn't help him. In our church we have a prayer of confession—we have sinned by what we have done, and by what we have left undone."

"Hmm. Confession, sin, and guilt. That seems to be the triple burden my conscience is laying on me."

Father Whitmore smiled, shrugged, and said, "Pax vobiscum."

THE PALAVER with her priest cast a shadow over Faith as she drove back to the condo. When she got there, she went straight to her underwear drawer and fished out her journal, taking it to the lounger. Flipping to the first blank page, she penned,

CONFESSION. *Sin. Guilt.*
    Trouble?
    Unanswered question.
    Pax vobiscum was nice, but insufficient.
    Will meeting Jim make a difference?
    Or will it make matters worse?

SHE CLOSED the notebook and returned it to its hiding place.

Bored and lonely, she longed for the companionship of Scott, or the camaraderie of the academy. Faith slipped on a jacket and headed for the elevator and the beach, to enjoy the company of her old friend, the lake. It occurred to her, she had not taken a solitary stroll on the beach since she and Scott married.

The lake seemed to welcome her presence, with its calming

slursh-slursh. As she walked, Faith reflected on her priest's three-word benediction: confession, sin, and guilt. She decided to ask her pk husband how he saw the situation.

On her way back from the beach, Faith picked up fixings for supper from a deli. When Scott walked in, he announced, "I'm bushed. A busy day. Didn't even have time for lunch. I'm too tired to go out."

"I have our dinner in the fridge."

"Hmm, do I notice a dark cloud over your head? Usually your priest-confessor sessions leave you more upbeat."

"I told Father Whitmore that I felt bad about Jim and all his problems, and he dumped a triple load of problems on me—confession, sin, and guilt."

Scott chuckled. "So that's what's dragging you down. Welcome to the real world."

"It's not funny, it really bothers me."

"Hey, I'm not laughing at you, just laughing with you. All of us have pangs of guilt, but it's only the honest and good-hearted souls who really pay attention to their shortcomings."

"Maybe my Christian upbringing makes me focus on my flaws."

"Well, it's not only Christianity. One of my Jewish co-workers told me this joke. What's the difference between Judaism and Christianity? Basically they're the same, it's just guilt with different holidays."

Faith snickered. "I wish I could banter about it like you. It really disturbs me."

"Hah. The people you should worry about are those who feel no guilt, who do all kinds of bad things with no shame, and when they're caught, show no remorse."

She gave Scott a kiss. "Thanks for helping me see through my own self-doubt."

WHEN FAITH WENT to the academy, she felt better about herself, but still wondered about Jim, and the three-pronged dilemma of confession, sin, and guilt. After breakfast and chatting with residents, she decided to call Frank Middleton at police headquarters. She figured this detective might tell her enough about Jim's actual situation to help clear her mind.

"Middleton here."

"Good morning. This is Faith Armstrong. I wanted to call early so as not to interrupt your day. Ever since the fire and the extortion attempt, I can't help thinking about Jim and where he is in the legal process. Can you—?"

"Funny you should call. I've been thinking about contacting you. Uh . . . have you been in touch with Jim?"

"No! Not at all. The police told me I shouldn't, and I haven't. Why do you ask?"

"Well, glad you didn't connect with him, because he's gone through some radical changes. It's not unusual for arrested people to undergo mood swings, but he's had more shifts and reversals than most."

"Uh, like what?"

"When he was nabbed getting off the bus in Springfield, he acted like a whipped puppy, and we thought he'd be easy to indict and try. But when we got him back to Chicago and started interrogating him, he turned hard ass and wouldn't cooperate. So, we threw the book at him, and threatened to haul in his wife. That got his attention, and he insisted on talking to a public defender. After that he asked for a minister."

"An odd combination."

"He had a plan. He got confirmation from the public defender that the courts couldn't force him to testify against his wife. That took away some of the leverage we had over him for any trial. We don't know what he discussed with the reverend—you know, like a prisoner's lawyer, that's confidential. Even so, after talking to Jim, the minister tipped us off that it would be good to question Jim about his intentions. We went to his cell, and found a different person. He had done a hundred and eighty-degree switcheroo from hard ass to soft soul. Said he would plead guilty to all charges and take responsibility for everything if we wouldn't charge his wife."

Faith sighed. "I thought he'd come around."

"He used the info from the lawyer that we couldn't make him testify against his wife. He laid his cards on the table, saying he had ruined his life, but at least he could help keep his wife out of prison so she could take care of their kids." He kept saying, "'I just want to do the right thing.'"

Faith sighed. "Wow."

"We thought maybe you had gotten to him and used your do-good charm on him."

"No, whatever he did was on his own. Hmm, maybe that's what he talked about with the jail minister."

"Uh, Faith, what I'm telling you is strictly confidential. Because you put your skin on the line during the stakeout, I'll let you in on the deal. Bottom line is that he's in negotiations with the district attorney, he's fessing up to everything, will plead guilty, and save the state the expense and trouble of a trial. The tradeoff is he wants his wife to go scot free, no charges."

"Can they do that?"

"Well, the case against his wife—Janine—is rather weak, based on hearsay, what Jim told you and your board. They can't force him to testify against his spouse. She didn't write anything down or make any phone calls, so it would be hard to prosecute. The DA is probably glad to get such a flimsy case off his desk. What surprises all of us is the complete turnaround. He threatened to burn down a facility with young mothers and kids, a real nasty crime. Now he's becoming the nice guy, sacrificing himself to save his wife."

"That's more like the Jim I knew before he went rogue. What about his wife?"

"From what we gather, she's started divorce proceedings."

"I never knew her that well. Gee, that means Jim is all alone. What does his sentence look like?"

"Hard to tell. Depends on the judge, but because it's a double crime of arson and extortion—well, make that a triple crime with the threat of burning down the academy—he's probably looking at five to seven years."

She fell silent.

"Faith, you still there?"

"Uh, yes. 'Five to seven years.' That threw me for a loop."

"The DA will probably allow you to speak at the sentencing. You could put into the record how you and all the people at the academy were terrified. That might make the judge rachet up the sentence."

"I don't think I—or others at the academy—want to make things worse for Jim. But please keep me informed. Let me know when he's sentenced and sent to prison."

"Sure. I've got another call, have to ring off."

38

F aith mumbled, "Five to seven years," and put the receiver back on the cradle, staring at it, as if the phone would help her comprehend the enormity of the sentence Jim faced.

She squinted her eyes, gritted her teeth and thought back to the long years—decades—she had been separated from her children. She turned her chair to the lineup of photos and made another virtual reality tour of her life, culminating with the two pictures on the far wall of moms and kids eating, and kids at playtime.

Then her mind's eye saw another image slowly take shape underneath those two pictures. It appeared as a grainy newspaper illustration of a burned down building. Above the illustration was the title of a newspaper article: "Multiple deaths in fire at moms and kids home." Faith's heart pounded at what might have been. This portrayed the potential catastrophe that the judge and society would consider as more than sufficient cause to incarcerate Jim for many years, separating him from his family.

Faith, always honest with herself, knew that her separation from the twins was different from Jim's situation. During those dark years she didn't have the twins, but she remained a free person, and had the hotel to keep her busy and motivated, moving up the ladder to an executive position. Jim would have just a cramped cell, an occasional glimpse of blue sky, and only fellow criminals as companions.

Faith shuddered at the prospect of Jim's lengthy confinement behind thick concrete walls. A shiver ran down her spine. She spun around in her chair and retrieved her jacket from a peg on the wall. The jacket helped break the chill, but she still felt cold. She shoved her laptop against the wall and folded her arms in front of her, putting her hands in the opposite jacket sleeves, laying her head down on her arms resting on the desk. Slowly her body warmed and she relaxed, dozing.

She woke with a start to hands touching her shoulders. Faith turned to see Felicia.

"Are you okay?"

"Uh, I will be."

"If you want to tell me about it, fine. If not, I'll butt out."

"Do I look that bad?"

"Like maybe you had a falling out with the most important man in your life."

Faith shook her head. "No, everything's fine on the home front."

"Problems with the academy?"

"Not really, but—"

At that moment Agnes opened the door, and did a double take. "Oops, am I interrupting a private moment?"

"Not at all. Well, pull up a chair and I'll tell you what's bugging me, but it's absolutely QT, not even repeatable to husbands."

Agnes frowned. "Sounds mysterious."

"Well, it is deep. You know I'm still concerned about Jim."

Agnes shook a finger at Faith. "Don't let that skunk bother you. PU, it stinks even hearing his name."

"I can't help feeling for him, like the Bible says, about the lost sheep. I've discussed Jim with Father Whitmore, and he doesn't fault me for being bothered by Jim's situation."

Felicia frowned. "But Jim deserves what he gets, after all he did."

"Yes, of course. But let me tell you more about his present predicament. I just got through talking with Detective Middleton, who leveled with me, telling me not to make this public. Jim's probably up for five to seven years of jail time, which I know you think he has coming to him. The situation is that he confessed to all the crimes in a plea bargain, in exchange for them not charging his wife. Here's the irony—his wife is divorcing him, and yet he's sacrificing his life and career for her. Well, and for the sake of his children."

Wrinkles spread over Felicia's forehead. "Why would he do that? Didn't you say his wife put him up to stealing from the academy? She's what a prosecutor would call the kingpin."

"Yeah, but the evidence against her is hearsay, so they'll settle for a stiff sentence for Jim."

Agnes frowned. "Once before I got nasty and called her a bitch on wheels. She's worse than that. Maybe she's Lucifer's bitch."

Felicia snorted. "Jim takes the fall, and his wife gets away without even a slap on the wrist."

Faith nodded. "You know, this is the Jim I remember before he went bad. He was a good guy. Jeremy taught me a lot about human nature, that even bad people have some good in them, some redeeming features. He showed me that with Doug, the twins' father, who was a hopeless Casanova, but at the end of his life did try to make amends."

Agnes repeated slowly, "At the end of his life. You don't mean . . .."

Faith held her hand to her mouth. "I don't know if this is Jim's last gasp of altruism."

Felicia hugged Faith. "Don't you worry your pretty head about him."

Agnes joined Felicia in the hug. "What are you going to do?"

"Well," Faith took a deep breath, "I may visit him in prison.

Father Whitmore quoted the words of Jesus in Matthew: 'When I was in prison, ye came to me.'"

Felicia smiled. "You *are* remarkable. A lot of people read and repeat the words of Jesus, but you put those words into action in your own life."

"Give the credit to Jeremy. He showed me it's not what you say you believe, but what you do, that counts. Let me tell you a story about Brigitte, one of our first residents, at the old hotel. Jeremy and I interviewed her, and she was completely honest with us. As a teenager she lived with her divorced mom, and money was tight, so she didn't have nice clothes like the other girls. She became friends with a bunch of girls who shoplifted. Brigitte went into a store with a large purse, tried on a nice dress that was on a mannequin, with no security tag. She put her own clothes into her purse and walked out wearing the store dress. Her not so good friends dared her to do it again. She felt so empowered by this successful theft that she repeated it a few months later. But she forgot to take the paper sticker off the dress, and was caught. This gave her a juvenile record, yet she was fortunate to get off with probation as a first-time offender. Then she became pregnant, and did try to put her life together, not associating with her former friends.

"The reason I'm telling you this is that when Jeremy and I discussed whether to accept Brigitte as a resident, I was against accepting a "juvie," while Jeremy was for her. He said these are exactly the kind of young women who need a second chance. He said we should look at the potential good in Brigitte. He talked me into accepting her, and I'm glad we did. Moms and Kids helped Brigitte turn her life around, and now she has a good job in a department store.

"That's one reason I got so mad at Jim for blackmailing Brigitte into the kickback scheme, forcing her to accept a check for six hundred transition money instead of five hundred, and then to hand over the extra hundred to him. You may recall when we harangued Jim in the office, I called his taking advantage of Brigitte's juvie record a 'despicable' act. Anyway, that's one reason I worked hard with the police to keep Brigitte out of any official records.

"Julia, our social worker, has talked to Brigitte a number of times, and heard the rest of this gal's story. Bottom line is that Brigitte showed us she has a good side, and is making good in her life. Jeremy taught me that every person has some worth, even Jim. And remember, Jim did have remorse for blackmailing Brigitte. Now Jim is taking the blame for everything, letting his wife go free, even when she's divorcing him. He does seem to have a good side."

Felicia nodded. "Yeah, but it takes someone like you to not just say it, but to act on your belief. I think this is the homespun philosophy that helped you start Moms and Kids."

"When I look back, it seems that little things, seemingly unimportant circumstances, can determine your whole life. In my case, if I had not been so headstrong and insisted on not being a counselor at church camp, I wouldn't have worked at Pappy's Pizza Parlor. And I wouldn't have met Doug. And if my folks had allowed me to date in high school casually, I wouldn't have been so overawed by this college hunk, and gotten pregnant. If my parents hadn't been so pious and sanctimonious, they would have let me keep my twins and raise them. Well, those circumstances led to my twin destiny, and here I am today. I want to do what I can to see that women who made a mistake or two don't let these kinds of circumstances separate them from their children.

"Our residents here each have their own story of how trivial decisions or events can shape your entire life. In Brigitte's case, she fell in with the wrong crowd, and made a few foolish choices. That could have led her to a life of crime, pushing her to worse offences. If she had not gotten pregnant, maybe she wouldn't have turned away from those bad influences. If her mother had not been so hard on her, she might not have come to us. And if Jeremy had not persuaded me to accept her as a resident, who knows what she would have done. Just when she was turning her life around, Jim took advantage of her juvie record to force her into his kickback scheme. If we had not been able to persuade the police to overlook her part in Jim's thefts, she could have lost her department store job and become a welfare mom. A few minor incidents can turn into life-altering events.

"Look at Jim. He was always a good father and reliable husband, but the move to Chicago forced them out of the house market, and he let his wife talk him into getting back at the academy by stealing. One thing led to another, and now he's heading for long-term incarceration. There's very little we can do for Jim, but at least I can go see him."

Felicia nodded. "Honey, you've earned your angel wings by helping all these young women at Canterbury. You shouldn't feel bad that you can't save everyone."

Faith chuckled. "That's what Father Whitmore says. He reminds me the phrase 'The Lord is my Shepherd' means that the Lord takes care of his flock, and we shouldn't try to take the place of the Lord."

Agnes joked, "If the Lord ever needed a vice president, you'd be his first choice."

The three laughed, as they turned to their daily tasks.

A WEEK later Faith sat in the henhouse alone in mid-afternoon, when the phone rang.

"Hello, Faith, Middleton here. How's Moms and Kids doing?"

"Fine, thanks for asking. Let me cut to the chase. I know this isn't a social call. You have news about Jim?"

"Okay, you want it straight, here it is. He was sentenced to the lower limits, five to seven. First the judge gave him hell for putting your hundred residents in mortal danger. He said he was ready to give Jim seven to ten for such serious offenses. But because Jim was contrite, pleaded guilty, saved the government time and money not having a trial, and cooperated so fully, the judge let him off easy with the minimum five to seven."

"You know, Frank, the first time you mentioned 'five to seven years,' it shocked me to recognize the severity of Jim's crimes, and the length of his punishment. Now what you're telling me is that this is a good deal, the best sentence he could hope for."

"Hell, if you appeared for the sentencing, cried on the stand, and went on about how terrified you were, how you still can't sleep at night—and had young mothers tell the same story—the judge might have gone to ten plus years."

"So where is Jim now?"

"He's been transferred to Joliet, the Stateville facility."

"Joliet?"

"Yeah, not the old famous one, but the newer prison, a few miles from the old landmark."

"So I can see him there?"

"You still want to visit him?"

"Let me say that I'm considering it."

"Hmm, mind telling me why?"

"I'm not sure why myself. I've talked to my priest about it, telling him I think I should, and my conscience tells me to go. The priest and I considered the words of Jesus in the Bible—the book of Matthew—'when I was in prison, ye came to me.'"

"Holy Moley! I know a lot of people who claim they're religious —mostly words—but you *are* religious. You take Jesus seriously, and follow his teachings. Well, more power to you."

"Hey, I'm not so brave. Honestly, I'm a little afraid of entering a prison, and worry that things might not go well with Jim."

"If you're determined to do this, let me give you a few tips. You can't just waltz in the front door of a prison and ask to see Jim. They have a bunch of formalities, like asking permission to see him, and he has to agree to it."

"I figured it wouldn't be easy."

"I've got some other calls to make today, but let me close with the best tip. Look up 'Stateville Correctional Center' online, and read through the ton of conditions and warnings and rules. If that doesn't discourage you, then good luck."

"I appreciate the tips and the best wishes."

"Listen Faith, if you find this is just too much for you to go through, don't do it. And don't beat yourself up for not going. You're doing great work at Moms and Kids, a hundred times more than the average person does for others. You must have so many brownie points in Saint Peter's ledger that he had to start a new page for you."

"Thanks for the support. I'll let you know how things go."

39

E ven though it was getting late, Faith googled Stateville Correction Center, and began poring through the numerous conditions for visitation. As Middleton indicated, the prisoner had to agree to the visit. If the prisoner had broken rules, he could not have visitors.

Then the site specified numerous conditions for visitors. Restrictions on clothing seemed petty, especially no "see through" or sexually suggestive clothing. It shocked Faith that she would be required to wear a bra! Every visitor was subject to a body search. She certainly didn't want to be manhandled by some strange guy, so she called Stateville. After a rather brusque greeting, she was transferred to a guard. "Visitation Center, what did you want to know?"

"Uh, your website states that all visitors are subject to a body search. Will women visitors be searched by a woman?"

"Yeah. Of course. A woman visitor will be patted down by a female corrections agent. I should warn you that if a search turns up a weapon or potential weapon—a sharp object—or any contraband, you'll be escorted out the gate and your name permanently removed from visitation privileges."

"Thank you."

Faith returned to the site, and noted that 'contraband' even included cigarettes. She would have to leave her purse and belongings in a locker outside the visitation area, and was not allowed to hand over anything, even any papers, to the prisoner.

She first had to write to Jim to ask him to put her on his visitors' list. If he approved, she was required to fill out a Prospective Visitor's Interview when she showed up for the visit. She could not receive anything from the "offender." Jim would be strip searched before and after the visitation.

Slowly Faith felt the tentacles of the law encircling her, turning her into a suspect. The document called prisoners "offenders," and the more she read, the more she felt like an offender.

Middleton had been right. The conditions for visitation were numerous and offensive. She anticipated probing questions on the Prospective Visitor's Interview: Have you ever been arrested? When? Where? Were you convicted of a crime? Misdemeanor or felony? Specify. Have you ever been imprisoned? When? Where? Have you used recreational drugs? Are you on drugs now? Do you drink? Did you have anything to drink before entering the Center today?

Yes, the good detective had been correct that she might get discouraged by all the rigamarole, and give up on visiting Jim.

Faith went home, finding Scott had beat her there. "Long day?"

"I ended up looking at the Stateville Correctional Center site."

"Not exactly a friendly welcome committee, huh?"

"It made me feel like a criminal."

"Remember, dear, they're not running a day care facility. They have murderers, rapists, arsonists, con men, all of whom are desperate to get out. Reporters on the crime beat are so familiar with the rules that they just forget about them."

"Detective Middleton warned me that the rules are so onerous I might just give up on a visit, and not to blame myself for not seeing Jim."

"Did you ask Jeremy what he thought about you visiting Jim?"

"He quoted the passage in the Bible where Jesus said, 'When I was in prison, ye came to me.'"

She decided to sleep on it, and write the letter to Jim at the henhouse in the morning, when she was fresh.

The next day when Scott left, he said, "Good luck with your letter. Don't fret and spend too much time on it. Whatever you put down on paper will get the message to Jim."

Faith drove to the academy and breezed through an early breakfast, then headed right for her laptop.

Dear Jim,

It has been some time since we have been in contact. I would have been in touch with you earlier, but the police said that would not be appropriate until your case was settled. Detective Middleton informed me that the case is settled, and you will be at Stateville for a number of years.

This makes me think of the many years I was separated from my twins, a difficult time for me. I know this must be a difficult time for you. If you allow me, I am willing to visit you at Stateville. You know there is nothing I can do to change your situation.

We have been through some very trying times, on opposite sides. I remember in the past you were a vital part of Moms and Kids. I want to remember the times when we worked together to make Moms and Kids function.

I have no agenda in visiting you. My intention is to support you as you sort out your life and plan for leaving Stateville and restarting your life.

The authorities tell me that for me to visit you, you must put me on your visitors' list. Please let me know if you will do this, so that I can make a formal request to see you.

Thank you,

Sincerely,

Faith Armstrong

.   .   .

F AITH READ and reread the letter, which did not satisfy her, but she mailed it to Jim.

~

T HAT NIGHT she and Scott talked about her letter. She told him, "I haven't done anything wrong, but waiting to hear from Jim makes me feel like a criminal awaiting a sentence."

"Hang in there, babe, we've been through the waiting process before. You have plenty to keep you busy."

Faith kept her routine at the academy. The Canterbury trio slowly developed a pattern of a gabfest between breakfast and playtime, and often another session after playtime. The threesome shared family news and commiserated over ailments. They even traded shopping and cooking tips. While Faith waited to hear from Jim, the women spent a lot of time discussing how Faith would handle the proposed "interview" with Jim.

"I learned in the hotel business that there's such a thing as being over-prepared. The advice I received about interviews and dialogues—and later talked about when I did consulting—is just be yourself. Don't say anything you don't mean, or try to be someone that's not you."

~

F INALLY, the letter from Jim came, a short note.

Y OU ASKED to meet with me. I am willing to meet with you, and have put your name on my visitation list. Contact Stateville Visitation Center to find a time when you can come.

F AITH PHONED THE V ISITATION C ENTER, asked for available times, and then mailed a visitation request.

The day of the meeting, before Scott left for work, he enfolded Faith in a bearhug. "You'll do fine, dear. I'll try to get home early so we can talk." He shut the door and then reentered. "I won't tell anyone that my wife is going to prison today."

"Funny, funny."

Faith drove to Stateville Correction Center, feeling a twinge of nervousness as she passed through the huge gates. Walking to the entrance, a guard asked if she came to visit, had proper ID, and was aware of all the rules.

"I've read the visitation information on the website, and brought two forms of government ID with me."

The guard allowed her to enter, where she was directed to the lockers to store her purse and all personal items, then shown where the restrooms were located. "Best to use the restroom now. No restroom breaks during interview time."

Faith left purse, keys, and all metal goods, even pens, in the locker so as not to set off the metal detector she was required to pass through. Then she cringed as she faced a burly woman with rubber-gloved hands holding an electronic wand.

"I'm gonna give you a double check with the wand, and then will pat you down."

The woman thoroughly traced the seams of her clothing, bra, and underwear.

Faith instinctively moved away.

"Stay still, lady, or I'll have to do this again."

When the guard started feeling her chest and breasts, Faith flinched and stepped back.

"Lady, if you don't cooperate, you don't visit. I ain't havin' any fun. Some gals hide ten dollar bills or a stash of weed in their bra or undies. Hold still and we'll be done here."

She closed her eyes and frowned, feeling violated.

She suffered through the visitation form, which was as probing and offensive as she had expected.

The heavy-set guard told Faith, "Sit in this chair until you're called."

Faith didn't know whether to cry or scream. She was ready to turn tail and drive back to Chicago.

The guard returned. "You ain't got any matches, do you?"

"Uh, matches for what?"

"For startin' a fire, honeybun. The word came down that you're visitin' a firebug, and we want to make sure you don't slip him any matches."

"No, I don't have any matches."

"Okay, you can go in now. Sit on the chair opposite the offender. Hands on the table. Don't drop anything. If you do, a guard will pick it up. No contact with the offender. Nothing passed between the two of you. Video cameras will record your visit. If you break the rules, both you and he can be barred from future visits. You can talk to him over the phone on the wall."

The guard punched in the code for the door and ushered Faith in to the interview room. Jim sat on a chair in a cubicle, behind a long since new sheet of plexiglass, its cloudy appearance making Faith think of Jim's unclear future. Jim had his hands on the table, staring into space. He didn't look at her as she took a seat in a chair on the other side of the cubicle.

The guard announced, "You have one hour. Watch the time."

40

F aith did an instant look-see. She noticed especially Jim's skin color. He had always been on the pale side, but prison detention had turned him into an ashen semblance of his former self. He had lost weight, making his cheeks hollow and his eyes seem deep set. He had his head slightly lowered, gazing over her at the wall.

She picked up the phone and broke the silence. "Hello, Jim."

He paused, reached for his phone, and mumbled, "Hello, Faith. Thank you for coming to Hotel Hell. That's what my buddies call this place."

"I would have come sooner, but the police told me to wait until you were sentenced and had a permanent residence."

He grimaced. "Yeah, once I got my head straight, I decided to plead guilty, and make the best of a bad situation. I confessed to everything, and my public defender helped me arrange a plea bargain to keep Janine out of it. That way she can take care of the kids."

"I heard that. It was good of you."

He half smiled. "The kids are all I have left. You know Janine filed for divorce."

"That's what I understand. Sorry."

"My wife divorced me. My son is old enough to understand my predicament, so he disowned me. He wrote me, 'If you were going to set fire to a building and burn up a hundred people in it, you're not my dad.'"

Faith gasped.

"Yeah, I figure my life is over, but my kids are young, so they can make the most of their lives."

Jim lowered his eyes to look into Faith's. "Well, we only have an hour. I could talk all day about what's happened, but you've come all this way, so you should have a chance to say something or ask questions."

"As I mentioned in my note, I don't have an agenda, I just wanted to come and give you support."

"Well, let me plow ahead. If I have to say it a million times, I'm sorry for all the trouble I caused you, Jeremy, the academy, the staff, and all the residents. I've confessed and taken the blame for what I did, so I'm not going to try to weasel out of that. But when we moved to Chicago, I was up against it. Being a downstater, I had no idea how much money a house cost in the Chicago area. Janine was so unhappy she said she was going to leave me if we couldn't have a house. She blamed the Moms and Kids Foundation, and said when companies relocate staff to expensive cities, they provide a housing allowance. That's how we started talking about ways to get hold of some of the Foundation money we thought we had coming.

"I started out skimming money from the meat man, and from transition payments, but Bill Ludwig was right, I had my sights on the Foundation endowment. I kept the 'misappropriated' money in a separate bank account, and as it was accumulating, Janine stayed with me. Then she got impatient, and that's when I sent a thousand dollars to my wife's sister.

"I should have known this wouldn't work, and I'd get caught. When Felicia discovered the kickback scheme with Otto the meat man, I panicked. Janine was ready to leave me, and said if I didn't go ahead with the fifty thousand blackmail scheme, she definitely was taking the kids back to Springfield.

"I have to admit that you, the academy, and Bill Ludwig were more than fair. You let me off with just paying back the money, and no criminal charges. I was ready to accept that and start over, but for Janine that was the last straw, and she moved with the kids to Springfield.

"The word was out at One Way, and everyone they knew, that I had stolen money from Moms and Kids, which kept me from getting a decent job. I was desperate, figuring I'd never find a good paying position to support my kids in college. That's how I came up with the crazy idea combining arson and extortion.

"One thing I'd like to make clear to you. I knew no one would be in the maintenance building at the academy in the early morning hours, so nobody would be hurt. It was far enough away from the main building that it wouldn't set it afire. Also, after I started the fire in the maintenance building, I parked about a block away, and waited until it really got blazing, then I started to dial the fire department. To my surprise, I heard sirens. Someone saw the flames and called it in before I did. So I left the area. That's when I called the academy and left the text message making the hundred thousand demand.

"You should know the hundred grand was for my kids' education, fifty grand for my son, fifty for my daughter. We had a small fund started for each of them, and I planned to deposit the money in their accounts. I've never gambled or run around with women, so the money wasn't for me or something foolish. And I want you to know the threat to burn the main building was complete bluff. If the academy had refused to pay the hundred thousand, I simply would have gone back to Springfield.

"Hey, I've chewed up much of our hour, but I want to be sure to ask a favor before we're done here. Even if I've given you my version of the story—you know, I never intended to burn down the academy main building—that doesn't excuse me. My life basically is over, but my son and daughter should have a chance to grow up and make good. My son has already disowned me, and my daughter probably thinks that way, even though she didn't write to me.

"I want to send letters to my kids, but my wife simply returned unopened the envelopes I mailed to her. Today you and I can't exchange any papers. But I'd like to mail you two short letters, one to each kid, telling them how sorry I am to have messed up the family, and how they should forget about me and make the most of their lives. If you would send those letters to Janine, maybe she'd soften up and give them the letters."

Jim began hyperventilating, and started to sob. "I never intended for it to come to this. It's just that ever since we left Springfield for Chicago, one thing led to another, and . . . here I am."

"Jim, I know deep down you're a good person. You took all the blame, to let your wife go free. I feel bad, because if I'd known you needed that house down payment so bad, I could have loaned you —long term—some of my retirement money. Then you wouldn't have fallen into this irreversible tailspin."

Jim had been looking at the floor as he rambled on. Now he opened his eyes wide, staring directly at Faith. He sat back stiffly in his chair, dropped the phone, and raise both fists, pounding them on the table. "What? You would have?"

He started to say more, when the guard approached the table. "Settle down, mister, or this interview's over."

He kept his hands in front of him, clenched into fists, sobbing uncontrollably. Choking, he looked again at Faith. "Promise . . . you'll send the letters."

"Yes. I promise. I'll send the letters."

Jim turned sideways in his chair, struggling to get to his feet.

The guard rushed over to him. "Are you through with the interview?"

"Yeah."

The guard led him to the opposite door, punched in the code, and pushed him through it. Faith knew the next step for Jim would be a strip search.

Stunned by this climactic conclusion, Faith stayed glued to her chair.

The guard reentered the interview room, announcing to her, "The interview's over. You need to leave because we've got other visitors scheduled."

Faith found her way to the restroom, then retrieved her possessions from a locker, and walked to the car. Her body trembled, realizing at that moment Jim probably had been deprived of clothes, undergoing a humiliating strip search.

Still a little dazed by the ordeal, Faith locked the car doors and rested her head on the steering wheel. After a few minutes she regained her composure, and drove through the massive correctional center gates. She breathed a sigh of relief, as if escaping from confinement.

41

S cott kept his promise, returning from the newspaper early to help Faith recover from her brief prison stay. He had the wine glasses out. "Some vino?"

"Uh, no."

"Not up to a celebration, huh?"

"I usually don't go for Seagram's, but today's an exception."

"Coming up, on the rocks with a little water. Well, tell me about it. You look like you've been run through the wringer and hung out to dry."

"Middleton warned me it would be rough, but there's no way to prepare for the architectural despair and institutional deprivation that pervades the place. Jim said the prisoners there call it 'Hotel Hell,' and that's the best two-word description."

"What was the worst?"

"The body search, even patting down my undies and bra. They had a woman do it, but still I felt violated." She took a big swig of whiskey, coughing.

"Hey, take it easy, that's strong medicine. Go ahead and tell me about Jim."

She summed up quickly Jim's backstory of how he and Janine

slid into the 'misappropriation' scheme and from there it was downhill all the way, even though he made sure nobody would be hurt in the fire at the academy. She mentioned the plea bargain that kept Janine out of prison.

"Let me get this straight. Janine was the mastermind of all of Jim's crimes, and he has to pay the piper, even though she's divorcing him."

"That's the bottom line."

"Shrew is a nice word for her, I won't mention other terms that come to mind."

"Scott, I started to cry when Jim pleaded with me to send the letters for his kids to Janine, telling his son and daughter to forget about him and go on with their lives."

"Well, dear, I'm not your father confessor, but he's acting out a self-sacrifice for the benefit of others. Although he may be a convicted criminal, he's an unrecognized saint."

Faith nodded, almost spilling her whiskey. "And that makes his wife, to put it politely, an unindicted co-conspirator or the devil's accomplice. Give me another drink."

"Coming up. I've never seen you like this."

"It was totally humiliating. They strip searched him before and after the interview. When he had his emotional meltdown, he seemed to be totally defeated, barely able to raise up out of his chair and retreat to his concrete cell."

"Hey, let me fix us some sandwiches."

"I'm not hungry."

"Listen, you need something to soak up that alcohol. You're not used to drinking hard liquor."

They ate and then returned to the loungers, as Faith sipped a third whiskey. She leaned back in the recliner and fell asleep. Scott waited until bedtime to rouse her and lead her to bed.

∼

THE FOLLOWING morning Faith slept in, not hearing Scott get up. She woke to his kiss on her forehead. "I left a morning cocktail for you."

She rubbed her head. "A cocktail is the last thing I want."

"The cocktail prescription for a hangover is orange juice for sugar, to speed up your metabolism, and two aspirins for the headache."

She followed his advice, downing the aspirins with OJ. A hot bath helped her combat the aftereffects of the whiskey. She arrived at the academy much later than usual. Felicia and Agnes were already perched in their nests. Faith walked into the kitchen. "Maisie, if you have a few minutes, come to the henhouse and listen to the story of my prison experience. I only want to tell this once."

Faith retold her tale, punctuated by the gals' gasps and muttered cursing.

"I never thought I'd feel sorry for Jim," Felicia admitted.

Agnes snorted, "And I didn't think my opinion of Janine could go any lower. She should be in prison."

Faith held her hand out in a stop motion. "She deserves to be in prison, but her kids don't deserve to be deprived of a mother."

Maisie nodded. "Yeah, forget about that bitch-witch. Think of the children."

They talked about Faith's ordeal, the pathetic situation of Jim, and the plight of his children, until Maisie said she had to get back to her lunch. Agnes and Felicia went to playtime, but Faith stayed behind to make a phone call to Frank Middleton.

"Hello, Frank, it's Faith Armstrong. Do you have a few minutes?"

"I've got about ten minutes before an appointment. What's up?"

"I went to see Jim, and want to thank you for tipping me off to the horrors of Stateville. Just going through the screening process and the rigorous questionnaire—and then the humiliating body search—made me feel like a criminal."

"If more people passed through the gates of hell like you did, we'd have fewer people risking prison."

"I guess you know the inmates call the place Hotel Hell."

"That's what I've heard."

"You don't have much time, so I'll give it to you short and sweet. Jim's a broken man, resigned to his punishment, and desperately reaching out to his children, who are alienated from him. Jim told me how his wife egged him on to steal, and threatened to leave him if he didn't come up with the fifty grand. He did set fire to the maintenance building, but stuck around to call the fire department once it was in flames. And he said setting fire to the academy was all bluff. He never would have gone through with it."

"Well, you learned the backstory, what seldom comes out in police interrogations or judicial proceedings. Where does that leave you?"

"I'm glad I went. It proves what Jeremy taught me, that every person has some good. And I'll forward the letters from Jim to his son and daughter, that tell them to forget about him and look to the future."

"Well, I think the department should consider you for a counselor and parole officer for inmates."

"It was a sobering event, one I'll never forget."

"Sometimes school classes go on field trips to prisons and the students listen to prisoners explain how they went wrong, and how young people shouldn't make the same mistakes. I wish more schools did that."

"I know you're busy, so I just want to thank you again for helping me prepare for the interview with Jim."

Faith hung up, then went to catch the last of playtime. The kids spotted Faith and insisted she lead them in a singalong of Inky Dinky.

After playtime she walked back to the henhouse and called Church of the Redeemer, asking the secretary to arrange a ten o'clock appointment for the following Wednesday.

FOR FAITH, the next week became a blur. The traumatic prison visit kept replaying in her mind. Then she tried to anticipate the letter from Jim, along with the notes to his son and daughter. She tried to frame a message to Janine, diplomatically urging her to pass on Jim's notes to the children. Also, she would have to be careful writing to Jim, letting him know she forwarded his notes, without guaranteeing what Janine would do with them.

Finally, Wednesday rolled around, and Faith made her way to Church of the Redeemer, arriving just after half past nine. She needed extra time with Saint Harriet and Mary. First came prayers of thanks for helping her survive the prison ordeal, then petitions for assistance in handling Jim's notes to his kids. Then she prayed to her saints for Jim, asking them to strengthen and guide him during his difficult years of incarceration.

A little before ten she left her pew and walked into the open door of Father Whitmore's office.

"Good to see you, Faith. I noticed you had a long session with your saints."

"Heavy duty prayers, Father, but first thanks to you. For years you've been counseling me and guiding me along the straight and narrow path. Your best advice has always been to follow my conscience. That hasn't been easy, but it provided the personal compass that enabled me to navigate some difficult times. You know I had been thinking about seeing Jim, even though the police, friends, and my lawyer questioned that move. I considered coming to see you, but knew you would tell me to listen to my conscience."

"And you did."

"Yes, and frankly, it turned out to be one of the most disturbing events of my life. I've had serious problems before, like confronting Doug. But then I had a clear adversary and could fight against him. With Jim, there's no clear foe, and no winning. It's such a hopeless situation, and no resolution in sight."

She quickly retold the nightmare of the prison visit, ending in Jim's emotional breakdown and hangdog retreat to his concrete cell.

"Faith, that is a sad tale. I've heard similar stories from prison chaplains. How can I help you?"

"My unanswerable question is how can I help Jim. He says his life is ended. He's given up on his family. He's all alone, defeated, in despair. I prayed to Harriet and Mary, both to assist me and to support Jim. I'm open to any suggestions you have."

"First, I commend you for listening to your conscience. Most people shut their eyes and turn their backs on these situations. You walked into that prison and faced Jim in the midst of his impossible condition. You've promised to send on letters to his children. I don't see what else you can do. Do you plan to see him again?"

"That's where I'm at. He's in a hopeless spot, and I don't have any hope to offer him. Another visit wouldn't change anything."

They talked for a while, until Faith excused herself.

Father Whitmore said a nice prayer to end the session, but Faith felt incomplete.

She knew some musical composers left unfinished symphonies. She felt her prison visitation, and also her church appointment, lacked a solid conclusion.

She was still sorting out her thoughts when she returned to the condo, and saw a blinking light for a message.

"Hi, Faith, it's Jackie. I knew you had a meeting with your priest, and didn't want to interrupt you. But you said to be on the lookout for a letter from Stateville, and I wanted to let you know that a rather thick letter came today."

Faith didn't take off her coat, just got back in the car and drove to the academy.

42

A t Canterbury, Faith rushed to Jackie's desk and got the mailing from Jim, taking it to the henhouse. She opened it and separated Jim's note from the two letters he had written to his children. She didn't want to intrude on his privacy by opening the two envelopes and reading the letters. Jim's note was brief.

FAITH,

Thanks for coming to Stateville. I know it wasn't easy for you.

And thanks for forwarding these letters to Janine. Maybe if they come from you, she'll let the children read them.

My son and daughter are all I have left in the world. All I can hope for now is that they will avoid my mistakes and lead happy lives.

Please let me know that you received this and forwarded the letters to Janine.

Jim

. . .

FAITH WENT to the kitchen for a cup of tea to calm her jittery nerves. Bringing the cup back to the henhouse, she reviewed in her mind the message to Janine she had been thinking about. Finishing her tea, she wrote,

JANINE,

I am sorry to hear that you and Jim have separated, and hope that you are able to find your way into the future.

Recently I visited Jim at Stateville. He seems to be adjusting to life there. During our talk, he asked me to forward to you letters he has written to your son and daughter, asking you to pass them on. I include them with my letter.

Good luck to you in Springfield. Maybe returning to your hometown is the best for you and your children.

Sincerely,

Faith Armstrong

SHE TRIED to come up with a better letter, but felt the important thing was to send it out immediately.

Her note to Jim was brief.

JIM,

Your letter, with the letters to your children, came today. I put the letters to your son and daughter in an envelope addressed to Janine, asking her to pass them on.

Good luck settling into your new surroundings.

Sincerely,

Faith Armstrong

She put stamps on the envelopes, and placed them in the outgoing mail on Jackie's desk.

∼

THE NEXT TWO weeks Faith had to play the waiting game to see if Janine would reply. Then the expected letter, with the anticipated response, arrived.

FAITH,

I know you mean well by seeing Jim, and forwarding his letters. What you do with Jim is up to you.

My children and I left Chicago, and also left behind Moms and Kids. We want to go beyond these things. Jim is no longer a part of our lives. We need to focus on the future, not dwell in the past.

Jim probably told you I returned his earlier envelopes to our children, unopened. I am doing the same thing with the envelopes you sent, unopened.

We would appreciate it if you did not write us and remind us of what we would rather forget.

Janine

JANINE'S LETTER disappointed but did not surprise Faith. She half expected Janine to simply disregard the request to forward Jim's notes. The return of the unopened envelopes left Faith in a quandary. She needed to let Jim know she had kept her promise of forwarding his letters, but couldn't bring herself to write him about Janine's refusal to give the letters to his son and daughter.

After waiting a few days, she sent a noncommittal note to Jim, letting him know Janine had received the messages to his children.

SCOTT AND FAITH talked about Jim and Janine every evening. Scott scolded her, "Don't obsess on Jim. You can't change anything there. Look at what you have, a lively, successful Moms and Kids Foundation with a flourishing academy. You're helping many young mothers and their kids enjoy a better life."

"You're right, Scott, it's unfair to you, getting so preoccupied with Jim's hopeless situation. Thank you for being so patient with me."

The next Wednesday morning she walked to her bookstore and asked the clerk to recommend a good novel. She bought the book and went back to the condo, ready to settle down in the lounger for a relaxed reading session.

The phone rang.

"Faith, it's Frank Middleton."

She dropped her book. "Frank, you have news of Jim?"

"I'll give it to you straight. He's dead."

"What? Killed?"

"No, he died in a fall."

"What kind of fall?"

"Well, Stateville is calling it a fall, but it sounds more like a jump. They don't like to report a suicide."

"What else can you tell me?"

"Jim had volunteered for the library, and was delivering books to prisoners in their cells. That gave him access to some upper floors of the prison, and apparently, he was alone, found an unprotected area and dived head first onto the concrete on the first floor, died immediately."

Faith blurted out, "Oh, my God! I realized things weren't going well for him, but there was nothing I could do."

"Sorry to give you the news, but knew you'd want to hear it."

"What will happen now?"

"A lot of bureaucratic mumbo jumbo. An autopsy. Cause of death. Ambiguity about fall or jump. An administrator's statement about their safety precautions in the past, and heightened security in the future."

"I mean, they'll have to notify his wife, won't they?"

"Sure. They already did. Looks like it's gonna be messy. She says with the divorce, she's done with him."

"What does that mean?"

"I guess she won't claim the body and arrange funeral or burial arrangements."

Faith sobbed, "Even in death . . . .."

"My understanding is that Jim has, or had, a brother in Pennsylvania, so if Janine refuses to take care of Jim, it will be up to the brother."

"Frank, keep me informed. I still feel bad that I didn't help Jim with a house down payment. If his brother doesn't claim the body, let me know, and somehow we'll make sure Jim is put to rest in a decent manner."

She called Scott and told him about Jim. "Hells bells, you were spot-on that something wasn't right with him."

"Yes, and if it's the last thing I do for Jim, I want to make sure he has a proper farewell."

She called Bill Ludwig's office and left an urgent callback message.

An hour later Bill called. "What's up?"

"Jim died in prison, apparently a suicide, and it seems his wife Janine refuses to claim the body. The next in line apparently is his brother. I want to make sure Jim has a respectable service. If necessary, I'm willing to pay some of the expenses. Upfront, let me say that cremation might be the best procedure. What I'd like you to do is get in touch with Brad Ashford or whoever could represent me to Jim's brother and Stateville as willing to bear expenses and hold a funeral ceremony."

"Sorry to hear the bad news. And you're right, Brad is the one to handle this. I'll have him get right on this."

"Thanks, Bill."

"Hey, young lady, are you alright?"

"No. I had a humiliating trip to Stateville to visit Jim, and knew things were bad, but hadn't anticipated a suicide. I worried more about him being killed."

"I have a client waiting. You're going to have to come in to see Brad. Let's talk then."

WHEN SHE HUNG UP, she sorted out some priorities, and decided first to call Father Whitmore.

"Father, I want to make a request of you. If you can't honor it, let me know. I just learned that Jim is dead, maybe a suicide. His wife refuses to claim the body. If Jim's brother doesn't want to be responsible, I'm willing to pay for expenses, maybe cremation. No details are available now, but what I'm asking is if you could dignify Jim's passing with some kind of brief memorial."

"Sorry to hear about Jim. Your conscience, as always, is your best guide. I don't know what we can do, but we'll do something. Probably not in the church."

"No, not in the church. We'll work something out later.

WHEN THE CALL came from Frank Middleton, she set aside the novel she had started to read, and could not return to it.

She walked into the bedroom and pulled her journal out of the dresser drawer, taking it to the lounger, opening it to the first blank page.

JIM.
   A lost sheep.
   A lost soul.
   All alone.
   Where is his soul now?
   Is suicide a sin? A mortal sin?
   How will Father Whitmore handle the service?
   May God have mercy on Jim's soul.
   Harriet and Mary, guide me through this rough spot.

43

Faith felt alone and lonely. She longed for Scott's comforting embrace. The company of the Winnetka duo would be reassuring. She thought about driving to the academy, but came up with a better idea. She disrobed and slipped into thermal underwear to ward off the spring chill, put on warm clothes, and took a hoodie out of her closet, then headed for the beach.

The crunch-crunch of her shoes on the sand and the splish-splash of the waves reassured her. No matter what humans did, no matter how bad they messed up their lives, nature remained a constant. She didn't talk to the lake, but it seemed to commune with her, soothing her jangled nerves. Refreshed, she returned to the condo and the reality of people and problems.

Faith had avoided calling Jeremy, knowing Jim's death would upset him, but she needed to contact him before he heard it from others.

"Hello, Jeremy, it's Mom."

"Hi, enjoying your day off?"

"Uh, it's not that kind of day. I have bad news. Jim is dead."

"In prison? How—?"

"The authorities haven't officially announced it, but detective Middleton is sure it's suicide, diving from an upper story head first onto the concrete."

"Oh . . . that's terrible."

"What makes it even worse, you know his wife divorced him, and turned the kids against him, and she's refusing to claim the body."

"But what will happen?"

"I hate to dump so much on you all at once, but you know me, the executive planner. If Jim's brother doesn't want to handle it, I've offered to pay for expenses and plan a funeral service. Things will happen very quickly. I already asked Father Whitmore if he'd conduct a service, and he agreed. Here's one part of the ceremony I'd like you to think over. If he's cremated, we could have a service at the academy and deposit his ashes there."

"Uh, I don't know, this is so sudden."

"Yes, you don't need to give me an answer now, just think about it."

"Gee, Jim dead, I can't get over it."

"There's more to tell you, but I need to call Agnes and Felicia, and also Father Murphy. I'll be in tomorrow and we can talk more then."

She hung up, took a deep breath, and dialed Felicia.

"Hello, Felicia. Is Agnes there, and can you talk together on speaker phone?"

"Yeah, we're here. Something important?"

"Jim's dead. Suicide. Died doing a header from an upper floor of the prison."

Felicia moaned, "Oh, no, and you just saw him."

"Yes, I knew he was depressed, but worried more about him getting killed."

Agnes wondered, "What happens now?"

"It's complicated, because Janine won't accept the body, and it's unclear if Jim's brother in Pennsylvania will take over. I've gone out on a limb, contacted Bill's office, and offered to cover funeral

expenses. I also got Father Whitmore to agree to a simple ceremony. Here's the rest of the plan. I just asked Jeremy if we could
have the service and scatter Jim's ashes on the academy grounds.
How does that sound?"

Both of the Winnetkans agreed to that idea.

"Felicia, would you mind passing on this information to Father
Murphy? My head is spinning from everything that's happened,
and I don't want to tell this story another time."

"Sure, dear, you get some rest."

FAITH WAS GOING to lie down, but her stomach reminded her she
had been so busy she had not eaten. She put two slices of bread in
the toaster and boiled water for tea. That would tide her over til
supper. After her snack she drew a hot bath, got out of her beach
clothes, and soaked.

Her mind would not turn off, reviewing the prison visit with
Jim, and visualizing him making his death leap onto the concrete
floor. In spite of the hot water, she shivered.

She directed her thoughts to what she had done, and what she
needed to do. She had made the immediate necessary notifications.
Tonight, she'd have Scott's efficient brain help her make plans.
Tomorrow if Brad didn't call her, she'd phone him for an update on
negotiations with Stateville.

When she got out of the tub she put on pajamas and got in bed.
She didn't wake up until Scott came home.

"Sorry to hear about the bad news. Glad you got some shuteye.
You must have been in emergency mode all day."

Faith got out of bed. "I'm still discombobulated. It seems unreal.
I had just visited Jim, and was wondering whether to go back."

"You did the right thing."

"I need to ask you about funerals, something I know about only
from my parents' services, when I was too upset to notice. Maybe it
wasn't fair of me to ask Father Whitmore to conduct a funeral. You

know, Jim was never Episcopalian, and after all . . . he committed suicide. Your dad was a preacher, so what are the rules for non-church members? And can a minister or priest hold a Christian ceremony for someone who killed himself?"

"Those are two knotty questions, with diverse answers. Let me tackle the suicide issue first. In earlier times, suicide was seen as a sin against God, trying to destroy what the Lord had created. That meant no service in the church, and no burial in hallowed ground. Gradually most churches have eased up on that strict interpretation, and let's face it, most cemeteries today are not church territory, hallowed ground. They're municipal or corporate properties.

"The first question is mostly a local matter—depending on each congregation. I see no reason why Father Whitmore couldn't conduct a ceremony. And with suicide, most churches just overlook it."

Faith put her hand on her chin. "I think our Lutheran church in Canton would only allow a funeral in the church for members. I recall my dad complaining, something like, 'If they don't support the church while they're alive, the church won't honor them while they're dead.'"

Scott chuckled. "I never knew your dad, but from what you tell me of his bean-counter mentality, his objection was probably more financial than theological."

Faith grinned. "Don't get me started on Dad. When Jesus spoke about moneychangers in the temple, I think he could have been talking about Dad."

"Let's face it, with undertakers and funeral homes, death has become commercialized."

"And cremation is not a problem?"

"No, for a while there was resistance, but nowadays the movement to avoid embalming fluid and save valuable land has overcome earlier resistance to cremation."

"Thanks a lot, Scott, you've cleared up a lot of questions and concerns I had on the religious side. Now we have to wait to clear up the legal issues."

THE NEXT DAY she and Jeremy had a long talk. She confessed to him that he had changed her mind about people, forcing her to realize that every individual has some good inside. Jeremy agreed to her plan to have a funeral and ash-scattering on the academy grounds.

She called Brad Ashford and got an update. He had contacted Stateville and conveyed Faith's offer to cover funeral expenses, even cremation. The prison authorities were noncommittal, just told Brad they would let Jim's brother know of Faith's generosity.

44

F rank Middleton was right about the bureaucratic mumbo jumbo at Stateville. The only clear and prompt determination was that Jim suffered a skull fracture, blunt trauma, and broken neck which resulted in severed spinal cord and immediate death. All of this they attributed to a fall from an upper story onto the first-floor concrete.

The prison administration danced around the cause of the fall, running a number of reports through several committees. They considered whether he fell accidentally, was pushed, or jumped. With no eyewitnesses, their findings remained inconclusive. Jim had found a gap in the protective netting on the third floor, under a surveillance camera, which captured the downward path of his body and its crash onto the concrete, but not how he began his "fall."

Faith told Brad Ashford those legal niceties did not bother her. She was more concerned with the disposition of Jim's body, being held in a morgue pending internal prison procedures. The prison administration informed Brad that Janine had refused to have anything to do with the cadaver. Through some legal negotiating, Brad found out that Jim's brother in Pennsylvania, a construction worker, did not welcome the liabilities of funeral expenses. The brother readily accepted Faith's offer to assume responsibility for Jim's final resting place.

Finally, the prison committee reached an ambiguous conclusion that the cause of Jim's fall was unknown, whether an accident, involving another person, or self-motivated. Brad forwarded papers to the brother in Pennsylvania to transfer responsibility for cremation and final rites to Faith.

Two weeks later Brad told her he had received the signed papers, and thought they should have a face to face meeting. Faith said to alert Bill to see if he wanted to sit in.

FAITH WENT to Bill Ludwig's office to meet with Brad Ashford. Bill greeted her with a warm hug. He stood back, and wondered out loud, "Is it proper to embrace a saint? I can't believe all you've done for down and out moms, and you went way beyond the call of duty to visit Jim after all his threats and shenanigans. Now you're going to make sure he has an honorable sendoff. That's the work of an angel."

"Save some of your praise for Jeremy and Father Whitmore. Jeremy showed me that even the worst human being has some spark of goodness in him. And my priest said to follow my conscience."

"Well, your mentors should be proud of you. Now let's hear what Brad has to report."

Brad began, "All the formalities have been taken care of. Jim's wife, Janine, wrote the prison that she accepted no responsibility, and Jim's brother has signed the agreement for Faith to handle last rites, including cremation. Next, I'll contact a crematorium, and they may have some papers to sign. Other than that, I think we're in good shape. Uh, Faith, you wanted to receive the ashes?"

"Yes. We don't need a fancy urn. Any receptacle will do, because we're going to scatter the ashes at the academy."

WHILE BRAD HANDLED the details with the cremation, Faith had a meeting with her priest.

"Father Whitmore, I had a discussion with Scott, who you know is a preacher's kid. He said that most churches nowadays have no problem with funerals for suicides, and for people who are cremated."

"Mm, that's right, 'most churches.' The Episcopal church is more lenient and accepting than some."

"I've told you all about Jim, and although he did some bad things, he also had a good heart and did some good things. I actually believe he committed suicide so that Janine and their kids could get on with their lives, not have a jailbird husband and father."

"That occurred to me, too. In some ways, he was sacrificing himself for the good of his family. The ideal of sacrifice is at the heart of the Christian message."

"I'm glad you put it that way."

They planned a simple ceremony, with an opening prayer, then a brief bio of Jim, a scripture reading, and ending with a funeral prayer from the Book of Common Prayer.

Faith thanked Father Whitmore and drove back to the condo. On the way she had an idea she wanted to try out on Jeremy. When she got home, she called him.

"I want to run something by you. Father Whitmore has the ceremony planned, brief and simple. I think one way of memorializing Jim would be to plant a tree in his honor."

"That would be most appropriate."

The Crematorium included delivery of ashes as part of their service. Jim's remains arrived at the academy in a plain ceramic urn. Faith arranged a convenient day for Father Whitmore to come at one o'clock for the ceremony. The small gathering included Faith, Scott, Jeremy, Felicia, Agnes, and Maisie.

Father Whitmore's abbreviated bio mentioned Jim's upbringing in Springfield, marriage to Janine, and two children, and his long service at One Way as well as Moms and Kids. To close the ceremony, he quoted a funeral passage from the Book of Common Prayer:

"In sure and certain hope of the resurrection to eternal life through our Lord Jesus Christ, we commend to Almighty God our brother Jim; and we commit his body to the ground; earth to earth; ashes to ashes, dust to dust. The Lord bless him and keep him, the Lord make his face to shine upon him and be gracious unto him and give him peace. Amen."

Faith stepped forward with the ashes and dumped them in the prepared hole. Father Whitmore used a shovel to sprinkle some dirt on the ashes, and each one present took their turn with the shovel and dirt.

Faith had picked out an oak tree to be planted. The maintenance man placed the tree in the hole and filled it with earth.

SCOTT NEEDED to go back to the newspaper to finish several stories. Maisie had prepared some light refreshments which they ate while talking. All present gave thanks to Father Whitmore for a tasteful and moving ceremony.

He commented, "Funerals are for the sake of the deceased, but also for the benefit of the mourners, providing closure and an opportunity for healing."

They talked for a while before heading in their individual directions.

Faith thought about the service as she drove home. She had some time before Scott would return, so she took the opportunity to write an entry in her journal.

JIM.
A lost sheep, who has returned to the flock.

Ashes to ashes, dust to dust.
The Lord bless him and keep him.
Harriet and Mary, thank you for your support.

As she stuck the journal back in its place, she recalled the Biblical passage she wanted to quote to Father Whitmore when they planned Jim's service: Greater love hath no man than this, that he lay down his life for his friends.

Scott had mentioned that Jim sacrificed himself for the sake of his family when he plea-bargained his wife's freedom. And Father Whitmore had said Jim's suicide was like a sacrifice to enable his family to better move on without him.

Faith was not happy, but felt satisfied with what she had done to make a bad situation acceptable.

Scott came home and asked Faith, "Vino or Seagram's?"

"Neither. Tonight, I'd go for chamomile."

"Faith, my dear, I don't know how you do it. You've been under tremendous stress since the fire, all the stakeout detective work, and then you had the cojones to go to the prison to see Jim."

"Hmm, 'cojones.' Does that mean what I think it does?"

"The polite translation would be courage. Well, on top of all that, you finessed complicated interpersonal and legal matters to arrange diplomatic and sensitive final rites for Jim."

"I had a lot of help."

"Face it, without you, Jim would have ended up in what they call a pauper's grave."

"Oooh, don't even mention that."

Scott fixed a light supper, and then they gravitated to the loungers. Faith snuggled against her hubby, and soon was sound asleep. Scott woke her at eleven to go to bed. She had slept so much she couldn't fall back asleep. After Scott started snoring, she returned to the lounger, looking up at the stars in the sky. That reminded her of Dan McLean's ballad, "Starry, Starry Night." She dug her smart phone out of her purse and played it. Phrases in the song seemed to echo Jim's sad situation. People, especially his family, would not listen to him, and he struggled for his sanity. Finally, when no hope was left, he took his life.

Faith felt a chill travel up her spine. She remembered all too vividly during the dark days of her pregnancy when she felt her family would not listen to her, and all hope was gone. She considered ending her life, as van Gogh did, and as Jim did. The memory of that struggle for her own sanity frightened her.

She couldn't tell anyone else, but the words Father Whitmore recited, ashes to ashes, dust to dust, conjured up her nightmares when Jim threatened to burn down the academy. He warned he might reduce the building, and maybe the people inside, to ashes. Now his own cremated remains were the only human ashes on the premises.

She carried to bed with her the words Father Whitmore had intoned: "Ashes to ashes, dust to dust."

45

T he funeral ceremony for Jim should have marked the end of a chapter in Canterbury's history, yet the scenes and events lingered in Faith's memory. She tried to bring closure to this episode by having a brass plaque made, "In Memoriam, Jim Anderson," and asked the maintenance man to install it on a metal stake in front of the oak tree at the burial site.

Standing in front of the nameplate, Faith felt more satisfied that Jim's passing had been properly memorialized. Faith wondered if, years from now, when Jim's children became adults, they would want to know more about their absent father. If they did, at least the bronze plaque would be a place where they could pay their respects. She supposed that his son and daughter would never hear the backstory of Jim's sacrificial suicide.

Pondering these undisclosed facts about Jim's life, she could not suppress a twinge of anger and resentment toward Janine. This woman bore a double debt of guilt. First, she urged her husband to commit several crimes. Then she deserted him and turned his children against him, pushing him to the hopeless predicament that led to his suicide.

If the prison really wanted to get behind Jim's fatal fall, they would find that someone did push him off that upper story of the prison. Janine was the pusher.

Turning away from the marker for Jim's final resting place, Faith felt a vague sense of unease. She walked into the academy, stopped in the kitchen to get a cup of tea, and went to the henhouse to gather her thoughts. She asked herself why she had lingering reservations about Jim's passing. After all, people praised her for going the extra mile to put Jim to rest, even after he had given her so much trouble.

Her mind moved on from Jim to his wife. Janine had been the real antihero of this tale, who was mean to Jim even after he passed away. Faith's eyes glanced at some papers on the corner of her desk, seeing the unopened envelopes Janine had returned to her. After Jim committed suicide, Faith didn't know what to do with his final writing. They were almost like a last will and testament. Picking up these letters, she realized the source of her discomfort—she might feel anger toward Janine as a vicious villain, but the real victims were the children. They had been deprived of their father, and probably would never know that he sacrificed himself so they could have better lives. Even in his last desperate extortion fiasco, he was trying to set up funds for their education.

Faith had experienced pangs of remorse for not helping Jim with the down payment for a house, that eventually led to his downfall. Now she suffered from a double dose of regrets. Indirectly she had played a role in the separation of a father and his children. And she had not made good on the promise to Jim that she'd pass on his farewell letters. The two envelopes, light in her hand, weighed heavily on her heart.

Swiveling her chair toward the gallery of pictures on the wall, she saw all too clearly what had been bugging her. She had devoted her life to keeping mothers and their children together. In Jim's case she had been instrumental in separating a parent and his children. Ironically, Jim had his own sacrificial strategy for making sure his children would be raised by their mother—rather than being separated by years of Janine's incarceration. Faith and Jim shared a commitment to the mother-child bond.

She remembered, and then said out loud the New Testament phrase, "Greater love hath no man than this, that he lay down his life for his friends." With Jim, it was for his own children. Turning back to her desk, she cried softly as tears trickled down her cheeks.

Jeremy knocked and entered, then walked to her desk and asked why she was crying. She shared with him her concerns for Jim and Janine, and especially the children. "Jeremy, I have an idea. It's risky, but I think it's worthwhile. Usually I try out my hare-brained schemes first with Scott, but you came in just as I happened upon this possibility, so I'll share it with you. She explained a rather daring proposal, which he encouraged her to run by Scott.

FAITH WENT HOME EARLY that afternoon, stopped by the deli to pick up the fixings for a meal, and waited for Scott to appear as she rehearsed the plan she would set forth to Scott. After the meal, Faith made a pot of tea and carried cups to their loungers.

"Scott, I need your input on something that has to do with Jim."

"I thought the memorial put Jim to rest—you know what I mean."

"Looking at his memorial plaque today, I felt good that we gave him a decent sendoff, yet I have conflicting sentiments about Janine, on the one hand, and their kids, on the other hand."

"I see where you're heading. Resentment toward her, sympathy for the kids."

"Right. And I won't beat around the bush with you. I'd like to contribute some money to the education funds of Jim's daughter and son."

"Sounds good to me. Where's the obstacle?"

"Janine. She told us to stay out of her life."

"That's touchy."

"Yeah. What I'm considering is a double delivery—in person—of Jim's farewell letters and two checks—ten thousand for each child."

"Uh, how would you do it?"

"I'd run the money through the Foundation, so we can treat it as a belated severance package for Jim."

Scott laughed. "I understand. Dealing with Janine, you have to be devious in order to be generous."

Faith kissed Scott. "I'm glad to have your support, and will go ahead with setting this up."

She resorted to her hotel executive efficiency mode, clearing the financial arrangement with the academy board. On Wednesday she had a session with Father Whitmore, who admired her compassion and perseverance to care for Jim and his children. He gave his usual advice for her to follow her conscience, and sent her on her way with a prayer.

Then she penned a letter to Janine.

Janine,

I think you know we had a memorial for Jim and buried his ashes on the grounds of Canterbury Academy. The last time I contacted you, you said you did not want to hear from us again, but I want to let you know about a proposal approved by the Moms and Kids Foundation.

When Jim left our institution, we did not have in place a severance arrangement. In lieu of a severance package, the Foundation would like to present a check to each of your children toward their education. When I visited Jim at Stateville, he mentioned that the two of you had started education accounts, one for your son and one for your daughter. I would be willing to drive to Springfield to give you these checks.

The unopened letters from Jim are still on my desk. I would bring them with me for you to have, and maybe some time in the future, you would consider passing them on to your children.

If you agree to this plan, mention a time when I could come to Springfield. Given a little advance notice, my schedule is rather flexible.

Sincerely,

Faith Armstrong

THREE DAYS after Faith mailed the letter, she got an email from Janine, who must have looked up her address on the Moms and Kids site. Short and to the point, Janine said they should take care of this quickly, once and for all, and meet Saturday noon at a McDonald's on the north side of Springfield.

Faith agreed to the meeting, and began rehearsing how she would approach Janine. She talked it over with Scott, and had a heart to heart phone conversation with Father Whitmore. With both of these confidants, she admitted the most difficult part of talking with Janine would be getting past her intense anger and resentment toward this cruel woman. She told Scott and her priest, "I have to keep repeating, 'I'm doing this for the kids.'"

SATURDAY MORNING on the drive to Springfield, Faith felt relaxed and composed getting ready to talk with Janine. She had gone through much worse when she ran the gauntlet seeing Jim at Stateville.

She followed Janine's directions to the McDonald's on the north edge of Springfield, and walked in, immediately seeing Janine in a corner booth, sipping a drink. Faith noticed that the past few months had taken a toll on Janine, worry lines creasing her forehead, bags under her eyes.

Taking a seat opposite her, Faith broke the ice, "Thanks for coming."

"I don't know why we had to meet."

"I go back a long way with Jim, from the days of his work with One Way, and I wanted to make this contribution to your children's education in person. The last time I talked to Jim—you know, at Statevile—he was quite concerned about their education."

Janine frowned. "He pretty much left us in the lurch. It will be hard for me, as a single mother, to get them through college."

Faith opened her purse and took out two business envelopes. "Here are two cashier's checks, each for $10,000, made out in the name of your son and your daughter. I hope that eventually this will help in their schooling."

Janine's mouth opened, but no words came out. She gasped. Recovering, she mumbled, "Thank you ... that will help."

Faith retrieved from her purse the two unopened envelopes from Jim that Janine had returned to her. "I also brought these letters, which I thought you should keep, and when you find an appropriate time, pass them on to your son and daughter."

"You know what's in the letters?"

"No, Jim just said he wanted your children to forget about him and go on with their lives. He didn't show me the letters."

"As I told you when I wrote you, that's what we're trying to do, make a fresh start and put him out of our minds. Meeting with you doesn't help."

"I know this is difficult for you, and appreciate you taking the time to see me."

Janine put her hands over her face, muffling a scream. When she uncovered her eyes, she glared at Faith, shouting at her. "You have no idea what it's like, the hell I've been living in! Trying to move into a small apartment and keep up with expenses while putting up a brave front for my children."

"How are your kids doing?"

Janine's eyes widened in surprise. "As well as can be expected. New neighborhood, new school, no father."

"At Canterbury we try to help single moms get back in the swing of managing by themselves. It's difficult, and I wish you well."

Janine shook her head vigorously, her mouth distorted in a scowl. "Hah! You think I'm a dumb shit like your Canterbury Country Club prima donnas? I see right through your fake severance pay maneuver. You've got the money and just used the Foundation to hide behind your charity. Where were you when we needed you for a house down payment?"

Faith paused. "I regret we didn't know about your house situation."

"You were too caught up in your do-good, feel-good activities to see the hurt right in front of you."

"Unfortunately, all we can do is try to help you in the future with your children."

"Okay, Faith Armstrong, you came to Springfield with your soup-kitchen mentality, but let me dish out a serving of the facts of life. You probably look at me as the devil's handmaiden, pushing Jim into his life of crime, and then abandoning him. Well, you don't know where I came from.

"I grew up in Kentucky, just over the border from southern Illinois. Me and my sister and two brothers. We were dirt poor. My dad was an alcoholic womanizer, and as soon as my brothers were old enough, followed in his footsteps. Mom tried to protect us girls. My sister and I vowed we would escape the life of 'hill people'—what others called us. We lived in old farm houses up in the hills. Every few years, when we owed too much back rent, or the sheriff evicted us, we moved to another dilapidated place. Somehow my sister and I managed to do well in school. She graduated a year ahead of me, and with the help of a counselor, found an office job in Springfield. I graduated the next year, and got a job in the same office. We shared an apartment. It wasn't great, but we were independent, self-sufficient, and felt we had made a permanent escape from 'hill country.' We shared the dream of owning our own houses.

"We went to church, where sis met a nice guy. That's where I ran into Jim. He seemed to be a good man. Most of the young fellows I had known in high school, like my brothers, were just interested in girls to get them in bed. Jim was different. He didn't come on strong. He had a college degree, and a steady job with a religious organization. I told him about my dream of being married and raising children in our own house. He shared that dream. We got married, started raising our family, and before long we moved into a small house. Nothing fancy, but it was ours, with a small patch of grass for the kids to play in.

"When Moms and Kids shifted their operation to Chicago, we had the opportunity to move to the big city and thought we'd be able to enter the paradise of suburban America. We had no idea what it took to buy and live in a metropolitan area, and after only a few years in our Springfield house, when we sold it, we had very little equity to take with us. We couldn't afford to buy even a small house in Chicago, and had to settle for a dinky apartment in a crummy neighborhood. I felt like I had traded the nickname of hill people for urban hillbilly.

"That's when our marriage went down the toilet. Jim had promised me a house of our own, and I thought we were trapped forever in rundown apartments. I told Jim that the Foundation should have helped with moving costs and made up some of the difference for housing costs in Chicago. I warned him if we couldn't have our own house in Chicago, I'd leave him and take the kids back to Springfield. That's when he agreed to siphon some of the Foundation's money that he—and I—figured they owed us. Well, I guess you know the rest of the story. Anyway, Jim and I had always worked hard, and didn't deliberately set out on a path of crime, we were just trying to find a way to get what we thought was ours. And look where we ended up."

Janine buried her head in her hands, sobbing and whimpering.

Faith had listened patiently, and waited until Janine lowered her hands and looked across the table. Faith reached in her purse for a handkerchief and held it out to Janine, but she ignored the gesture and wiped her eyes with the sleeve of her blouse.

Janine began again. "Well, I've kept that bottled up for months. My sister doesn't want to hear any more of it, I can't talk about it to my kids, and I don't want to blab it at work."

Janine's expression changed into a half smile, half smirk. "How do you keep your cool? Here I've been reading you the riot act, badmouthing you, and you just sit there and calmly take it in. Waiting for you today, I really expected you to walk in and start criticizing me, and we'd end up in a shouting match. Don't you ever have problems and get mad?"

"Everyone has problems. At Moms and Kids, I listen to the stories of many young mothers, and believe me, some are worse than yours. Most of these women have problems, or they wouldn't be with us."

Faith hesitated, pursing her lips. "Yes, we all have problems. You ask me how I handle them and keep my cool. My priest helps me maintain my balance."

Janine's eyebrows raised. "You're Catholic?"

"No, Episcopalian. What about you?"

"Mom called us 'Thumpers.' She was such a strong Fundamentalist and believer in the Bible that others called us Bible-thumpers, so she shortened our religious name to 'Thumpers.'"

Faith and Janine shared smiles at this first glint of humor in their conversation.

"Janine, do you still go to church?"

"Yes, not every Sunday, but we go when I don't have to work."

"You have a rough road ahead, and most ministers are good listeners and will help you find your way through difficulties."

"Our minister is not really a Bible-thumper like the ones I knew back in Kentucky, and he's easy to talk to."

"I don't want to take up a lot of your time today with the story of my life, but I did have serious problems with my father and forgiveness. Jim probably told you my parents—especially my father—insisted that my twin sons be adopted out and split apart."

"Yeah, I heard some of that. Too bad."

"It took me years to forgive my dad. Well, I won't go into details, but hope that as you try to work out your life with your children you make the most of it. Because of my father's insistence on adoption, I didn't have the opportunity of raising my sons. That's why

I'm so dedicated to helping young mothers keep their children and raise them."

Faith paused. "I know that Jim did what he did . . . and protected you . . . so that you could raise your boy and girl."

Faith slid out of the booth. "I wish you and your children well."

Janine stayed seated. "We'll do the best we can."

Faith turned toward the exit.

Janine called after her. "I do appreciate the checks. Thanks."

"You're welcome."

As FAITH WALKED to her car, she had several competing sensations. Because when she entered McDonald's, she saw Janine and walked directly to her booth, she didn't get a drink. An hour of talking left her thirsty. Her stomach reminded her it was hungry. And, although she began the conversation in a relaxed mood, Janine's outbursts made her uptight.

Faith got in the car and entered the freeway, eager to return to Chicago. She needed caffeine to keep her alert, so she stopped at the first fastfood restaurant. "Boy, two McDonald's in one day." She grabbed a burger and fries with her coffee. Attacking her meal, she noticed kids on the indoor playground equipment. That made her think of Moms and Kids, lifting her spirits. A little girl tripped and skinned her knee. Without thinking, Faith grabbed her purse and pulled out a small bandage and handed it to the kid's mother. "I always keep some handy."

Finishing her meal, she watched the little girl with the bandage on her knee cheerfully clambering around on the playground equipment. Faith was glad she had first aid supplies with her, so she could take care of the girl.

Faith thought about her conversation with Janine.

Yes, today all I did was give Janine a temporary bandage for her problems, but her difficulties are more than skin deep and can't be handled by a quick fix of gauze and tape. She has major difficulties that

will keep her busy for a long time. Her biggest hurdle will be forgiving
herself for the way she treated Jim. She led him to crime and then she
pushed him to suicide.

ENERGIZED WITH CHOLESTEROL AND CAFFEINE, Faith got in her car
and headed toward Chicago. She laughed at herself, knowing that
her decades of hotel negotiations and business consultations would
not let her leave a tense discussion without doing a follow-up
analysis.

She used her executive skills to dissect the meeting with Janine.
It was smart to let Janine set the time and place, on her home turf,
making her comfortable. And it had been wise to give the checks to
her right away. From past labor negotiations, Faith knew that
sessions beginning with demands usually ended up contentious
and unsatisfactory. Not making any conditions Janine had to agree
to before receiving the checks was an act of good will, a gesture of
trust.

Faith had expected some emotional fireworks from Janine, and
bit her tongue rather than trade insults with her. This caught
Janine off guard, enabling her to open up, and they found common
ground talking about religion. Faith saw her opening and could
suggest Janine find help from her minister.

Faith realized she couldn't expect too much from one meeting,
and made her exit while she was ahead. Faith knew, but did not
need or want to state, her objectives for the meeting. Short term,
she hoped Janine would accept and pass on the letters from Jim.
Long term, she shared Jim's goal of supporting the mother-child
bond for the son and daughter.

She had made progress on those two concerns, and felt she
couldn't do anything more. Better to leave on good terms, and keep
the door open for contact or a meeting in the future. Faith wished
she could have exacted a promise from Janine to hand the letters to
her children, but that would be too much to expect.

Faith's quickie review of the session left her satisfied that she had avoided a major confrontation with Janine, and had made a small contribution to help this woman face the future with her children.

Her big victory for the day was managing to keep under control her anger and contempt for Janine, reminding herself to do what was best for the children.

Finishing her analysis, she allowed herself to vent the pent-up feelings she had restrained while seated across from this foul-mouthed woman.

Faith filled the car with a raging howl. "Janine, you're a mean, selfish witch. You let your obsession with a house destroy a family. A house is just a collection of wood and bricks, held together by nails and mortar. A home is a bond of living people, supported and maintained by feelings of love and acts of care. I hope, for the sake of your children, that you straighten out your life and redeem yourself."

Faith's heart pounded. She turned on the radio and tuned in music to soothe her mind.

Approaching Chicago and seeing the skyscrapers on the horizon reminded her of her first car trip to Chicago, more than thirty years ago, a newly minted high school graduate, escaping Canton and the misery of losing her twins, hoping to find her way in the Windy City. Faith sighed.

Today I'm escaping Springfield and another miserable situation, but hope that my trip makes a difference.

WHEN FAITH OPENED the condo door, Scott was waiting for her. "How did it go?"

"As well as could be expected. She did turn defensive and attacked me for being a goody-goody two shoes with our mothers and kids, but overlooking Jim's need for a down payment."

She summed up the meeting quickly, ending with, "It was a

good thing I went. Not easy. Like with visiting Jim in prison, something I didn't want to do, but my conscience told me was right to do."

Scott cheered. "I hope that's the end of the saga with Jim. Want a drink? Wine or Seagram's?"

"It's not an occasion for a celebration. I'm just glad it's over."

46

The following Monday, Faith went in early to the academy, had a quick breakfast and schmoozed for a few minutes before she dropped her purse at the henhouse. Then she went out the back door and walked across the grounds to the marker for Jim's remains. She spoke to the bronze plaque as if he were present.

"Jim, I kept the promise to deliver your letters to Janine. She's going through a rough patch now, but I think eventually she'll mellow and hand over the letters to your son and daughter. It was a courageous and selfless act for you to assume all the penalties for the crimes so that Janine would be free to raise your children. I borrow the words of Father Whitmore from the day we buried your ashes: The Lord bless you and keep you, the Lord make his face to shine upon you and be gracious unto you and give you peace. Amen."

∾

EVENTUALLY FAITH MOVED past the emotional upheaval of Jim's passing, settling into a comfortable routine at the academy, reserving Wednesday for her personal time. One evening as she and Scott talked, she joked, "This is the ho-hum boring life I've been looking for."

Scott agreed. "Canterbury runs like a well-oiled machine."

"Jeremy does a good job, and Maisie, Felicia, and Agnes, along with my own volunteering, provide him with much needed support. We supply the oil that keeps the machinery operating smoothly."

"Every time I'm in your henhouse, I marvel at how Moms and Kids started from one corner of a desk in a rundown former Montgomery Ward store, and morphed into a major institution with first class facilities."

"Okay, Mr. *Trib* reporter, that's my cue to clue you in to my latest idea for the academy. I remember when we vacated the old rickety hotel, we all piled into school buses, and moved to Canterbury. Because public school was out, the bus company gave us a good deal on their idle buses. Now we're coming up to summer, the anniversary of our move, and I think we should have a big celebration. Invite everyone on our mailing list—donors and supporters, other agencies we work with, volunteers, and our growing number of transitioned residents. If we set it for, say two to four on a Sunday afternoon, we would bring in quite a crowd. Jon can announce it in the Canticle, and then send out a reminder just before the day. What do you think?"

"Great idea. Why don't you propose it to Jeremy and your Winnetka buddies?"

"You're my in-house sounding board. If you like it, I'll run it by the others."

She talked to Jeremy, who liked this plan.

Felicia babbled, "Oh, that would help me connect with past donors, and cultivate new prospects."

Agnes nodded. "I'm sure that would present an opportunity to recruit volunteers for our instructional programs."

The prospect of a party excited Maisie. She mentioned the

event to Otto, who offered ten pounds of cocktail wieners for appetizers.

Jeremy got out of the way and let the women plan the shindig. They had a loose format of schmoozing two to three, then a prayer from Father Murphy, and brief remarks from Jeremy and Faith. They agreed not to have any long speeches. Bill Ludwig emailed that he would attend, and he wanted to bring along a representative from the mayor's office to give congratulatory remarks. People could snack and talk until the affair wound down at four.

When the appointed day arrived, it turned out to be a glorious sun-filled June day. Faith reveled in the festive atmosphere. Jeremy and Melanie brought Mark and Beth. Mark and Leonard put together a ball game; Beth hooked up with her best friends. Jon and Rachel showed up with Stephie and Jeb, who hung out with their cousins.

Felicia and Faith kept busy greeting people and giving visitors a tour of the henhouse, with Faith narrating her well-rehearsed travelogue of the career of Moms and Kids. Agnes talked with her instructors, and was on the lookout for new volunteers.

Melanie and Rachel mixed with residents, holding babies and infants. Jon and Scott jotted notes on their smart phones. Scott had his boss at the newspaper agree to a brief article in the *Trib*, and Jon gathered information and photos for a major piece in the next issue of the Canticle.

Jeremy circulated, greeting as many people as possible. Bill Ludwig showed up shortly before three, with the mayor's representative in tow. Faith and the Winnetkans corralled the residents and guests into the all-purpose room, where Father Murphy gave a standard prayer of thanks for Canterbury Academy and its continued success. Jeremy and Faith made brief remarks, thanking all the people who helped fund and run the foundation.

Bill Ludwig introduced the mayor's assistant, who walked to the front of the group with several large envelopes. "The mayor regrets that other commitments prevent him from attending, but he sends his congratulations to this very important organization in our community. The fame of Moms and Kids Foundation has spread across the country, and the City of Chicago takes this festive occasion to recognize the dynamic duo of Faith Armstrong and Jeremy Goodman, co-founders of Canterbury Academy for Moms and Kids."

He paused, to pull out a formal certificate. "The City of Chicago recognizes Faith Armstrong and Jeremy Goodman for their untiring and longstanding service to young women and their children. We could draw up a long list of 'whereas' phrases, but I don't want to detract from the main purpose. The City of Chicago designates these two people as recipients of the Citizens of the Year award, and honors them with keys to the city."

He pulled from envelopes two huge gilded keys and motioned for Faith and Jeremy to come forward and receive them.

They walked forward and accepted the certificates and keys, as the audience rose to their feet, clapping and cheering.

Jeremy, and then Faith, gave thanks to all who had made Moms and Kids possible.

Felicia and Agnes rushed in front of the audience and announced, "The kids have prepared a closing. They want to sing Inky Dinky, twice." First, they sang it with the "I love you" phrases punctuated with shouts of "JEREMY," and the second time through with shouts of "FAITH."

After the song, well-wishers mobbed the two recipients. The grandchildren had to hold the keys, asking where the big door was that needed such large keys.

By four o'clock the crowd had thinned out, and Maisie and her volunteer crew cleared up the remainders of the refreshments and the dirty dishes. She wouldn't let Faith help.

Faith turned to Jeremy. "This is the most satisfying recognition I've ever received. A complete surprise! Bill didn't tell me anything about it."

Jeremy choked up. "Well deserved, Mother. This must be the crown jewel of your life."

"I couldn't be happier."

SCOTT AND FAITH headed to their cars to go back to the city. He turned to her. "Well, Miss Celebrity, what's your pleasure? The condo and a much needed rest? Or the restaurant of your choice."

"You may think me crazy, but I'd like to stop at the condo long enough to change, and then take a walk by the lake. All those years when I was alone, Lake Michigan was my companion. I want to share the celebration with my old friend."

They went to the condo, slipped on casual clothes, and then walked to the beach. Faith held Scott's hand, but was not talkative. She gazed out over the waters, as the sun lit up the waves. They returned to the condo and sat in the loungers, watching night settle in over the lake. Suddenly Faith realized the fatigue from the day's excitement, and closed her eyes, sleeping for an hour.

She woke with a start, surprised to see Scott still sitting beside her, reading. He laughed. "You needed that, running at full speed all day."

"Sorry, I didn't realize how tired I was."

They ate some leftovers, and watched some news before going to bed.

Faith's mind replayed the day's events, and the long-ago memories that led up to the Moms and Kids Foundation. She couldn't get to sleep, so after an hour of tossing and turning, got out of bed.

EPILOGUE

F aith went to her underwear drawer, started to open it, then quietly shut it. She didn't need to write anything.

As she walked to her lounger, many stars greeted her. She thought of calling up Dan McLean's "Starry, Starry Night," but knew it so well she didn't need to hear the music.

The sky and the water remained silent, yet they seemed to be communicating to her. The glints of light above reminded her of recent encounters with people. Somewhere out in that void, Jim resided, thanking her for the burial and wishing her well with the academy.

Doug did not appear as an image, but seemed to be in the background, glad to know that she and their sons were doing well.

Even Faith's parents seemed to be present. They offered their best wishes for the foundation, her father grudgingly, her mother with heartfelt love.

The scene shifted to the past day's events. Her beloved twins Jeremy and Jon and their wives warmed her heart. The grandchildren and the residents' kids playing together delighted her. Felicia, Agnes, and Maisie comforted her. Scott's support pleased her. The tune that accompanied these figures was Inky Dinky. Jon would write in his newsletter about this memorable day, but the stars and the lake provided a preview of the next issue of Canterbury Canticle.

The End

PRAISE FOR H. BYRON EARHART

For No Pizza in Heaven

In *No Pizza in Heaven*, H. Byron Earhart uses his vast knowledge of comparative religion to craft a compelling study of how belief can both destroy and heal.

—*Richard Lederer, best-selling author of books about language and history*

For Faith Finds Forgiveness

Faith's quest for forgiveness is matched only by her professional expertise which becomes a part of her spiritual journey. This journey is especially challenging when she faces decisions about the twins' father. The reader is drawn convincingly into her struggle and the conflicting emotions that result after she takes action. Faith's saga examines religious beliefs, soul-searching, and the power of understanding and compromise when finding common ground. This is a thought-provoking read that leaves one fully satisfied.

—*J.T.*

For Meeting the Devil

Growing up in the 50's, I remember my mother going next door to have coffee with Betty. Betty and mother would share the ups and downs and little ordinary details of their lives. Years later when Betty passed away my mother shared with me the details of her friendship with Betty. They were ordinary women. They did not blast dragons from the sky or hack zombies or machine gun terrorist hordes. They were not prostitutes or princesses draped in diamonds.

This book is about one woman sharing with the reader the ups and downs of her life without machine guns or magic. There isn't blood and guts oozing from the pages. We share with her hope for better times. We don't want her to lose her moral compass. This book is sharing life with a friend. It is warm, satisfying, and a pleasure to read.

—*Sara Allen, Attorney*

For The Devil Déjà Vu

After devouring the first three books of the Twin Trilogy, my wife and I couldn't wait for a fourth book to appear on the scene. We weren't disappointed! The Devil Deja Vu is another terrific read that we both thoroughly enjoyed. Now we're hoping to see a fifth book in the series to be published soon.

--James H. Smith

ACKNOWLEDGMENTS

I would like to thank those who read early drafts of this novel, especially Caroline McCullagh.

I would also like to thank my publisher, Rick Lakin, at iCrew Digital Publishing, and D.J. Rogers of Justwritedesign.com for finishing the cover.

ABOUT H. BYRON EARHART

H. Byron Earhart, born in central Illinois, attended Knox College, and received a doctorate in History of Religions from the University of Chicago and was awarded a grant as a Fulbright Scholar. He began writing fiction as a teenager, but as a professor at Western Michigan University, published books on religion, especially religion in Japan. After retiring to San Diego, he returned to his early love of writing fiction. *Canterbury Chronicle* is Book Five of The Twin Destiny Series.

His latest book is "At Grandma's House: The World War II Homefront in Havana, Illinois," a memoir/documentary of the life his family and other Americans experienced living through World War II.

Visit his websites at byronearhartauthor.com and byronearhart.com.

www.ingramcontent.com/pod-product-compliance
Lightning Source LLC
Chambersburg PA
CBHW061942170626
46813CB00006B/2507